Trick or Treat?

by

Simon Bramhall & Fionn Murphy

Scalpel Stories

www.scalpelstories.com

Dedication

To all those who have given so much support to Simon through very difficult times

ISBN: 978-1-9161915-0-1

Disclaimer

Trick or Treat? is a work of fiction. All characters in this publication are fictitious and any resemblance to real persons, living or dead, is purely coincidental.

www.scalpelstories.com

Chapters

1	Singapore 1973	6
2	Glasgow 1973	9
3	Wyeminster. Halloween 2017	10
4	Same Place, Same Night	29
5	Endless Night	40
6	Endless Night Continued	49
7	All Saint's Day	59
8	Two Days Later	67
9	The Same Week	83
10	The End of the Same Week	92
11	Monday Morning	101
12	Friday Morning	110
13	The Beginning of December	120
14	The Following Morning	131
15	The Same Day	140
16	What Happened Next	157
17	Later That Day	175
18	Down	183
19	Forward	193
20	Following	203

21	The Next Day	212
22	The Day After	219
23	All the Next Day	225
24	That Night	243
25	The Next Day	264
26	What Followed	279
27	The Week Before Christmas	310
28	Christmas Eve	334
29	Singapore 2018	338

Acknowledgements 341

Chapter One

Singapore 1973

Sweat or humidity? It was impossible to tell. Edible air. Suffocation born of heat and unfiltered cigarette smoke. Lizard-tongue roll ups dangling like serpent breaths, licking Chance, tasting Fate.

Four men sit at the square table in the small room, playing Mah-jong. Eyes open, faces closed. Everything that matters is in the dry, bone tiles chattering about them – stippled white noise in a dim room. It is scene from forever set down here, now, for the men in singlets and flaccid shorts. Three are young and the other is slightly older, but none as far as middle aged. They gamble in the present for their future and the tiles will decide. An unholy way to choose, perhaps, but as sacred and binding as the discreet tattoo they all wear on the soft skin of the inner right elbow, where with every bend and crease the silent black lines shriek out their allegiance as the tigers' jaws blend with their bones. They were born and then they chose. Now they belong until they die.

They sit in the half light at the sides of the square table, hunched forward on abused rattan chairs dark from age and suffering, the tops of their heads illuminated by the bulb-eye. Light dribbles downward, shiny with perspiration soaking darkly into saggy fabric under armpits and sticking to the spine. The whole world is in this small room where Mah-jong Winds blow through the Seasons and order is adorned by flowers amongst which dragons cavort as the sparrows chatter. Time waits, patiently, outside. Finally, at the North point of the flat-earth table the tiles are tired. They have had enough of being fingered by soiled hands, the sweat and stickiness. A clicking flurry of blue, red, green. Then it happens. The Nine Gates of Heaven open and everything stops. There is silence. The others look at The One. Stare their acceptance.

"It has been decided." It is said in Cantonese by one of the unchosen who speaks, needlessly, what is already known. It sounds trite and unnecessary but marks the moment. There is no rancour, no envy. Their turn will come, maybe, one day, if the game decrees. This is not gambling. It is Fate.

A scrawny apology for a man has won. An unlikely champion in his stained vest and shapeless shorts he has no musclebound shoulders to carry the burden and only bent pin legs to tread the path. Troglodyte feet in flattened flip flops; toes stubbed and ingrained with the language of the streets; toe nails broken working for others. Under a shaved head – long hair is illegal in Lee Kuan Yew's emerging economic miracle – the victor's face is non-descript and expressionless. Only his eyes move as he glances at the insignia in the tender cradle of his inner arm. Then by unspoken cue the four men move closer to the table and gaze down at the decision in silent homage. Each man extends his right arm out over the discarded tiles and places his right hand, palm down over them in unholy blessing.

Ring finger and thumb embrace against the palm of the hand as the middle, index and little fingers extend themselves away and the sign of the Heilokbaat floats over the tabled earth.

“Go. Now.”

Someone speaks. He nods, serpent’s eyes flicking fork tongued around the room towards the door that leads to the outer world, where Time is waiting.

Chapter Two

Glasgow 1973

Glasgow in winter is monochrome. The man blinks as if it is night and his eyes must adjust to the dingy twilight. He is a forlorn figure, standing on the platform as the train gently hisses and pants itself into rest after grinding through the cold landscape. Around him people move and jostle and hurry with purpose - somewhere to be, someone to see. He is oblivious to them all as they twist about him, swerving past his meagre suitcase as water flows around a stone in a stream. His face is expressionless. Above him the girded ceiling blends into a steel grey sky and no light unveils the gloom below.

Away from the small room the man is even more scrawny, crowded into a heavy coat designed by someone in the tropics to keep him warm in a climate that neither could ever have imagined. He is freezing. He has come from a vibrant world of porous dark and intense light without seasons where it is always hot and moist, the colours sing and even the rain is warm. He has travelled across the world and ended up in Glasgow because the tiles told him to. Never once has he questioned his destiny until now, in this granite-grey place with steel bars above and dirty smooth travel-stained stone below where everyone speaks in coughs and splutters. He knows no one; he has no-where to go.

He picks up his case and leaves the station.

Chapter Three

Wyeminster; the West Country. Halloween 2017

White, ultraviolet fractured light, vibrating flesh, sweat. The smell of cheap scent mingled with alcohol masked by sugar and synthetic fruit for kids who pretend to be adults; Haribous with attitude; teenagers too young to like coffee but old enough to have sex. Halloween in the provinces and they are determined to have fun, ostentatiously happy, outwardly confident, desperate to be liked and to fit in.

Taya had dressed with agonising care. It had taken most of the day to achieve the just-thrown-together-nothing-special outfit she was barely wearing. At least it was warm in the night club. Well, not a real night club, not like in Bristol or London, but the best that Wyeminster had to offer teenagers for the closest thing to a rave that they could get away with. She had nearly frozen when they had walked through town but had not dared shiver or bleat. God. Being cool was really tough. Kezia and Courtney were so sophisticated so she was determined to prove that she was ace enough to be seen with them. Her clothes were just right and she was secretly proud of herself. Not fancy dress – that was for kids – but themed and on trend. Black tights under a red bodycon sleeveless dress that showed off her slim frame and not quite flat chest, her hip bones jutted out like a supermodel's and she loved the cavities in her collar bones when she hunched forward. Sort of elfin and dramatic at the same time, like something out of Lord of the Rings. In her ears were red chandelier earrings that bled into her neck from below her corn-rowed hair – vamp and elegant. She loved the way the earrings swung as she walked and tugged at her ear lobes. Amazing. Irresistible. Her feet had nearly been her undoing though, until inspiration struck and she wore her black Doc Martens. Better those than tacky versions of something impossibly uncomfortable with pencil heels. She wanted to look sexy not tarty and anyway, she knew she wouldn't be able to walk on the cobbled city centre streets in high heeled, high end knock offs. Courtney and Kezia seemed to manage fine but they'd had practice and were so classy. No, the Doc Martens looked good in a chic boho sort of way and reassured her; at least she wouldn't twist an ankle. Besides she'd read somewhere that successful actresses worked from the feet up: if they walked in character, they would become the character, live the role rather than just play the part. That's what she would do. She'd ignored the bit that said Greta Garbo always wore slippers for comfort. The last thing Taya wanted was to be alone.

The three of them were in the middle of the night club dance floor, facing each other in a triangle but not self-contained. It was essential to be available for lads who showed interest – lads were okay of course, but older than that would be much better. Real men. There were plenty of lads around, most of whom were known to them from school or were local to the city where Taya had spent her whole foster life. Which was her whole life, more not less, and she never saw her father out of disinterest rather than choice even though he lived quite close. Her foster mothers were pretty awesome actually. They were the ones who had paid for her hair to be corn rowed and it was cool that they lived together; they were even planning to get married which made them even more cool, especially in the eyes of her mates.

"D'they like kiss in front of you n'stuff?" was almost the first thing Courtney had asked when she found about them.

"God, no. D'your parents?" Taya had replied and Courtney had laughed.

"Ugh. My parents don't even speak 'cept to argue. Old people kissing – gross." She had shuddered. "They're old, right?"

"Yeah. Old enough. Been together for years. Same as everyone else really." And nothing more had been said, but Taya knew they were not quite the same: they liked her.

Their dancing was self-contained but public: eyes furtive, kept to themselves but noticing everything male. They moved together but separate; accessible, ready, prepared. Kezia and Courtney were also in red and black; bewitching and enticing with long legs that shimmered over spiked heels, rooted to the dance floor as they shook like reeds in white water through the noise. Sensuous, rippling, melting into the pulse of the room.

"Six pack. Six o'clock." Kezia mouthed the words so the other two thought they heard and immediately jerked their eyes in the given direction.

"Tackle that!" Courtney meant it.

"I wish". Taya did not but said it anyway. She would say whatever she had to. She did not know that sharper eyes had noticed.

"Looking for some fun, girls?" He was tall and disfiguringly thin. He too had hip bones that protruded out into his low-slung jeans like hooks upon which empty trouser legs hung, leading to soiled trainers that had collapsed under fallen arches and trailed the ground. So angular and brittle he might break if his concave chest in the baggy grey T-shirt inhaled too deeply. But it was not his body that commanded attention. Over his head he was wearing a rubber Donald Trump mask, grinning wildly, boiled yellow rubber hair combed and set forever. His simulated throat was cut. It gaped, leering at the girls as blood dripped in latex down his creased, one-size-fits-all mutilated neck which ended abruptly at the top of the T shirt where his torso began. He spoke to the three of them but it was Taya he wanted.

They squealed in mock horror for attention and effect. People turned to look and laugh so they squealed louder. Kezia and Courtney tried to look shocked; Taya did not have to.

"Whatcha' offerin' bro?" Kezia was flirting, snaking her shoulders around him as she shimmied closer. Courtney and Taya maintained vigil a little further off, circling, watching. Listening.

"Best night of yer life" he promised. The smiling mask was grotesque and unchanging, still bleeding as far only as the top of the T shirt, but the voice had life and depth. It was a local accent but deep, male and therefore of interest. Kezia was almost touching him now as she gyrated with the rhythm of the music; he followed her like a mirror reflection, as if tied by invisible strings.

"Oh yeah?" She teased. Come on, impress me. If you can. Courtney seized the gauntlet and slapped the challenge across his smirking face:

"Nah, all talk. What ya got to show?"

The figure twisted slightly to bend to the pull of Kezia's movements then swung itself away and edged towards Taya. A thin arm, tattoo sleeved, bony wristed, nicotine fingered stretched forward and the hand opened, an unlikely bud blossoming in a heavy metal jungle. On the palm of the hand was a plastic sachet, compact, clear, clean, within which sat a nest of orange pills, tiny and round. They glowed with promise; the colour flowed into the noise and shone with allure. Like a magician pulling silk from a pocket he opened the sachet and pulled out a single pill; pollen on a stamen, waiting to be sucked and savoured. There for the taking.

Courtney screamed with derision. "That your idea of a six pack?" She and Kezia laughed at his emaciated frame, his absurd face, his audacity. They have seen it all before; nothing here for them. Now if he had a better bod, or was wearing an expensive watch like a Rolex or something, or even if he spoke with a different accent, they might have been interested.

"Try before you buy, girls. Go sky high!"

"Na. Not me."

"Piss off!"

"I will."

"Taya! No! Don't be stupid." But Donald Trump has chosen well and Taya has fallen for it. She has swallowed the orange promise by the time Courtney has finished speaking and was standing motionless on the swirling floor in her sensible Doc Martens, waiting for Paradise to arrive. And as she stood there with her appalled friends, no one heard the neoprene Donald Trump saying,

"Fly, sister, fly" as he dissolved into the vortex.

On the other side of the city in the Wyeminster Royal Infirmary, Debbie Crawley had just emerged from operating theatre number two. Wide eyed in the suddenly less glaring light of night-time Men's Surgical, she and the ward sister were peering at the patient on the bed below them who had just been delivered like a badly-wrapped, overdue parcel from the recovery room.

"He's lucky I was on call." Debbie's voice was hushed and unexpectedly deep; plump with well-rounded consonants and buttery vowels. It was her one great, alluring quality – gravelly yet smooth, like an enticing stream tumbling seductively over a bed of precious stones, rich, caressing and lustrous. Infinite promise, crumpled bed sheets and tousled hair. Colorectal colleagues from across the country would call her in quiet moments just to hear her speak rather than to use her advice which was although always requested, was rarely implemented but often cited in surgical anecdotes. It was a voice almost impossible to place; carefully bred by a second-rate private school with aspirations to class but no breeding. Much like Debbie herself. Thin rather than slender, potentially tall but habitually hunched she appeared older than her 52 years and a great deal more dated. Her over-long mousey hair, untainted by colouring or conditioner, was tied back at the nape of her neck into an apathetic pony tail that did its best to conceal itself ignominiously between her shoulder blades and to blend in with her black polyester jacket. Ironic really, as the cat hairs from home clung tenaciously to every synthetic fibre, resisting all attempts by washing machine and Sellotape to dislodge them. Her suits have become their permanent abode; they accrue gently as each week progresses, starting hesitantly on Monday but glorying in their abundance by Friday. The reception staff used her as they would a calendar;

clinics on Fridays were always the hairiest day of the week when extra tissues are kept at reception for patients prone to sneezing. The possibility of an anaphylactic reaction to cat hair had been considered but never voiced; she is the self-appointed Head of Department and therefore on the Management Committee by default, because nobody else wanted it. Debbie's own hair was confined within a rubber band of exactly the same stretched, lifeless consistency as the strands within its grasp. Both seemed determined to keep as low a profile as possible, anxious to avoid attention. If they could have escaped they would but alas, both were inextricably and hatefully attached. It's not that she did not have alternatives – senior consultants were well remunerated and she had no one with whom to share her income; this was just more convenient. One year the hospital Secret Santa had presented her with an assortment of clings-like-magic-never-a-stray-hair tie backs which she had every intention of using until her cat had started playing with them and so they immediately became feline property. Sacrosanct. The rubber band had stayed, to the mortification of the hair in its stranglehold. And the split ends despaired and tried to pretend they did not exist, trying hopelessly to escape down the plughole when she washed them on Sundays but succeeding only in angling themselves in pointless swirls over the basin as the water ran away and they were left behind to straggle on for eternity.

The Ward Sister, shorter, plumper, cleaner, older but noticeably more fecund, studied the patient's notes. Debbie spoke for her.

"Gavin Mitcheldean. 63. Mr Yeo's patient. Emergency second colonoscopy to investigate suspected cancerous growth. Mr Mitcheldean is lucky it was a false alarm."

"So is Mr Yeo." The women avoided each other's eyes as they gazed thoughtfully at the prone body, breathing steadily beside their thighs. There was a brief silence before Debbie chirped in, a little too determinedly.

"Mr Yeo is a very busy man, Sister, with a great many private patients to look after in addition to his numerous responsibilities in our own hospital. We must allow for the occasional oversight. After all, consultants are only human." Did she mean that? Was it a flippant remark? Should she laugh? Smile even? The Ward Sister was not sure so decided not to respond. She sighed. It was always so difficult to tell with Miss Crawley and it was going to be a long night. God, how she hated Halloween and Christmas and bank holidays and New Year. Especially New Year.

"Does Mr Yeo know about the admission?" He would not be happy that was for sure and she really did not want to be the one to tell him. Let consultants fight their own battles. God knows, there were enough of them – consultants and battles. No wonder Miss

Crawley's nickname was Creepy. Not even vaguely funny anymore.

"I'll take care of that. Leave the paperwork to me" Debbie reassured. She would indeed. Paperwork was her speciality.

At the same moment Taya was also comatose, badly wrapped and straddled across a pavement kerb in a dim Wyeminster back street where she had collapsed. Her breathing was irregular, her unseeing eyes dilated empty black and her red painted lips were turning a deep bruise purple. The red bodycon dress had become a jeering shroud.

"Taya! Taya! Look at me! Stay awake!" Kezia was frantically shaking the unresponsive body, too heavy to lift, inert and cumbersome. Courtney, the sensible one, was on her phone.

"Breathing, yeah... No, not responding ...Kezia. Where are we?"

"Dunno". Both the girls look around them. Everything looked so different in the dark when the shops were grilled shut and the street lights little more than a blur to save money for resentful rate payers by a politically insecure county council.

"Behind that posh outdoor country shop place with the dead animals in the window." Kezia was really trying to help. "Y'know, opposite the smelly bath bomb shop".

Courtney waited; the emergency services' operator waited; Taya's breathing faltered.

"Lower Aldgate! Yeah, that's it. She's really ill, Courtney. Tell them to hurry. I think she's dying."

The ambulance arrived in a rush of light and noise, unearthly, haloed in blue, a white knight in street-streaked armour panting heavily on wheels while the bulky green men loaded the red girl into its belly. It left with a roar and screamed into the darkness. Kezia and Courtney stood spellbound; bystanders in a still life as the dimly lit stillness settled once more into darkness and silence.

The rocking of the ambulance on cobble stones distorted everything except Taya who lay inert, oblivious to her body straining inside the straps holding her onto the trolley.

"Bugger!" the paramedic grunted as he was flung across his patient as the vehicle lurched to avoid a coven of witches and a red light. That was good news though, one more violent lurch and they would be turning sharp right into the narrow lane leading to the Wyeminster A&E department. Ever since the new hospital had been built close to the railway station and the out of town shopping mall, the access road had been a source of contention, not least to the occupants of the houses alongside who could not park their cars on the street and who impotently objected to the noise and commotion of endless traffic. The ambulance drivers also hated it: narrow, confined and necessary to cross the drop off circle outside the main entrance before they could reach the Holy Grail of ER medical assistance.

“Nearly there! Hold on.” So came the violent swerve and they were on a straight run home – no one visiting or dithering in the turning circle at this time of night. Suddenly there was a screech. The wheels squealed. Squawked. And stopped.

“What’s happening?” Why’ve we stopped?”

“There’s a bloody queue.”

“A queue? How long?” The paramedic with Taya was looking at her with increasing concern. She was on a drip and oxygen; her pallid face has folded away from the mask clamped to her nose, her eyebrows were forgotten lines falling into her ears, her once red mouth was thin and darkly purple. He looked at the screen charting her blood pressure which was spiralling downwards. Now the ambulance was still but it was Taya who was moving, jerking, writhing in spasms, her chest pulling away from her limbs which stiffened and twitched and all the time her eyes were blank, black holes in her contorting head.

“She’s fitting! We need to get her in now. Do something!” Then, in a quieter but even more desperate voice,

“Stay with me, Taya. Stay with me.”

The belly of the vehicle opened with a metallic clatter, the doors were slung apart as the face of the driver appeared in the widening gap.

"We'll wheel her."

"We're losing her."

"No bloody way. Not on my watch. She's just a kid." The trolley was flung from the back of the van onto the black road and landed heavily with a thump, wheels spinning as the two men hurled themselves behind it. They propelled it past the line of panting ambulances, smashing into the kerb and bouncing towards the disabled ramp leading into the side of the emergency department entrance, ahead of the careful unloading of the ambulances waiting ahead of them. The paramedics were sweating; Taya was twitching like a marionette on strings pulled by an invisible hand: a dance macabre on an NHS trolley, performing on a moving stage illuminated with blue and red and white lights flashing like an old-fashioned picture lantern where dark figures dart and jerk into life.

She knew it was wrong and totally against hospital policy but if she did not have a fix soon, she would expire. Her shift had started at 8.00 pm but had forever to run. There had been no time for even a cup of coffee, never mind something to eat – what was the hospital policy on that she wondered – so if she had to have a slug of nicotine to keep her going, well, that wasn't her fault was it? Lizzie Gilbert was the

Emergency Department Sister and was well fed up with the evening. Hallow bloody 'een. Everyone else out having fun and she was working, again. It wasn't even as if the money was good. Hell, she wondered, why did she bother? But she already knew the answer so no point in going on about it – nothing else in Wyeminster and at least she liked the people she worked with. Mostly. Besides, it was her home town, familiar, safe and most importantly, where Andy lived. The main reason for staying there in fact. Andy. Her Andy. Not the greatest man in the world but her man. Just the thought of him made her smile as she exhaled, forcing her mouth into an ungainly grimace as she tilted back her head and watched the smoke dissipate into the cold air. The end of the cigarette glowed warmly beyond her fingers with the promise of calm and relaxation. She felt her nerves quieten as she leant a little further back against the wall outside the heaving innards of the ER department. Screened by a strategic hedge this was a popular retreat for those members of staff who still smoked and, she smirked, had they known, the Hospital Board would have been mortified by the number and seniority of those who did. She inhaled deeply, felt her taut nerves untangle and relaxed a little more. Obviously, she should not have left Analyn to cope on her own but it was only for a moment. Not her fault if the agency nurses could not understand English. It was bad enough that she had to double check everything they did: took twice as long to do anything and always on the busiest nights. Through the hedge she could see the ambulances waiting to disgorge their cargoes. It was never ending.

Her phone began to vibrate against her leg. Thank God it was still on silent so no one would detect her; she needed a few more minutes to herself. As she fished in her pocket with her free hand to retrieve it, the sleeve of her uniform shifted upwards revealing the snarling Salamander dragon descending from her shoulder towards the soft white flesh of her inner arm. The tattoo had been Andy's idea. He had, over time, covered almost all his torso with exotic beasts and coiling reptiles. They nested and crouched in every crease, displayed themselves over smooth flesh and writhed alive with every twist and turn of their hosts' narrow body. People mistook Lizzie's Salamander for an ordinary dragon and she rarely disabused them. No, he was her creature, hers and Andy's and she liked to keep it that way. Since knowing Andy, she had progressively covered her body with inky art but only within the borders of the Wyeminster Royal regulation blue uniform. What went on within those borders was nobody's business but her own and Andy's. She would do anything for him.

"Hi Babe." She loved it when he called her, especially at work. "You OK?" She beamed into the phone.

Yes. Fine. But he had a request. Something she could do just for him. The smile on her face fell away as she listened and the cigarette burned forgotten between her fingers.

"Andy! I can't do that, even for you."

Didn't she love him?

"Yes. Of course. You know I do."

Then she wouldn't mind doing this one thing for him, would she? It wasn't much to ask.

"But Andy. This is Fentanyl we're talking about." Hastily she dropped her voice and looked around to ensure no one was within hearing. All clear but she hushed her voice, just in case. "It's not like it's aspirin or Gaviscon." A brief pause then her voice became high pitched and pained. "That's not fair! You know I do! You're the best thing that ever happened to me."

Suddenly the trolley carrying Taya propelled by the sweating paramedics hurtled into view on the other side of the thin hedge. Lizzie's voice became assertive and proactive. "Got to go." She snapped Andy and the phone shut, lobbed the dying cigarette to the ground below to be trodden into the detritus of other clandestine smokers and flung herself in the direction of the approaching trolley.

"This way, boys. Follow me." Grabbing the metal to help accelerate the pace she glanced at the patient beside her hand. Purple lips, dilated eyes, irregular breathing. It looked like an opiate poisoning but whatever it was, the girl was obviously in a bad way.

Like a monstrous 'Open Sesame' the Emergency Department doors swung themselves open to reveal the grotesque fairy tale world of an NHS Hospital on a busy night. Timeless but of its time; pain and suffering the same the world over; the smell of fear, anguish and chemicals. It was pandemonium. Dante's Inferno in medical form and fancy dress. Even the seasoned paramedics were halted momentarily by the sight before them: every seat in the waiting area was occupied; people sat on the floor or leant against the walls; some lay on trolleys lined up in the corridors like customers at a drive thru' MacDonald's. Many of the patients, and even more of their companions were drunk and oblivious; there was little blood but a great deal of anger. At the unenviable eye of the storm was the hapless Analyn de Rosales, the innocent victim of a national nursing agency that specialised in providing well qualified personnel for any medical situation, even at the shortest notice. She was doing her best but her limited mastery of the English language, especially in this provincial part of a strange country with an impenetrable accent was deeply perplexing. She knew she could be a good nurse; she just did not know what they are saying.

"Please. All must wait." They were flooding through the system; Reception has processed them and now they all wanted to be seen, at once.

"Please to wait."

"Wait? Wait? My girlfriend can't wait. She needs help now." Analyn turned around to address the voice behind her. A man, dressed as a zombie, white faced, black eyed, dripping blood from a crudely ink-stitched mouth above a torn ketchup-encrusted shirt was supporting a similarly attired girl, except that her face was even whiter than her make-up and her eyes were mascara laden slits in a face hanging as if by a thread to lank, vomit-stained hair.

“She’s really ill. Look! She’s unconscious.”

She was incomprehensibly drunk but Analyn cannot say this, even if she knew how.

“Many people. Please, sit.”

“No, I won’t bloody sit. I want to see a doctor!” The zombie was shouting and heads turned with interest.

A skeleton took up the cudgels.

“We all do, mate. You’ll just have to wait, like the rest of us.” Analyn looked gratefully at the man dressed in black with a perfect anatomical representation of the human bone structure about his person. His head was concealed inside a rubber skull through which his eyes weirdly flickered; his words were a little muffled but perfectly understood by the zombie who muttered and grumbled but slumped down onto the floor with his girlfriend on his lap. No sooner had they descended into their putrefied pieta than Taya was rushed through the doors.

“Out the way, everyone! Coming through.” That was the Emergency Department Sister wasn’t it? With the young girl on the trolley. It must be bad. People parted seamlessly like water.

"Crash Team!" The doors to Acute Care were closing behind them even as Lizzie called out.

Chapter Four

The Same Night. Wyeminster.

"Trick or treat?"

Fun not a threat. No one ever refused anyway. The small groups of wildly dressed kids would not know what to do if they did; it never occurred to them. No, this was an opportunity for an uncontrolled free sugar fest as well as the chance to metamorphose into the acceptably unspeakable, the coveted nightmare world of video games and the HD screen. Glorious hours had been spent in the preparation and planning, trawling the charity shops for garments to dismember and maim, begging, stealing and borrowing garish make up with which to disfigure their faces and decorate their bodies. Blood, gore, scars and weeping wounds: a parody of the surgeon's art; sick cosmetic surgery. Perverted, abnormal, innocent and adored. All the horror and none of the pain, with confectionary as a reward.

The five boys – not old enough even to be proper lads – Year 7 pupils and inseparable in spite of streaming in Maths and English, have planned their outing down to the last, bloody detail. Their route will take them away from their homes into streets just a little way removed, with the obligatory parental consent of course, but not a single adult with them. Curfew is 10.30 which is OK. Half an hour later would have been better but by then the occupants of the chosen streets would probably be sweeted out so they would only get manky fruit or biscuits hastily salvaged from the bottom of tins. Probably not even chocolate biscuits at that. Last year someone in desperation had slipped them some loose change but it had not amounted to much when split five ways. Comestibles were always better. The trick was to target streets less likely to be visited by other erstwhile bands of marauders or at least to get there before they did. So far, their haul had been good and even though they had already ingested a great deal of sugar, there was plenty more to go. In the distance could be heard intermittent police sirens and the constant low grumble of traffic on the ring road, even at this time of night but in the street, it is quiet and the boys have a clear run.

"Knock and then we'll say it again."

"Go on Josh. Your turn." The smallest of them, dressed as a diminutive Incredible Hulk without biceps or shoulders but sporting disproportionately large amounts of blood on his face and arms steps up to the Victorian door and hammers his knuckles ineffectively against perfect paint. Fortunately, he is expected. Jennie Parrish has been waiting with almost as much anticipation as the boys themselves. She loves events like this; they alleviate her loneliness and remind her of the grandchildren she never sees. Since her marriage broke up twenty-five years ago and she left London for Wyeminster with the proceeds of a terraced house in Richmond, sadly before it was worth millions, she has led a largely solitary life. By choice in the main, but it hurt her far more than the loss of her husband when her daughter joined forces with a Canadian, produced three children then departed with him to his home country. Not just Canada, as if that was not bad enough but the farthest west she could go, to Vancouver Island. On Jennie's income it might as well have been the dark side of the moon. So, she looked forward to the company of Trick or Treaters, carol singers, cold callers, Mormon missionaries and even Jehovah's Witnesses with pathetic enthusiasm. She was ready for the juvenile extortioners with a stock of sweets accrued weeks in advance. The boys had struck lucky.

As the petite Incredible Hulk flung his smooth knuckles against her front door she waited, just a moment, then opened it with a flourish and assumed an expression of fear well practiced in front of the bathroom mirror.

"Trick or Treat?" they shouted at her in unison.

"Treat!" she responded with girlish horror. "Treat! No tricks!"

The boys smiled ingratiatingly behind their masks. Jennie also grinned at the motley youths pertaining to be icons of terror and stepped back into the hall to collect some of the confectionary amassed on the table. She selected a family size pack of Skittles – enough sugar and e numbers to keep them on the ceiling for several hours – and was about to hand them over when she hesitated, seeing their small hands clad in clumsy gloves, plastic dead men's fingers and curled against the cold.

"Want me to open it?" she asks.

"Yes please." Such nice, polite boys she thinks. Probably from the Grammar School. She enthusiastically pulled the top of the packet apart and handed it over into the green digits of the Hulk.

"Don't eat them all at once. Have a nice night."

"Thanks, Miss." They were already starting to shovel them down as she shut the door, hoping that another set of petty blackmailers would assail her very soon.

The high produced by the illicit nicotine had long since worn off and Lizzie battled on. Thankfully the queue of ambulances has finally been cleared and the onset of patients has steadied to a constant flow rather than a tsunami. For the present. There was quite a party atmosphere amongst those waiting; an air of raucous macabre enjoyment of their joint plight as they were forced to sit apparently endlessly until it was their turn to be treated. A perverted Blitz mentality; zombies, witches, ghosts, several Frankensteins, one partially unwrapped Mummy and assorted criminals all waited, mostly cheerfully and extremely noisily, for tetanus shots, stitches, X rays and in one case, almost certainly a stomach pump. Leaving them for the moment in the care of the hapless Analyn, Lizzie headed down the corridor towards Acute Care to get an update on the young girl who had been brought in earlier. Although not strictly in her care, having helped the paramedics wheel her into the arms of the Crash Team and a chance of life, Lizzie was curious to know what was happening. Taya she was called. Nice name. A bit unusual for round here. Wonder if she's local thought Lizzie as her thin legs in dark tights and sensible flats trod the familiar hard hospital floors.

"Lizzie Gilbert! Light of my life!"

Oh God. Rohan bloody Patel. Lizzie smiled mirthlessly and tried to look pleased to see him. Rohan. Affable, plump, soft bodied and mushy, prone to sweat and always profusely. A Trust Grade Anaesthetist and competent medic, his unwanted attention to anything remotely female – no matter how remote – was matched only by his resolute lack of ambition. Political correctness and the emancipation of women have completely passed him by but his fleshly intentions were so innocuous and ineffective that he had earned the dubious distinction of becoming a laughable sex pest, an endless source of denigration and entertainment; a sort of carnal class clown. He liked to look but never got the opportunity to touch. There was no one that would be that stupid or desperate and everyone knew he would not know what to do anyway. Good old Rohan they said. What a jerk! It was only during Ramadan when hunger made him ratty rather than just a pest that he actually annoyed people. The fact that he had a wife and several children produced incredulous laughter rather than sympathy. It was impossible to take him that seriously.

“Hi Rohan.”

“Ah, Lizzie. Always so alluring.” Rohan had by now sidled up to his colleague and was sweatily close to her; she could see the moisture on his upper lip and he exuded an old, wet dog smell.

“Andy wouldn’t like to hear you saying that.” Lizzie had decided to implement the ‘when in doubt bring in the boyfriend/husband/male partner’ tactic which generally convinced Rohan to back off to a more comfortable level of lechery.

“Your boyfriend is a very lucky man” he responded wistfully. Are you seeing him tonight?”

Lizzie had to give the man marks for persistence but not logicality: weren’t they both on duty in the hospital?

“Not tonight, Rohan. Not with that lot out there. Quite lively this evening, aren’t they?” As if by answer, Analyn could be heard vainly entreating everyone to be patient and to wait, please. They ignored her.

“Anyway, he’s working too.” Lizzie was not entirely sure about that or indeed, exactly what the nature of Andy’s current employment happened to be, but it was enough to keep Rohan at bay. Andy was an entrepreneur. He saw opportunities and took them. Lizzie was proud of his initiative and spontaneity. His income was variable but hers was not, so together they made a good team. She liked to think of herself as the stable foundation upon which he would build his economic empire; she was his rock and he, her inspiration and vocation. Her misgivings about the phone call earlier began to be appeased. Andy knew what he was doing. She trusted him. If he wanted Fentanyl it must for a good reason.

True to form, Rohan was persisting.

“How about a little party of our own, out here?” He edged closer to her. Any moment now she expected to see him dart out a wet tongue and lick his lips. Well, two could play at that game. Sensing an opportunity but not the opportunity that Rohan had in mind, Lizzie leant into his softness so that she was almost touching him. Close enough for him to smell her skin, for her straw-bleached, blonde hair to tickle his tawny ear, for the echo of nicotine on her breath to vibrate the black wiry hairs in his cavernous nostrils.

“Oh, Rohan! Where everyone can see us?”

He was astonished. Was she serious? This was unprecedented. Unexpected and highly gratifying. Go with it he told himself.

“Well, not here but, maybe, later?” A deep look into her watery blue eyes which, he noticed, contained flecks of grey like dust beams. Charming. “Anything I can do for you, Lizzie, you just have to say. You know that, don’t you?”

“Oh, Rohan, I do. I do.”

For a moment Rohan was suspicious but lust overcame caution and he began to play the game in earnest, marvelling at his own wit and ingenuity.

"Trick or treat, Lizzie?"

Her head had archly tilted to one side and she was looking at him sideways, eyes narrowed, mouth tantalisingly half smiling, lips slightly parted.

"You'll have to find out." Then she had winked at him and was walking back towards the waiting area where Analyn's tones of entreaty were becoming more desperate as the volume of noise increased to raucous.

"Please to sit" she was imploring. "Everyone. Patience."

"Yeah, we are! Tell us something we don't know!"

The subsequent laughter officially raises the level of disturbance to that of a near riot. Much more and the police would have to be called. Again.

Huddled around the open bag of Skittles on the street outside Jennie's house, the boys did not see the tall, thin man in the Donald Trump mask until he was standing over them. The light from the street lamp cast his grotesque shadow and contorted features over the hands they had plunged into the packet of sweets and when they looked up to investigate the shadowy intrusion, they were struck with a delicious horror. Donald Trump with his fixed blood and gaping neck let them gasp and exclaim before they started laughing, a little too loudly to disguise their discomfort.

Joshua was transfixed and said nothing. His friend covered in a once white sheet with small round holes cut out for eyes and a crude black, open mouth howling silently aloud painted below spoke for the group,

“Cool, man!”

“Yo! Trick or Treat?” Donald focused on the grubby phantom but his question was directed to them all.

No need to confer.

“Treat!”

“Yeah! Treat!”

Then in unison as at a football match,

“Treat! Treat! Treat! Treat!”

Like a benevolent uncle at Christmas the tall man put his hands enticingly behind his back. In a tacitly understood gesture they knew that one of the closed fists would contain a hidden delight. Now they had to choose, and choose well.

“Which hand?” the alluring benefactor teases.

A moment’s hesitation and this time they did confer, heads together, murmuring agitatedly, greedily. Who would take the responsibility?

"You do it." The phantom had been given the voice but did not use it. He pointed instead at Donald's right arm and the boys held their breath.

"Yo! Treat! Good choice! Boys done good".

They grinned and waited for their reward. The man's right hand appeared before them and he uncurled his closed fist, palm up. Two small, smooth, orange orbs glowed in the semi-light, fluorescent, innocent.

"One for you" the man said and handed one to Joshua "and one for the bag". He dropped the other into the bag of sweets and began to retreat. "Yo, bros. Adios." Then he had turned and was rapidly striding down the street away from the city centre, out into the dim suburbs, a lanky figure with an over large head receding into the darkness.

Again, the boys were huddled together but now they were examining the single pill on the unlined open palm of their friend. His hand is barely out of childhood, soft, virgin, yet to experience blistering hard work, the clasp of a lover, the pain of growing up. On its top it has been coloured green as part of the Incredible Hulk costume but underneath, it remains pure and unblemished.

"What is it?" Not the phantom this time but a skinny zombie. "A sweet?

"Dunno." The ghost was squinting through his eyeholes and bending down over the luminous temptation for a better view. Joshua decided to seize the advantage.

“Only one way to find out.” He snatched it away from the scrutiny of the group and directly from the palm of his hand, cast it into his mouth and began to chew.

“Josh! Don’t!”

Too late. He already has. It tastes foul.

“Ugh!” Inside his mask his face has twisted into a far more horrifying mask than the one he wears and he spits out the small portion of the pill he has not swallowed. “It’s disgusting.”

Now the zombie is the group spokesman.

“You’re a bloody moron, Josh.”

Chapter Five

Endless Night. Wyeminster

The self-importantly labelled Laundry Room in Wyeminster Royal was more of a cupboard than a room but it was warm and dry, quiet and comforting, far removed from the clamour and chaos of the Emergency Department. It smelt of starch and childhood. Lizzie relished the rare moments when she was obliged to visit. Her mission this evening was an unexpected pleasure, a welcome respite and she had seized the moment ahead of anyone else – not many perks to being a Sister but this was one of them. Only she could disappear from duty with good reason while the other nurses had to stick it out. They were completely out of clean sheets for the narrow beds in the consultation cubicles thanks to the influx of clients as the Hospital Trust liked to call them. Usually the supply of linen kept up with demand, even on very busy nights, but thanks to the fancy-dress costumes of the occasion the bed linen was rapidly becoming soiled with fake blood, garish make up, inexpertly applied temporary hair dye and a palette of other unfixed colours that were being transferred on to the white NHS cotton sheets with the energy of a Jackson Pollock painting.

The overhead light was calmingly low wattage and she had shut the door behind her. Taking her time, luxuriating in the solitude, she sauntered over to the far side of the room where spare sheets were stored in regimental rows, straight from the external laundry, clean, machine pressed, tight and heavy. One of the enduring pleasures of her profession was the act of shaking out a newly laundered sheet before putting it onto a mattress. She loved the wind-blown sound of the fabric unfolding itself with a crispy slap, like a flag in a stiff breeze. The soft smell of fresh cleanliness reminded her of summer, the outside world, freedom. She inhaled deeply as she stretched up to one of the higher shelves, standing on her toes within her sensible shoes. Then shock nearly caused her to topple over.

Two hands were clasped around her waist, slithering upwards towards her breasts. Pudgy, soft hands, damp and determined. From close behind she felt rather than heard words being whispered into her ear.

"Trick or treat?

"Bloody hell, Rohan! What are you doing?" Vainly she tried to disentangle herself from his creeping hands. She dropped back on her feet and tried to twist herself downwards and sideways but clearly, he had anticipated such a manoeuvre and met it head on, limpet-like. Indomitable. The hot, wet words continued.

"What about a treat for me, eh, Lizzie?" Had he been able to see the expression on her face, Rohan might have desisted but lechery and opportunity had for the first-time crossed paths and Rohan was tenacious.

Lizzie grimaced. Then resolved. It was for Andy, after all.

"You'll have to do something for me."

"Oh Lizzie! Anything." The words were a little indistinct as he was trying to nibble her ear as he spoke, but Rohan meant what he said. His idea of anything however was not quite the same as Lizzie's. With difficulty she managed to rotate herself until she was looking at her suitor. They were face to close face, his hands firmly rooted to her waist having been equally firmly pushed away from her small but out of bounds breasts. She leant forward, her hands over his to prevent further roaming about her person, and whispered into his ear. She felt him tauten and retract himself a little, although he never let go of her or even relaxed his grip.

"I don't know. It's not right. And it's risky. What if we got caught?"

"But worth it? Or don't you think so?" A challenge. Twisted courtly love; faint heart never won fair lady. Or Lizzie. The plump knight in crocs hesitated, just for a moment, then assented. Wholeheartedly.

"Yes!"

Outside the hospital it continued deep dark, in spite of the orange glow of the halo of city lights in the night sky, visible for miles above the black stone of the cathedral but not enough to illuminate the kerbs and paving stones at its feet. In the street outside Jennie Parrish's house four boys were standing over the lifeless body of Joshua, green, incredible but not hulk, straddled over the kerb edge. His mask has been removed and his face, strangely pallid, glowed with the reflected colour of his costume with an unearthly translucence that accentuated the deepening purple of his lips. He was breathing, erratically. One of them, the zombie, was panting with uncharacteristic vigour having run to the summon help from the last house they visited. Jennie had opened the door with anticipation, prepared for more mock horror. Instead she found herself now out in the cold street on her mobile phone summoning an ambulance. The phantom had removed Joshua's mask and held it, flaccid and rubbery in his hand as he stared down at the body through the eye holes in his costume. It looked as if he was holding a shrunken severed head, blood drained, toxic green, shrivelled. The only movement was from Jennie's voice: assertive, sensible, grown up.

"Emergency. Ambulance ... A child." Not even a boy now. "Yes, he's unconscious. About ten or eleven?" She looked at the others for confirmation of his age and they nodded as she continued talking into the mobile. "He's breathing, just. Not regularly. I think he's dying."

Blue lights, white noise, black noise, paramedics in green, more lights - white, red, green, squealing brakes and protesting tyres, metal against metal slamming doors, the sigh of the opening Emergency Department doors that never rest and their exhalation as they shut and inhale before their next breach. Then the fluorescent overhead lights inside Wyeminster Royal and the rubbery hiss of trolley wheels on hard polished floors as Joshua is propelled through the waiting area directly into Acute Care where the Crash Team are waiting. They fall on him as vultures over carrion, blue clad, wielding monitors, tubes, masks, electrodes, syringes in a determined routine that puzzles and stuns unfamiliar onlookers. It looks like chaos but they know what they are doing; have done so many times before it is almost routine except that each time it is a different life and someone else's world that might implode. The team concentrate; they have a job to do. They care, but concentrate more; sentimentality merely gets in the way. Emergency Department Consultant Sesi Adebayo has full control of the situation, again. It was turning out to be quite a night. She had trained in Birmingham where an evening like this was normal but in Wyeminster it was unprecedented. Sleepy Wyeminster; a step down in her career in order to take a step up; E.D. Consultant in her early 30s with a few years in a relatively small department before applying for a much more succulent appointment in a big city, in a centre of medical excellence. That was the aim so an evening like this one was to be relished, if that was the right word. She did not want people to be critically ill, obviously, but it was so much more interesting when they were.

“Resus stand by. Blood pressure, Lizzie?”

“Low and falling.”

“Bloods please. We need liver and renal function and a tox screen on this one. Intubation done? Okay, ventilate him, Rohan... Rohan?”

“Yeah. Sorry. On it, Sesi.” Rohan has been mesmerised by the sight of Lizzie drawing blood from the cannula in the unconscious boy’s inner elbow, white and pale against the hastily rolled up lime-coloured sleeve of his costume, filling three phials with the sticky red lifeline. The arm lies small, thin, motionless and limp, the hand slightly curled as a baby’s at rest but the finger nails bitten short and smeared green, especially on the on the cuticles where his makeup has caught and clung. His eyes are open but unseeing, the pupils barely discernible pin pricks within huge black empty orbs.

“What’s the story?” The words are thrown over Sesi’s shoulder towards the paramedics who have brought him in.

“Joshua Critchley. Aged 11. Unknown ingested substance. Parents on their way.”

“Any idea what he’s eaten?”

“Not yet. Some sort of pill apparently but don’t know what. Police are on it.”

“An opiate by the look of him”. Amidst the humming, buzzing monitors, wheezing ventilator, raucous decibels of the reception area, padding feet interspersed by swishing curtains and Sesi's instructions, Joshua lay oblivious. His lips and nails were darkening into purple splodges, the green on his cuticles like grass verges beside murky pools of polluted water. No sound or touch was within his reach. His breathing inside the ventilator was laboured and painful. Sesi's beautiful, seamless, ebony face was creased with concern.

The police officers, all four of them for an incident involving a minor who has now been blue-lighted to hospital, were indeed on it. They were all over it. Two of them were taking details from Joshua's friends; a theatrical parody as the boys in blue interviewed creatures of the night, on a night-time stage illuminated by the dim lights of a narrow city street. Jennie has stayed with them, rung their parents and fretted. She knew the sweets she gave them were fine; no, the packet had been closed until she herself opened it. No one could possibly have tampered with them. How could they? They had gone straight from the supermarket – she had the receipt somewhere – onto her hall table. It must have happened after they left her house. It had. The boys said so. Holding the open bag of Skittles tentatively between finger and thumb tips, one of the police officers dropped it into a transparent plastic evidence bag and sealed it while his colleague stared.

"What do you mean, Donald Trump? The President of America? Are you sure?"

Vigorous nodding.

"With his throat cut?"

More nodding.

"Well. That narrows the search a bit, in one way, but rather widens it in another." He looked at his colleague holding the Skittles in their plastic casing and then at the other two officers investigating the spot where Joshua had been found. "We have absolutely no idea who we're looking for."

Sesi had taken Lizzie and Rohan to one side. Joshua was still lying on a trolley in Acute Care, insignificant, green and purple, intubated, ventilated.

"We need that blood report as soon as we can, Lizzie. Can you chase it up? I'm going to page Miss Crawley in Colorectal and Mr Alsop in Imaging for a scan. And then Toxicology. The parents?" This to Rohan.

"Outside. I'll see them if you like."

"Yes, that'd be good. Thanks, Rohan. I'll talk to them properly when we've got something to report. There's nothing to say yet and we've got the police in on this one."

"And on the girl in Critical Care who came in earlier" added Lizzie.

"Yes, same presentation." Sesi had an earnest glint in her eye. "I think we may be dealing with something big."

Chapter Six

The Same Night

Debbie Crawley liked being on call with Nigel. It brought them closer together, she felt, so she doctored the on-call duty roster wherever possible in her capacity as self-proclaimed Head of Colorectal, (she had often been heard to assert that she was the most senior surgeon) so that she and he could share an out of hours timetable. Nigel's office in Imaging was cosy somehow, especially late at night. It was so comfortable, so personal to be sitting with him, sharing a cup of coffee in the small, quiet embryonic office nestled within the noisy bustle of the rest of the hospital. Imaging was always a quiet place; calm, unhurried, people secreted in cubby holes and behind screens away from their patients while the discreet noise of technology whirred and clicked. She envied the unobtrusive largely sedentary control Nigel wielded as the Senior Consultant Radiologist, all from this small room. He watched, studied, decided, reported and recommended; never a raised voice or a hurried moment. She had never been able to interpret an X-ray or scan and relied so much on the skill and reporting of people like Nigel. That was what she liked about him she mused as she gazed at him in the almost romantic light of the lamp on his desk. They had eschewed the harsh overhead lights in order to enjoy an unobtrusive, undetected cup of coffee. Maybe even a biscuit. Nigel was so dependable. Steady. Just the sort of man her father would have approved of. It was a pity about the ex-wife and adult children but they were long ago and Nigel, being such a gentleman, had such a civilised relationship with the ex-Mrs Alsop. Who still persisted in calling herself Mrs Alsop. And Nigel did not mind. Such a long-suffering man, so forgiving. If Debbie had known how much of his income Nigel still invested in the ex-Mrs Alsop, she might not have been so sanguine, but Nigel kept money matters to himself. Besides, he liked his ex-wife. Had always liked her and now that sex was not required, liked her even more. Debbie could learn much from her about how to present herself he often thought. All those cat hairs! And those terrible polyester suits which never looked quite clean. She was earning enough to buy decent clothes so why didn't she? His ex-wife had always looked so ... fragrant; fresh. Smart but not showy, she worked wonders on her clothes allowance which, even he had to admit with the benefit of hindsight, had been a little on the ungenerous side. Debbie on the other hand had a used, second-hand air about her which was odd as he knew that there had been no one in her life before him and certainly nothing carnal. Ugh. The thought of it made him recoil. Even the word was enough to make him shudder.

"Are you cold, Nigel?" Solicitous, doe-eyed, grubby grey in the subdued lighting, Debbie had noticed her beloved shiver and was concerned. "You're not going down with something?"

Nigel shook his head slightly and grunted in the negative. A man of few words. Most of his conversations were internal.

“The hospital is too warm. I’ve often said it. A waste of resources and money. Patients expect too much.”

Nigel grunted but it was unclear whether or not he agreed.

“This is nice.” Debbie again, coyly. Nigel ignored her and took a sizeable slurp of his coffee. The sound resonated around the room and seemed to make the light flicker. Anyone else and Debbie would have made a sour remark about noisy eating and reprehensible table manners. No matter that she nibbled her food at the front of her mouth with sharp little bites of her incisors like a rabbit.

“Just us. A moment of P&Q.” Nigel took another hefty draught of the supermarket brand instant coffee and swallowed it loudly in a single gulp.

“Halloween!” Debbie spat out the word. “I don’t understand this obsession for dressing up. So puerile. Is that what one has to do to have a good time?” It was not meant to be rhetorical but Nigel offered no reply so she answered herself. “They look ridiculous. So vulgar.”

A grunt of assent so she continued. “I’m glad we’re not like that.” He sighed. She misinterpreted it. “This is so much more enjoyable but,” and here she sighed in sympathy, “so much paperwork. Always so much paperwork. I really don't know what the NHS is coming to."

Now Nigel spoke. Non-descript, accentless but not privileged, ordinary. "Notes from the Multi-Disciplinary Team Meeting? I haven't even looked at them yet.

"No, an incident form on Tommy Yeo."

"Another one?"

"He's a menace, Nigel." She loved saying his name and did so at every available opportunity. "Yeo ought to be stopped. I've lost count of the number of times I've had to intervene in his cases, invariably when I'm on call and there's no one else to do it. If he was as attentive to his NHS patients as he is to his private practice then none of this would be necessary. But it's all about the money with him."

If Nigel had a comment to make the moment was lost in the sudden, strident explosion of both their pagers going off simultaneously. Now they both sighed, in unison. Nigel put down his coffee and Debbie laid her biro on the desk and they examined their messages. Neither spoke, both casually finished their drinks and put their dirty mugs down, side by side on the desk alongside Tommy Yeo's almost completed incident form and stood up, resignedly, languidly. Another emergency. Without urgency or interest, they moved towards the door and their summons. Nigel went first and Debbie followed, having picked up the paperwork from the desk which she folded in half and tucked safely in the inner pocket of her hairy jacket. Then they headed off in separate directions, he to X-Ray and she to Colorectal.

Across the city other pagers were trilling and vibrating. Sesi had been right – it was big. The biggest thing to hit Wyeminster in years and surely guaranteed to bring them national recognition, possibly even international. The pagers were the advance guard, the scouting party for the onslaught to follow. In his wife's Chinese restaurant - Singaporean street food a speciality as stated by Trip Advisor - Tommy Yeo was helping out in front of house. They were always busy but occasions such as Halloween were frantic, especially as the night wore on and pubs and clubs closed. Alcohol served only to make people hungrier and less patient; the takeaway side of the business was working beyond capacity. Temperatures in the kitchen were reaching the unbearable but no one would stop or complain. They never did, not as long as there was money to be made. On the far side of the restaurant was a large group of medical staff from the hospital and he almost smiled as they all registered their insistent call to arms at exactly the same moment. Like a clutch of hens their heads bobbed down to read text messages then bobbed up again as they clucked to each other then bustled out of their seats to leave. As one, hands were thrust into pockets and handbags, money was hastily dumped in the centre of the table and then they departed, carrying coats they did not have time to put on, texting and phoning as they wove their way through the other diners and out of the double doors like fancy dress flotsam on a fast-flowing stream. There would be a substantial profit in the hasty overpayments on the table; everyone always wanted to be sure they had more than paid their share. However, no time to count the profits. He too had to go. Slightly built but deceptively strong and well-toned thanks to a regime of early morning running in all weathers, Tommy spoke briefly in Cantonese to one of the waiters then loped briskly after the exiting medics. The hospital was close enough to walk. All steps now led that way. A group of nurses, unrecognisable outside their uniform, heavily made up, slightly pissed and stumbling in high heels on the cobbled streets near the cathedral were rapidly sobering up as they answered the rallying cry and focusing on finding the hospital through poor light and alcoholic haze. When they arrived strong coffee and reality would restore them to full working order.

Juan Morales was comfortably settled in front of a computer screen playing online poker. He was winning but his face expressed nothing. Part of his strategy for success was the discipline he applied to his game. He would metaphorically recreate the game in his room; his opponents were seated around the table with him. To win he had to behave with consummate professionalism, absolute precision, without emotion or facial expression. And he did win. Not every time, but often enough to ensure a remarkably healthy bank balance and a portfolio of investments that surprised even him when he made his annual tax return. His finances were micro managed by only himself, with discretion and detail – his mantra. The online poker account was kept scrupulously discreet and separate from everything else. Profits were transferred out but additional money was never paid in. The account had to live or die by poker alone. No one could really call him a gambler, Juan had often thought - he was more of a mathematician, a connoisseur of the cards, a man of taste and discernment. His position at Wyeminster Royal as Associate Specialist Surgeon working alongside and, more often than not, instead of Debbie Crawley, was almost a pleasant distraction from his real vocation. He enjoyed surgery though, the frisson of the unknown and element of risk, the camaraderie of the operating theatre, being able to use his dextrous hands to heal and mend. Indeed, Juan enjoyed most things. Life was to be relished, embraced, savoured. It was too short to do anything else; anyone working in a hospital knew that. So, when his pager bounced into life on the desk beside his keyboard he obeyed, bowed out of the game, shut down the computer, picked up his mobile and car keys and headed downstairs towards the heavy front door of his substantial mid-Victorian detached house on a salubrious street on the outskirts of the city. Within minutes his Alfa Romeo had joined the torrent gushing towards the Infirmary.

Sesi caught the news bulletin when snatching a diet coke from the machine outside the closed canteen. It was on the central foyer TV screen which would normally have been switched off at this time of night but, in view of the exceptional circumstances, had been reactivated as a sort of information board for the off-duty staff now pouring through the doors. Sesi was a tall woman who struggled with her weight. No one knew just how much or how she had virtually starved herself as a teenager after an obese childhood. Variously described as statuesque, imposing, sturdy and big boned, all she sought was to be slim and accepted for her medical prowess. Her arrival in Wyeminster had been salutary. When asked from where she came, she knew Droitwich was not the anticipated answer and initially it had amused her, but now it was tedious. What did it matter if her parents had come from West Africa? Who cared? It was not prejudice that she experienced but curiosity; fascination with the different. The girl in Critical Care with her corn rows and coffee skin felt akin to an ally. What had happened to her was shocking. Sesi stopped, suspended, mid-gulp to watch the local Chief Superintendent of Police addressing the clamouring Press. Strange to think he was standing just outside the hospital as he spoke.

"... As a result, a state of emergency has been declared at the Wyeminster Royal Infirmary. The pills in question are small, bright orange and easily mistaken for sweets. Their street name is Tiger Bites. They are cheap and readily available and I must again stress, that they are extremely dangerous. If you, or anyone you know, has any relevant information please call the police, urgently, on 0800 787 8787." The number was now scrolling along the bottom of the screen as if to underline his words. "Your call will be treated with complete confidence."

No sooner had he stopped speaking when the gaggle of reporters began a barrage of loud, insistent questions. He responded to only one.

"How are the kids?"

"Critically ill. It's too soon to be able to comment otherwise."

"Will they die?" The Chief Superintendent looked scathing and ignored the interrogator. God, he hated the Press. They were always so crass.

"What does the drug do?"

"I prefer not to answer that at this stage." The reporters were becoming annoyed. If the police chose to make a public statement, they would have to come up with more than this.

"Haven't you just advertised Tiger Bites for every kid in the country?" A snigger of suppressed approval from some of the more seasoned reporters who rejoiced at any discomfort of the Police Spokesman.

"It's important that people know what to look out for. The public must be vigilant." Not a bad riposte but the Press were relentless.

"Where are the drugs from?"

"We believe they are part of a consignment from the Far East."

"Are you looking for anyone in particular?"

The question he had dreaded. Oh well. It had to be said; better to get it over with. With a deadpan face the Chief Superintendent delivered the fateful reply.

"A tall, very slim man in … ", a slight hesitation then, "a Donald Trump mask. With a simulated cut throat."

The silence that followed was profound but very brief. Then the clamour resumed with ferocity and incredulity. Everyone howled out together.

"Who? What? Donald Trump? Halloween disguise? Is this a trick?" And the rest.

"There will be a further statement later. That number to call again, if you have any information, is 0800 787 8787. Thank you."

He was gone. Only the telephone number continued its endless journey across the bottom of the screen as Sesi headed back to the Emergency Department.

Chapter Seven

The early hours of the following morning – All Saint's Day

Joshua and Taya were together in Critical Care but not in adjoining beds. Both lay nestled amongst a forest of machines, tubes, screens and concerned adults. The boy's parents had arrived in a flurry of agitation, fear and horror. They were sitting, with difficulty, beside their son's bed or as near to it as the medical technology would allow. Not quite gowned, they were wearing sterile face masks over their mouths and noses as a 'precaution' but no one had explained against what. Too dazed to question they simply sat and stared at their small boy, white, insignificant, now no longer so green but still streaked as if by grass stains which collided with his purple lips. His eyes were closed; his face expressionless. He could have been dead. His father kept looking anxiously at the pulsing on the monitor screen to the right of his son's head as if to check that he was still alive, the click and sigh of the ventilator providing scant assurance. The mother never took her eyes from Joshua's face, as she had done on the day he was born and she had been transfixed by wonder at his perfection.

The medical team were standing around Taya's bed like punctuation marks in a metal sentence of monitors and technology. Debbie had assumed the lead on the grounds of seniority and no one bothered to argue.

Juan, unperturbed and irritatingly suave amidst the general weary untidiness of everyone else was standing close to her on one side of the bed. Opposite them were Tommy Yeo and Sesi and then, fanning out behind them like deferential courtiers paying tribute to sovereigns from afar, were Rohan and Lizzie with an assortment of hastily assembled nurses and medics. Nigel had just arrived, unseen by Debbie, and lurked outside the gathering. Had she noticed him he would have been propelled to the forefront which was exactly what he did not want. Sesi was consulting Taya's notes.

"Severe opioid poisoning with copious colorectal bleeding" she concluded aloud. Debbie narrowed her eyes almost imperceptibly then fumbled on her mobile phone. After failing to find the speed dial and resorting to punching irritably at the keypad she finally got through and launched ostentatiously into her best 'I'm in control and taking command' voice.

"Miss Crawley here." Never Ms, she was always Miss. Independent, feminine and just a little too publicly proud of her single status to be fully convincing. "Prepare theatre for an emergency colonoscopy." There was a brief silence as they all listened for the reaction at the other end of the phone and Debbie, eyes narrowed now for all to see, had focused her gaze on Tommy. He returned the gaze with equanimity and concealed amusement. Stalin in a cat-hairy suit: Debbie in Generalissimo mood was always so ridiculous.

"Yes, I know." Debbie's eyes narrowed even more. "I know. It is the second one tonight." She stressed the 'second' with deliberate clarity and a sly look at her colorectal colleague. Tommy was puzzled and it showed. As she rang off Debbie leaned over the bed and the recumbent Taya and spoke to Tommy in a subdued tone, just loud enough for everyone to hear,

"Mr Mitcheldean."

A brief explosive silence. Tommy reacted loudly and incredulously, his pronounced Glaswegian accent strangely at odds with his Oriental appearance and slight frame. He had the voice of a Clydeside ship builder.

"Gavin Micheldean?"

Debbie met the challenge with a sorrowful shake of her head as if Tommy was a naughty school boy in whom she was more disappointed than angry. With palpable difficulty he repressed the urge to spit out a retaliatory remark but sucked in his breath as if fortifying himself for a full-scale attack. Juan's mobile burst into song, a jaunty, synchronised rendering of the 1812 Overture and halted Tommy in his tracks. Everyone turned their attention to Juan. How did he do it? His phone always went off at strategic moments. It was unsettling. There were some who were convinced he somehow called himself; you just never quite knew with Juan.

"Sorry" he said, without the least embarrassment. "Must just take this." And he did, moving aside slightly and speaking in such low tones that no one could hear what he said no matter how hard they tried.

Debbie looked daggers at him. Juan smiled sweetly and held up one hand to her as if to hail a taxi in the street. The other members of the group watched the scene with fascination, rooting for Juan to come out on top. Debbie had the look of an apoplectic kettle left to boil on the stove. Leisurely, Juan ended the call, snapped the phone shut and addressed her.

“Business associate. Unavoidable. My apologies. Would you like me to assist in theatre?”

“If you can spare the time.” Juan smiled assent, utterly unaffected by her cold demeanour and attempt at sarcasm. They both knew that she needed his surgical expertise far more than he needed her, in any capacity. He could push her as far as he liked, she would always depend on him no matter how much she remonstrated in public.

Sesi brought the meeting back to order and to Taya, lying oblivious and temporarily ignored.

“We’re still trying to contact her next of kin but she’s in Care so it’s taking longer than we’d like. Rohan, can you follow that up? Nigel, CT scan asap please? Toxicology and the police are working together to try and identify the constituents and exact nature of the drug, then we’ll decide how to treat her.”

“I hope they hurry”. Tommy’s rough, staccato Glasgow voice punched into the air, partly furious with Debbie

Crawley but more concerned for the sick teenager lying in front of him. Sesi agreed.

"Yes. She's critical. Stabilising her is the best we can hope for at the moment."

***

"Where is she? She should have been back hours ago."

"I've rung the social worker and left a message. Another five minutes and I'm calling the police."

"She was supposed to be back by 11.30 at the latest. It's gone 1.00. Where is she?" Annie Ghebo was peering through the white plantation shuttered bay window out into the darkness, seeing nothing. Her voice had risen to alarm pitch with anxiety and fear. She was the emotional one in the partnership; the one who spent endless hours encouraging troubled foster children to talk and unburden themselves; the one who gave advice, a shoulder to cry on, a constant presence in the comfortable, safe haven she and her partner, Ella, provided for girls like Taya.

Annie and Ella had been together for over thirty years. They had met when Annie's husband had abandoned her and their two children for his much younger secretary. Such a cliché but the pain was real enough, not to mention the financial hardship. Annie had got a job as a librarian at a local school in Bristol where she had been living and where Ella had started work as an NQT. Newly qualified and rather insecure, she had found friendship and solace in Annie and much to the surprise of the former and to the fulfilment of the latter, they had fallen in love. Annie's husband had gone berserk; it was fine for him to run off with a younger woman but he was outraged and emasculated when his wife did the same. Their divorce was bitter and cruel and he spent a fortune to ensure that she received nothing. Annie's children however, had accepted the matriarchal family unit without demur so the four of them had quietly established themselves as a permanent fixture. That was in the 1990s when it was all about Aids and discretion. Nowadays no one seemed to care. When Annie's kids had grown up and left home, heterosexual, happily married, independent and self-assured, the two women had wanted to continue their caring so had become foster mothers with the local authority. By this time, they were living in Wyeminster where Ella was a head of department and head of year at the Grammar School. She had started at the large comprehensive that constituted the 'challenging' comprehensive in the city but had been covertly head hunted to move to the Grammar School, in the interests of internal discipline which, contrary to popular belief, was not so very different to that of its comprehensive counterpart. The money was good for the provinces, the holidays welcome and the pension fund even better. They had bought a large, terraced Victorian house riddled with dry rot which they had rebuilt to their own minimalist, modern taste. Everything was in black and white, as if to declare to the world that 'this is who we are. No compromises or grey areas. Take it or leave it.' A statement of subversive rebellion: their lack of convention behind an oh so conservative Victorian façade. Ella was the more practical, less emotional of the two but no less caring. Although she did not show it, Ella was concerned. Taya was a good girl who liked to please and found security in conforming to their mutually agreed boundaries. It was so unlike her to be late. There must surely be a reason? But what? Wyeminster was such a backwater. Some of the kids were rebellious and belligerent, yes, most of whom seemed to end up in her classes at some stage in their largely fruitless education, but they weren't bad. There were only a few that she had actively disliked and most of those had ended up in Bristol, Birmingham or London. Wyeminster simply wasn't lively enough for their dubious talents. Not enough scope to get into real trouble.

"I'll call Kezia and Courtney. I'm Kezia's form tutor." Ella had already seized her smart phone and had located the contact number. She had it to her ear when the doorbell sounded.

Both women jumped. Surprise did not prevent Annie from passing judgement about Taya's friends however. Annie was a woman of strong opinions, not always diplomatically expressed.

"Those two are a bad influence and Taya is our responsibility. We're her foster parents and we have a duty of care. I don't like the company she's keeping." Ella smiled, as she so often did when Annie went off on one, and ended her call.

"That'll be her now. She's probably forgotten her key again. I'll go" she added, unnecessarily, as she was halfway to the door.

"Don't say anything, Ella. Leave it to me. Taya needs patient understanding and she's just begun to confide in me so I'll deal with it." Annie began to settle herself into a carefully relaxed pose of solicitous concern with which to greet their wayward foster child. But it was not Taya's voice which made her start, sit upright and grip the sides of the armchair.

"What's going on? Who is it?"

"It's about Taya."

"Oh God! What's happened?"

Ella was standing in the centre of the room with two police officers, one male and one female. Annie knew it was serious. The police officers had each removed their head gear and were clutching them with both hands as they stood uneasily, apologetically in front of her.

Chapter Eight

Two Days Later

When he went as lead surgeon into the operating theatre, Tommy put aside all his irritations and resentment with the insufferable Debbie to focus solely on the task before him. Today he needed all his faculties and a considerable amount of balls, as his father would incongruously say in guttural Glaswegian amidst the snap click of the Cantonese they spoke at home. Before him, prepared, ready, antiseptic pink, unconscious and waiting on the table was an otherwise healthy, active 55-year old man called Peter Lavery who had been the subject of much debate and contention within the hospital. The Multi-Disciplinary Team, of which Debbie was the self-appointed and rather derided leader had considered his case and ruled, on the grounds of budget limitations and uncertain surgical outcomes, that his care should be palliative. He was a no hoper; his rectal cancer had mushroomed and metastasized to his liver. No coming back from that one no matter how fit and healthy you might have been. However, Tommy was convinced that something could be done to halt and reverse the process. And that he was the man to do it. He knew it was controversial, that he was crossing a line - but it was only a financial and bureaucratic line imposed by complacence, lack of initiative and in Debbie's case he was sure, incompetence. If someone had asked him whether he was trespassing into a medical no man's land for the sake of restoring life to the condemned or to highlight his senior colleague's shortcomings, he might not have been able to answer.

"Our patient is a robust, active male in his mid-fifties with bilobar liver metastasis and primary rectal cancer. You may have heard that the Multi-Disciplinary Team decided on palliative care for him but a review of his CT scan by the European Liver Centre in Birmingham has said that if we remove the primary rectal cancer, they can then remove most of the secondary growths and ablate those that are left. We can give this man his life back. His name is Peter, Peter Lavery. I'd like you to think of him as Peter as we operate, not just an anonymous patient. It will remind us that we are working to restore a man's life." The harsh Scots accent seemed to resonate around the enclosed room, clanging off the metallic surfaces and ringing in the ears of those present. Tommy was well liked by his surgical team. He never lost his temper, never swore at them in times of stress, did not shout, panic or fluster them with contradictory instructions when things went wrong as Miss Crawley did. With the exception of the three anaesthetists who were seconded into theatre according to their own timetable, Tommy's team – even Rohan Patel who today was looking unusually alert - would follow and cross the forbidden line with him.

The anaesthetists. Always the anaesthetists. Tommy surveyed the room and finally let his eyes come to rest on their leader: Lesley Thomas. In her early forties she looked older, untidier and shabbier than her age, as if she was fraying at the edges and needed dry cleaning. Her stature and heavy frame did not help: not so much short as truncated. Her girth and substance suggested that she should have been at least 12 inches higher than she actually was; she had the appearance of bread rising in a tin too small to accommodate it which had been unsuccessfully trimmed at the edges to make it fit. Even in scrubs she looked lumpy and curtailed. Peering at him over her sterile mask with her thin hair tucked tightly into her elasticated theatre cap, Lesley looked like a hamster pouching food in its cheeks against imminent starvation.

"Who asked them to review it?" Her Welsh tones as opposed to his Scot's. Mellifluous and rhythmical, softer, but suspicious and charged.

"I did, Lesley." Consultant Surgeon speaking to Consultant Anaesthetist on first name terms; the opening gambit in the skirmish to follow. Everyone else watched with interest. Battles between senior medics were always so entertaining and this one had an added edge; as the anaesthetist in charge Lesley had the power to stop the procedure at any point and there would be nothing Tommy could do about it.

"Does the Multi-Disciplinary team know?"

"Let's operate first and sort out the formalities later. Time is of the essence." Lesley was dismissed. She smouldered behind her mask and sucked in her breath like a dragon preparing to ignite.

“Patient in position?” Tommy had already forgotten her; he had a job to do. Straddled in the unflattering Lloyd-Davies position, Peter Lavery had his legs firmly fastened apart and raised in the air on the specially extended operating table. The laparoscopic camera was in situ and all eyes had now focused on the image on the lap stack. His insides were clearly visible – colourful, over large, minutely detailed and strangely detached from the proceedings and rummagings in his green, shrouded immobile body.

“Legs up just a wee bit more, please... That’s it.” Tommy regarded the image with satisfaction. Anticipation. Excitement. On the threshold of the unknown, undiscovered, a world in which he was the first to venture, a voyage into uncharted territory, known but unseen, his to encounter and uncover, to restore and heal.

“Lovely. Aye. Cameras roll.”

***

Lizzie had been woken by the sound of dying zombies. Andy was on the Play Station again, racking up the levels of a new game at full volume with a dexterity that Debbie had never managed to achieve in 20 years of routine surgery. He was totally engrossed in the game, sitting forward on the sloppy sofa decorated with cigarette burns and songbirds hanging off branches in despair, decrepit with age and dirt. The sofa had been inherited from the street twelve months ago when they had moved into the small terraced house. Originally a late Victorian workman's two-up two-down, it had been updated in the 70s and a cold uninsulated bathroom added onto the kitchen at the back of the house. The front door opened straight into the living room, once the parlour, but now a place of combined slovenly living and eating. Meals were taken from the comfort of the sofa which bore testament to a lifetime of abuse and neglect. It would have liked Andy and Lizzie to be its final owners before it was laid to rest but could not be sure. Maybe exposure to the elements outside in the street beside another skip might be preferable to the endless singes, burns and spills that had remodelled its once chirpy, colourful patterned cover inside this squalid house.

Andy was as scrawny and dusty as one of the hapless cloth birds suspended around him. His long legs were drawn up towards his chest as his thumbs twisted and turned on the controls and the zombies fell one by one, sometimes two at a time. The room was awash with groans, screams, gunfire and explosions but not a word was said until Lizzie stumbled in, straight from their untidy bed in the cluttered room above. It was chilly; the heating had not come on again. Damn. The landlord said he'd sort out the boiler but, as usual, nothing had happened. She'd have to get onto him, much good it'd do. She rubbed her thin inky arms to try and warm herself as she stumbled into the furore of sound and death.

"What time is it?" Andy did not answer but another zombie bit the dust. Lizzie reached over to the sofa and retrieved a ten pack of cigarettes from which she took the penultimate precious stick and shoved it into her mouth with a deep expectant inhalation.

"Oi. Leave some for me." Andy barked, just audible above the sound of noisy slaughter, without looking at her. Lizzie rifled through the debris on the sticky coffee table in front of her beloved and found a cheap plastic lighter. As the cigarette glowed into life and began to darken at its end she breathed in deeply, filling her lungs, calming her soul, the nicotine smoking its way into her blood stream and hell, catching in her throat. She began to cough. Hacking and gagging but still inhaling.

"God. I've gotta quit." She looked at the cigarette smouldering between her fingers, swallowed down the cough with saliva that tasted of the night before and took another deep drag.

"Always like that. First of the day." Andy's words of comfort. Lizzie was satisfied.

"Coffee?"

Andy pointed to an open can of Special Brew on the table by way of reply. The noise continued. Lizzie wondered briefly where he had found the cash for the new game and the booze but let it go. He did not like being quizzed. Or being told what to do. On her way to the kitchen she shouted at him so as to be heard,

"You busy today?"

"Maybe. Dunno. You got that Fentanyl?"

She did not answer immediately but stood in the kitchen, cold and barefoot on the sticky lino that was lifting in one corner beside the chipped skirting board. She stared at the white salty residue on the wall above the wood where the damp had penetrated and was quietly fingering itself up and along the wall towards the stand-alone gas cooker. God. She really must clean those hobs she thought without thinking as she mused how to reply.

"I could lose my job."

"That sweaty lech Patel can get it for you. He's in and out of theatre all the time."

"It's not that easy. There are systems and records."

"Worth a fortune on the street." Andy let his words hang; gave them time to waft into the kitchen and steep the atmosphere, unite with the steam from the boiling kettle and pour themselves with the hot water into Lizzie's mug of cheap coffee.

"Could buy you that ring you're always banging on about." Her heart leapt. The significance of his words swirled round her head as the unsweetened soya milk coagulated in the too-hot coffee. They were vegans and could smoke and do weed but dairy and meat were worse than poison.

She was tempted and appalled. But mostly tempted.

"Andy!" He was proposing marriage! Wasn't he?

"On the street?" She paused. "I thought it was for you?"

"Yeah, Babe. Need to fly. Dance fever." She sighed, but with pleasure, relief or despair she had no idea. And did not ask.

***

Over Taya's bed the consultations continued as she lay, intubated and ventilated but comatose and limp, mouse-like, tawny, discreet and unnoticed against the white bed linen inscribed with Property of NHS written in faded blue letters irregularly folded around her. Debbie was leading the ward round. Juan, Tommy and Sesi were with her; the ward sister, staff nurse and medical students were also in attendance; the latter were hanging onto every word, the nursing staff had heard it all before.

"Her blood pressure is still a cause for concern. The colonoscopy," here Sesi who was delivering the update looked at Debbie as if for confirmation although she knew she did not need it, "identified severe colitis with ulceration and bleeding. She needs immediate intervention to offset the threat of perforation and on-going bleeding." A pause. Due deference required once more. She submitted to Debbie.

"Keyhole surgery?" she suggested rather than enquired. Miss Crawley looked at her. Tommy interjected.

"No other option given her condition."

Debbie glared at him before she spoke, quietly, defiantly,

"You'll have to do it then. I'm far too busy." For less than a moment they locked glances before he picked up the gauntlet and she glanced sideways to address the rest of the group. "Clinical governance and Multi-Disciplinary Team responsibilities" she explained, happily apologetic. "The price of seniority and experience I'm afraid. Something for you all to aspire to!" How pertinent and pithy, witty and amusing I am she thought to herself. So, she laughed, self-deprecatingly. Enough polite smiles emanated from the group of medical acolytes to afford approval.

"We'll schedule her in today. Right, let's move on."

The entourage shuffled on at Debbie's pedantic pace towards the next case. Sesi followed directly behind her senior colleague, expressionless, while Juan smiled almost imperceptibly at one of the prettier female trainee medics wearing a figure-hinting above-the-knee dress over legs clad in opaque black tights that shone in the brightly lit ward. He slowed his tempo to match hers and took an interest in the notes she had ostentatiously made whenever a consultant spoke.

Tommy stood where he was and the group moved away. Unnoticed by the others, visible only to the unseeing Taya, he said not one word but his face was a narrative of inscrutable fury. Impassive, fixed and tight, his features did not change, his mouth was closed, his lips thin and colourless. The only movement was in his eyes as he focused on the receding body of his colorectal colleague. Debbie was now barely visible to him through pupils contracted to the point of closure with venom and anger. He carefully raised his hands to the level of his chest and systematically pulled each of his fingers, one by one until the knuckles cracked. Then he clenched his fists until the same knuckles were white and bloodless, skin-stretched protuberances at the end of bony branches on the top of his hands striated by faint blue veins. When he violently slammed his right fist into the palm of his left hand four times there was only a soft thudding thump as bone met flesh. Only Taya could have heard him muttering in the language of his fathers.

"Cao ni zu zong shi ba dai.

The student medics were now standing respectfully, orbiting Debbie in the corridor outside the double doors leading to the Critical Care Unit where Taya still lay. Joshua was making better progress and destined for Men's Surgical as there was no designated children's ward as such and, if truth be told, no bed available anywhere else.

"And obviously he can't go onto a female ward," Debbie was saying. The students were nodding in agreement as if she had just said something profound or just told them how to turn base metal into gold. They had closed their files and notebooks and were preparing to depart, as one, in a group. No one liked to be the first to leave: safety in numbers. Miss Crawley was unpredictable and quick to take umbrage. Best to keep on the right side of her, especially as she dominated Clinical Governance and report writing. Not that she actually wrote the reports, but her input was essential and she invariably had something to say even if she could not always remember their names. As Sesi headed back towards the Emergency Department and Juan bowed out of Debbie's company to casually accompany the opaque-legged student down the corridor to wherever she happened to be headed, Tommy silently emerged from the doors behind. Unseen by Debbie, she started when he spoke to her and turned abruptly to face him. Eye to eye, balanced, the same height, he felt uncomfortably close so she stepped back. How dare he invade her space?

He followed her. And spoke.

"A word?"

She looked away from him at her watch, plain, scratched, inexpensive, not always accurate. A present from her father so priceless and beyond reproach. She pulled a 'I really don't have time for this but I suppose I'll have to' face and sighed out a begrudging

"If you must."

"In private." Not a request she noted, but an order. Well, she'd make him wait.

"Does it have to be now?"

"Yes." Damn him. Really, the man was intolerable. She sighed again, deeply, with the pain of a martyr contemplating immolation.

"Very well. If you insist. My office in 10. But this is most inconvenient" she added although she might as well not have bothered as Tommy was already walking away, insolence and contempt in every athletic step. Even the receding straightness of his spine was an affront. She seethed benignly as she padded flatly along the hard floor towards her office in the surgical admin block. It took her about five minutes, in which time she avoided eye contact and failed to acknowledge those she passed in the corridor as was her wont and thereby composed herself. Tommy Yeo was not a man to be feared; she honestly did not understand why she felt so discomfited. Perhaps it was his foreignness. Decidedly Oriental and that terrible Scottish accent. Just how had he acquired it? Now that she thought about it, what did she actually know about him? He never spoke about himself except in the most general non-informative terms. She knew his wife ran a successful restaurant in the city although she had never been there herself – eating out was such a waste of money and anyway, she did not like Chinese food - too bitty and salty. Juan had eaten there more than once and liked it, but Juan was easily pleased and sometimes she wondered about his moral rectitude. Nigel had been there too apparently but did not reckon it; said it was far too expensive for what it was. The ingredients of his entire meal could not have come to more than a couple pounds so quite how they had arrived at the fancy total bill was a mystery. And the cost of the wine! He had only had a glass of house red which had been almost undrinkable. God alone knew from which vineyard it had come...somewhere godforsaken like California or Chile he didn't wonder. It might be worth having a look at Tommy's file she mused as she unlocked her office door and went to the desk where she sat down in front of the computer, which she preferred off than on. However, here she paused. She would turn it on and be studying the screen when he arrived; then she could shut the lid in his presence and he would think she had been doing something confidential and sensitive.

A slight knock at the door which was immediately pushed open and he was there. She abandoned the computer and faced him. Before she could say anything snide about people waiting to be invited to come in before they entered other peoples' offices, he was standing on the opposite side of the desk and slit-eyed, addressing her.

"How dare you?"

She was astonished. In her office! She could ask him the self-same question but chose not to. Always the professional, she was also a lady.

"I beg your pardon?"

"How dare you interfere with my patient?"

"Are you referring to Mr Mitcheldean?"

"Yes. On this occasion. He's not the first."

"I had every reason to believe that the colonoscopy conducted by yourself had failed to fully investigate Mr Mitcheldean's condition. Fortunately, I was on call and able to repeat the procedure at short notice."

"And what did you find?"

"Thankfully nothing untoward. But I had to be sure." The still air, listening intently, had become as charged as Tommy's voice.

"There was nothing to find. I'd already determined that."

A slight pause which Tommy knew was hesitation before Debbie replied,

"We can never be too careful." Her piety almost sent Tommy into a maelstrom. His face twisted; he snarled at her.

"Is that why you make a habit of repeating routine colonoscopies on my patients when you're on-call and there's no one to gainsay you?"

Debbie decided to retreat into a position of outraged dignity.

"I don't like your tone, Mr Yeo. Or the implications of what you are saying."

"The you'll like my next question even less. Why won't you operate on that lass in Critical Care?"

“I have no idea what you are talking about.” A wall of icy, polite, formality. Tommy tore into it as if it were rice paper.

“It’s because it’s laparoscopic isn’t it? And you never do laparoscopic surgery d’you? And why’s that, Debbie? Because you can’t. You’re not capable.”

“Miss Crawley to you.” The wall was being rebuilt. “I have other more important responsibilities and demands on my time.”

“More important than retraining? Than keeping up to date with modern surgical techniques?” He was sneering. “Or is it just easier to hide behind Juan Morales in theatre. Och, I know. He does all the tricky bits while you ‘supervise’.”

Aloof disdain scattered like brick dust; Debbie retaliated.

“These are outrageous allegations, Mr Yeo and not to be tolerated. Be very careful. I am not without influence in this hospital. We don’t want your sort here.”

There was an awed silence; the air held its breath. Even the office furniture seemed to freeze in disbelief as Debbie heard her own words with a third-party shock, as if someone else had said them and she had been merely an unsuspecting witness.

Tommy fractured the room, quietly, the Scottish voice also seemed to belong to someone else, more malevolent, other worldly.

"So, it's like that is it? My sort?"

Debbie ignored the implications. She was not a racist; he was just an obnoxious, odious little man who happened to be foreign. No one could be less racist than she was. Why, she was good friends with Juan and he was from Madrid though you would never know it. She knew lots of non-English people, was the first to say how good the Phillipino and Spanish nurses were in spite of the language problems. She was even on familiar terms with some of the Polish doctors who had crossed her path, liked and respected Sesi and Rohan as valued team players, judged everyone by merit alone. Tommy just did not fit in. Everyone knew it. She struck back.

"You can't prove anything. But I can." Defiant. Self-assured. In control. For the moment.

"Och, I have friends too, Miss Crawley." He spat out her name like a foul taste. "Powerful friends."

Was that a threat? From him? An arrogant, jumped-up Glaswegian Oriental of indeterminate origins and dubious medical expertise? Her indignation was righteous and prim.

"You will regret this."

"Not half as much as you will."

He had gone, leaving the door open. The draught from the corridor felt like a fresh air.

Chapter Nine

The Same Week

It was business as usual. No more high-octane, furtive buzz in hushed voices, corners, corridors and clandestine huddles about illegal drugs and the destruction of innocent youth, both of whom were recovering well. After the initial furore the media had moved on to more recent dramas elsewhere and Wyeminster could relax and become once more its sedate, respectable self. The hospital had returned to its routine – steady, predictable, perhaps even a little smug now that it had achieved just enough national recognition to be remembered without being pilloried. Yes, it had acquitted itself well. The Hospital Trust were modest and self-effacing in their brief glory; they were also hugely relieved to have emerged unscathed by scandal, abuse, incompetence and public censure. They were no Stafford thank you very much. No, theirs had been a most commendable public performance but now it was time to step down into comfortable normality, like putting on a pair of slippers after a night out in heels.

In the Laundry Room Lizzie was once again looking for sheets. Leisurely this time, without the noisy out-of-hours Halloween service of before. No need to escape in quite the same way this time but even so, she savoured the warm starched smell and the folded order. If only she could get Andy to tidy up occasionally. Just to put things away would help instead of leaving them where they dropped or were abandoned, to settle in, take root and become long-term residents. As she perched on the lower level of the step stool and stretched up to the high shelf, she felt a familiar tentacle sensation around her waist. It stroked upwards, tickled over the bumps of her ribs then curved into her cleavage and moulded itself over the mound of her breasts which were cupped reverently in its moist palms.

"Rohan!" She squealed. He took it as pleasure.

"Lizzie" he murmured into her spine. She could hear the saliva and wondered briefly if it would leave a damp mark on her uniform.

"Get off!"

"Let me help you down. Don't want you to fall." The words were muffled against her back and she nearly gave him a nosebleed with the violence with which she turned around and descended to level ground. Her hands over his, she lifted them off her body and held them away and aloft, an outlandish tango. He was entirely unphased. Undeterred. Spurred on by lust and promise.

"Lizzie" He gazed her name with adoration. "My lovely Lizzie. Mmmmm." He sounded as if he just ordered something delectable from an exotic menu. "So sexy." This was exhaled rather than spoken and she averted her eyes to look heavenward but the clean laundry could not save her.

Now he was winking at her and getting even closer, his breath scorching her neck which tried not to flinch and retract. The tentacle hands, rubbery, suckered and sticky had evaded capture and were crawling under her uniform top and down into her trousers. Temporarily halted by hip bones they pressed on; her flat belly pressed itself against her spine in an attempt to escape and her legs were rigid with horror.

"Stop it!" She sought to grab and remove his hands again and was disgusted at the pleasure with which he enjoyed the ensuing tussle around her nether region and waistband. But the button held, the boarder was repelled. She extracted herself with some difficulty and flung herself to the other side of the room, closer to the door and freedom. He followed with delight and launched himself at her so that she was pinned against the wall alongside the door. If only she could reach the handle. Why were there no panic buttons in laundry rooms? There should be; she would suggest it.

Something small, hard, uncomfortable in her pants. It scraped her pelvic bone as she tried to wriggle free and pinched into her. Rohan was still too close but now she was the one who was squeezing a hand into the top of her trousers. He felt her moving against him and smiled knowingly at her. His secret. Her gift. As she fingered the phial of Fentanyl he had deposited in her knickers he almost swooned,

"And what do I get I return, eh, Lizzie? When?" Husky anticipation, eyes almost closed with imagined pleasure. She slapped him across the face. Flesh smacking into flesh, resounding, stinging them both. Lizzie's handprint on Rohan's cheek, red, throbbing, glowing. His eyes were wide with shock and incredulity, bereft. An outraged small boy about to be soundly punished for someone else's misdemeanour.

"Lizzie!" But she was on her way out, wrenching open the door, sheetless, retrieving the package from her underwear as she ran.

"What about our deal? Lizzie! You owe me!" Only the clean laundry heard him as the door slammed behind her.

Pulling herself together – literally when it came to her trousers and crumpled underwear - Lizzie strode to the point of a sprint in the direction of Women's Surgical. She needed a few minutes to regain her composure and to think, and to work out what to do with the Fentanyl in her pocket. She would have to get the syringe off hospital premises as soon as she could but that could not be until the end of her shift. No good putting it in a locker or handbag in case it was missed and people started searching but that was not likely; not yet, anyway. And no one would suspect her; she had not been in theatre and had no access to such drugs. Rohan had been clever; she had not credited him with such guile. He had kept the residue in the syringe from the anaesthetist's use of it in some surgical procedure or the other in the operating theatre. It should have been discarded as surplus to requirement; legitimately signed out of the drugs cupboard, he would have confirmed that the excess had been disposed of while removing the needle and pocketing the half-full syringe. For her. No, for Andy. That was why she had done it although Rohan did not know that. Nor would he. Getting rid of the Fentanyl would be easy in comparison to avoiding his sweaty advances. However, it would be the same sweaty fingerprints on the half full syringe so she would have to wipe it clean to get rid of them but mostly to erase her own, then handle it with latex gloves so that it could not be traced. Break the chain of continuity. Protect Andy. Burn the gloves in the infirmary incinerator via the contaminated waste system and it was done. And dusted. She was smiling with expectant relief when she found herself at Taya's bedside.

"Hello. How are you? It's good to see you sitting up and taking notice."

Taya was watching TV. Usually it had to be paid for by the patient on an extortionate pay as you watch tariff, but the Infirmary as a gesture of good will and because they felt guilty that she was on a ward with exclusively elderly women had given her free, unlimited access on the condition that she listened through ear phones. The other ladies needed their rest. Taya was almost certain that at least two of them had embraced it eternally and kept herself closely to herself. It was not just that they were all incredibly old, although that did not help, but they were all white. She felt conspicuous, highlighted, outlined against the snowy bedlinen, pale walls and bleached overhead lighting. Her mother had been white but Taya could not remember her. All her upbringing had taught her was how to feel different.

Taya was watching a local news broadcast. The Nationals, Red Tops and media big boys had left town leaving the playground to the smaller kids who were making the most of the space. Milking their coat-tails. On the screen was a detective inspector from the local police force. Contrary to adult belief, Taya could hear outside the ear pieces and was able to multi-task by listening to the TV commentary and answering Lizzie simultaneously. All teenagers could do it but adults never believed them, especially when it came to homework.

“Hi. Yeah. Much better thanks. It’s nice to see ya.”

“What’re you watching?”

“The news. They’re talking about those pills, the ones I took. Tiger Bites they’re called.”

Lizzie looked at the screen with interest. Obviously just the local news but the detective was directly addressing the camera and looked serious. It was dreadful. It had shocked everyone and everything possible was being done to find the perpetrators. They had to protect their youth. Nothing more important. Lizzie followed the ribbon of words across the bottom of the screen while Taya listened with a stricken expression creasing her young face. The police officer was identified as Detective Inspector Catherine Scott of the Wyeminster Constabulary. Taya was transfixed by her. Lizzie looked at the girl propped up in the bed then glanced back at the screen and suddenly understood why. The woman was taller than average and heavily built but not fat. She had short, wispy-fine auburn hair which clung to her head. Her fringe was functional, cut well above her eyes and seemed to float across her forehead. In her ear lobes were diamond studs, big enough to be fake but if they were real, to have cost a small fortune. But what had caught Taya's attention was the woman's complexion which was irregular, mottled, piebald. White on pallid; fair flesh made even fairer in ugly uneven patches which followed the movement of her facial features and bounced out of the screen. She had vitiligo. And she clearly did not care.

"What's the matter with her?" Taya was removing the ear pieces all the better to talk to Lizzie.

"I think she's got vitiligo."

"What's that?"

"When the pigment - the colouring - in the skin isn't even, so you get white patches."

"I've never seen it before. Is it common?"

"No idea. I can find out if you like."

Taya was thoughtful. She pointed the remote at the television and cut it dead.

"I've been lucky, haven't I?"

Lizzie nodded. "Yes."

“I could’ve died.”

“You were very ill for a while. But you’re okay now.”

“Yeah.” Taya was still looking at the blank screen.

“Are you alright?” Lizzie momentarily forgot the Fentanyl in her pocket.

“Yeah. Bit bored. That’s all.”

“Do you read? I could get the book lady to bring her library trolley round?”

“Nah. Not really. Well, only magazines and stuff.”

“I’ll see what I can do.” Lizzie smiled. Taya caught the movement of her mouth and turned to look at her.

“Would you come and see me sometimes? When you can? I’ve got my mobile but the signal’s crap and anyway my mates have been told not to contact me. Not even texts. My foster parents think they’re a bad influence” she added by way of explanation. “But they’re not. They tried to stop me but I wouldn’t listen.”

She was near to tears. Lizzie was touched. Taya looked so vulnerable. Small.

“Of course. Whenever I can. It’d be a pleasure.”

“Lush!” The girl meant it. Lizzie realised that she liked her. It really would be a pleasure.

“I’ve got to go now I’m afraid. I should have been in the Emergency Department a lifetime ago.” She paused. “But I’ll see you soon, yeah?”

Taya grinned. “Yeah.”

Chapter Ten

The End of the Same Week.

Debbie had chosen to live outside Wyeminster itself, in one of the satellite small villages that circled the mother ship. The city was attractive, historical and respectable, in parts, but since her arrival at the infirmary twenty years ago she had witnessed a sad decline in its character. Too many incomers who did not understand the culture of a provincial cathedral city; they brought their own customs, languages and food. The food! Where could you get a decent traditional meal these days without having to go to a pub? Falling educational standards – even the grammar school pupils went about the streets looking scruffy, blazer sleeves rolled up and the girls wearing skirts no bigger than pelmets. Rising crime, pollution from too much traffic and, to her horror last month she had stumbled, literally, over a beggar. Sitting in the pedestrianised centre with his dog, which looked better kept than its master. Using his mobile smart phone thingie so he probably had a contract, smoking and drinking takeaway coffee. It was all a scam; his house was probably bigger than hers and he would not be paying a penny in taxes. All undeclared income, cash in hand. It was outrageous. She had said so to Nigel at the time and he had agreed with her. He always did.

"Nigel." It was tenderly exhaled, barely audible. Debbie spoke, crumple-eyed, softened, fuzzy at the edges; her face like finger ends too long immersed in hot water. She was gazing out of the large, plate glass window at the front of her house, surveying her domain. Detached, spacious I-have-every-right-to-be-proud-of-myself middle class box built in the late 60s and entirely of its time. Style free, functional and identical to all its original smug neighbours, set sufficiently apart from each other to be exclusive but close enough to form a bastion of solidarity. Understated, tasteful, neat. Boring. Their only act of rebellion the appendage of the integral garage at each right side that jarred their rigid symmetry. Over time, innovative newcomers had stepped outside their box and made changes. Improvements. These made Debbie snort with derision. Shrubs, hedges, low walls to keep out the world of the pavement; crazy paving and even one concrete green-painted 'lawn' with gnomes. Double glazed porches appeared in the 90s after one disastrous attempt at stone cladding in the 80s but thankfully no one else had fallen so low. More recently, as their children became teenagers and prices rose so that new occupants needed two incomes to pay the mortgage, some had descended to replacing entire front lawns with block-paved car parks. No other way to describe the collection of assorted vehicles that seem to reproduce and multiply overnight. Appalling. Debbie now had the distinction of possessing the only original house, faithful and true to its conception. Shabby and dated according to the gospel of the street and badly in need of new gutters, but as she never communicated with her neighbours she continued to glory in its architectural integrity.

Nigel was expected at any moment and Debbie's look of love was for him. Would he be held up in the Friday evening traffic? She did hope not. No, there he was, edging methodically up the road maintaining a steady twenty-three miles an hour, following the line of the kerb exactly, always between one foot and eighteen inches away from it, never deviating. She watched him check his rear mirror, indicate, then slowly curl the Skoda Superb onto the car length drive up to her garage. The car stopped, exactly one foot from the up and over metal door and the engine was turned off. She smiled ingratiatingly, coyly but he was concentrating on the hand brake and did not see. She continued to smile, demure, lips slightly pursed in a frozen embryonic kiss. Nigel never saw. Never looked. Checked the car door was shut, locked, pulled the handle twice just to be sure, wiped a non-existent speck of dirt off the pristine white paint work and headed morosely towards the frosted glass front door. Debbie was now waiting on the other side, avid to open it but far enough away for her outline not to be seen through the glazed icicles. Should she pre-empt the door-bell? Or let it ring and wait just enough time for him to assume that she was elsewhere? She opted for the latter; they were adults. Mature. Professional. Besides, she did not want Miss Muffat to escape.

The doorbell toiled the same tired ringtone it had repeated for over thirty years and sighed into silence. Debbie counted to three, stepped into the light fracturing her shape through the door and twisted the latch. She smiled brightly at Nigel who was looking at his shoes, a pair of ancient Hush Puppies which he would wear until they wore out, no time soon.

"Nigel! Come in. You should use your key. You are welcome anytime, you know that." Nigel knew it all too well; she told him every time he rang the doorbell. Only he knew, regretfully, that he could not let himself in to a house where he had never even been upstairs, never mind arrive unannounced. He did not possess the spontaneity.

"Awful traffic" he grumbled by way of greeting. "Twenty minutes from the lights."

She clucked.

"Too many cars. How many times have I said it? There are people here who have two and sometimes three. Three cars! And they park them on the street. Ridiculous. Who needs three cars?"

Nigel chose not to comment. He, his strident ex-wife and his adult kids all had cars which he had chosen to finance. Couldn't manage without them. He stepped over the threshold into the stagnant-pond-brown hall, wiped his clean shoes on the bearded door mat and was assailed by the smell of cat. Debbie had swept up Miss Muffat in her arms and was rubbing her thin nose in the copious Blue Persian fur.

"Look, Miss Muffat. Look who's come to see us. Isn't this nice?" It was hard to say which of the two looked less enthralled, Nigel or the cat, but the feeling of antipathy was mutual. It had nothing to do with Debbie. Their intense shared dislike was boundless and satisfying; meat and drink to the soul. Miss Muffat was more malevolent but Nigel had the advantage of size. His tenacity was admirable; he would quite happily have glared her to death. Miss Muffat however had an enviable capacity for spite. The accumulation of her hairs over Debbie during the week made Nigel think of a venomous spider encasing its prey in a suffocating web. If she did not change her clothes, Nigel wondered whether one day his colleague would eventually disappear within the sticky threads.

Debbie and her hairy charge led him into a callous living room that ran the width of the house from front to back. It seemed endless: a beige carpeted desert punctuated by dark, dated furniture like forlorn water bores in an arid, sandy landscape. The low coffee table presided over the centre of the room, a boat in dry dock, abandoned by all but a couple of coasters left to languish on its deck.

"Take a seat. Make yourself at home, Nigel." He headed for the least hairy dralon armchair and sat himself down. He would not move until it was time to go home.

"Coffee?" his charming hostess enquired. He nodded glumly.

"Won't be a minute. Miss Muffat will look after you, won't she? Yes, she will!" Debbie cooed. Nigel felt slightly bilious. Miss Muffat was deposited in a chair opposite him and commenced a blinkless stare that would not end until he left. Even after he had departed, she would continue glowering at the spot where he had been sitting, as if her malice might pursue him. Against the backdrop of Debbie's happy coffee-making noises in the kitchen they continued their unarmed eyeball combat. He wondered, not for the first time, why he continued to visit Debbie's home and indeed, how he even had a relationship with her at all. In his own apathetic, high spectrum way he was very fond of her and enjoyed her company. And she idolised him, which was both endearing and irresistible. Also, he conceded, it was much better to continue the liaison than curtail it. No sex required, female company on tap, adoration to the point of servility: what was not to like? And her voice was beautiful. Besides, he did not want to risk alienating her at work. Debbie could be very obstructive if she chose, subtle and cunning; extremely clever. People who found themselves on the wrong side of her suddenly found that they had been side-lined or overlooked, or questions were being asked about their clinical outcomes. Nothing could ever be traced back to Miss Crawley who was always so helpful unless you happened to be a junior medic in which case, she was a mellifluous harridan in polyester with a cat hair problem. The school bully who loads the gun but passes it to someone else to fire. She had the ear of

Senior Management and People in High Places who understood even less about advanced surgical techniques than she did. Miss Crawley was invaluable. How would they manage without her contribution to clinical governance, auditing and monitoring of standards? So reliable, always willing, always there. What she did not know about her colleagues, their clinical practice and their patients was not worth knowing; and it saved them finding out for themselves.

"Here we are. Just the way you like it." Debbie was holding two mugs of coffee, one gripped in each hand, her body bent slightly forward as she entered the room with the exertion of not spilling them. Not that it would have mattered; they would have blended perfectly with the décor. She placed one of the over full mugs on a bandy-legged occasional table next to Nigel. He reached for it, took a sip and winced.

"Too hot."

"Oh, sorry! I'll put more milk in it." Up on her feet again, the coffee was immediately on its way back to the kitchen.

She's so attentive and caring, Nigel's internal monologue continued, as if to justify his presence both to himself and to Miss Muffat. The ex-Mrs A. would have told me to sod off and get my own. It's nice to be fussed over. Platonic, mature; two work colleagues being friends. He ignored the contribution made to the relationship by his apathy and her Electra complex.

The ancient chimes of the tired doorbell limped arthritically into action and echoed sorrowfully through the hallway. Neither Nigel or Miss Muffat moved, not even a flicker of an eyelid although the cat's irises had contracted to black nail clippings. They listened to Debbie patter down the hall to the door which was opened to reveal Lesley. Squat, stocky, chatty. Alexa and Amazon combined.

"Lesley! Do come in. Yes, through to the living room on the right. Nigel's already here. Coffee?"

"Lovely." More likely to a response to the offer of coffee than the décor, Nigel thought as Lesley bowled into the room.

"Hello!" Bright, chirpy and Welsh. Nigel's grunt was the 'on' switch for Lesley's chatter and she was off, straight into a hearty sprint as she negotiated her way to a marginally less hairy settee upon which she perched herself and drew a quick breath.

"Very comfy. Nice room. You won't believe what he's done now."

"Who?"

Nigel had spoken. Debbie was framed in the doorway holding his doctored coffee.

"Tommy Yeo!" Lesley proclaimed his name as if he just been announced the winner of a Golden Globe or an Oscar. Her Welsh lilt soared around the room. Even Miss Muffat turned to stare at her in the dramatic pause that followed.

"He's only gone and overruled the whole MDT! Blatantly disobeyed a clear directive!" Lesley was triumphant. She had barely been able to contain the news of the discovery but was immensely proud of her discretion until this chosen moment. Oh, but the relief of letting it out.

"Yes, overruled the entire Multi-Disciplinary Team!" Her voluminous melodic Welshness sounded as if it was about to become a Baptist chorus. She was known to comfort-hymn-hum when stressed, the prelude to tears.

"He can't do that." Debbie's disbelief was exactly what Lesley had counted on.

"He's already done it!"

"How?" Nigel, less emotional but no less interested.

"Peter Lavery. Remember him? Declared palliative by the MDT, and Tommy Yeo operated! Only sent Lavery's scan off to Birmingham for review in direct contravention of the MDT decision and then took it upon himself to remove the primary cancer. I was there."

"We've got him!" Debbie's beautiful voice; Tommy Yeo's death sentence. In the kitchen the kettle whistled a jaunty gallows anthem. Nigel and Miss Muffat stared, with Lesley, at Debbie, whose face was lit up like a rogue ray of sunlight.

Chapter Eleven

The following Monday Morning.

First things first, a slug of coffee. A prolonged healthy slurp to lubricate the senses then Clare Howard-Jones's forefinger poised over the mouse, tapped left and the auditor's report was on the screen. It was the annual report and as the Wyeminster Infirmary Chief Executive Officer it had come through to her ahead of everyone else. A deep breath and she began to read. She knew there were shortfalls – there always were – but it was finding a way to cut costs already cut to the bone that was the perennial problem. She did not want to have to amputate.

It was peaceful. Dark outside still, but muddy light was beginning to probe its way into the sky, stroking its way through the limpid water as it glided silently into view. Clare was engrossed in the figures on the screen, her chunky face aglow with its white light. Naturally blonde, which everyone assumed was from a bottle and then admired how her roots never showed, Clare was head girl. Solid, gamesy in a netball, hockey sort of way, she had always led, shown initiative, welcomed responsibility, had bags of potential and been a credit to her parents/school/red brick university. Now she was doing the same at the infirmary about which she really cared, possibly more than she did her almost grown up thank goodness sons and husband. She went to church on Sundays. Hearty and holy. Her devotion was comfortable, strongest on Sundays and as flexible as the demands of her job required. Elastic Christianity.

A determined rap at her door exploded the calm which jumped and shook itself with surprise. As it was shaking down its fur another louder rap made its ears twitch.

“Yes. Come in.” Absentminded. She could have done without the interruption.

Debbie appeared. Clare did not look up from the screen.

“You said your door was always open.”

“Good morning, Debbie.” No need to look; Clare recognised the voice and, as she repressed the urge to sigh, the tone. “It is, but there are occasions when …”

“It is closed. I understand that. But the hospital’s reputation is at stake. Otherwise I wouldn’t be doing this.”

Clare sensed danger, tensed. Tried not to gawk.

“I beg your pardon?”

“Tommy Yeo.”

It suddenly felt very cold.

“You’d better sit down.”

It was good that Lizzie was on an early Andy thought. If she had known he could get out of bed at this time in the morning, smarten himself up and go into town for business she would never be off his back. She was an okay girlfriend though. No trouble, really. Nagged too much but didn't all women? He took no notice of course. Wyeminster was surprisingly busy but perhaps this was normal for a weekday morning at about 9.30. He had no idea. The text had come from an unknown caller, number withheld. It had just dropped into his phone about an hour ago: The Nine Gates of Heaven. 9.45. So here he was, as smart as he knew how and early. If he had not been so nervous, he might have been amused.

No one took any notice of the spidery nicotine-fingered man loitering outside the Chinese restaurant. The shirt collar did not quite conceal the inky patterns clawing up to the ears and into the hairline. The hair was clean and brushed, strangely exuberant in its new-found state of hygiene, trying to break free and rejoice in its new grease free state. Andy kept patting it down. Lizzie had said she would trim it for him but as usual she had not got around to it. What did she do when she was at home? Not tidy the house that was for sure. He hitched up his trousers – his best jeans – pity he could not find a belt. If he bent over slightly, they seemed to catch on his hip bones so he could keep them up that way. Normally he did not care but somehow, today, it seemed important. He was hunched over in the cold contemplating a cigarette and balancing his trousers on his pelvis when an expensive – a very expensive- car drew up alongside the kerb edge. He did not hear it arrive; it suddenly appeared like a creature of the night, obscure, silent, ethereal. Shiny, mysterious. Eyeless; blacked out windows reflecting only his own lanky reflection framed by the red and gold exterior of the restaurant behind him. The car slowed and stopped precisely where he was standing, hummed his name, opened its rear door and beckoned him in.

He was gobbled up by the leather upholstery. The slick smell made him gag and revolted the vegan in him. He too was blacked out and eyeless, blindfolded with something silky and rich, taut and tight. The hard knot at the back bulged into his head so he leant forward in the seat to relieve the pain but was immediately shoved back and did not move again. No seat belt he noticed. Why?

Where was he being taken? There had been no time to register who was in the car when he was absorbed into it; as soon as he had entered, he had been forced back into the seat by soft hands which covered his eyes and twisted his head so that his body was forced to follow, doglike. His arms were pinned behind his back with pitiless hands which he would grow to fear. As he sat, immobile, between two sets of thighs and shoulders he sensed their warmth, heard one fatly breathing, smelt leather, opiate sweetness, fear. The car pulsed onwards. He wanted to shit.

“Where ya taking me?” Was that his voice? He could hardly believe he had spoken. Or maybe he had just thought it aloud? It made no difference; no one replied and the silence constricted his throat, stopped his nostrils, started to suffocate him. Just as he thought he would might die for want of air he was aware of the car slowing. It curved gently to the right, halted for a moment than crept a little further before easing itself into rest and cutting its engine. Then the movement began – the hard hands this time, propelling him clumsily out of the car onto unforgiving ground, level, concrete. Prodded and pushed like a beast in an abattoir he was compelled to walk – blindly - across an unseen land into some sort of building. It felt large, empty and cold. Draughty. Open but enclosed. His fear echoed alongside his faltering footsteps.

Then he was sitting on a chair – hard, upright. In chilly darkness. But not alone. Faraway, traffic murmured. A cold wind shackled his feet and neck, caressing the blindfold. His hair lay flat. Subdued. Frightened into submission.

What Andy cannot and would not see were the three men with him in the abandoned warehouse. One of them, an elderly scrawny gentleman – for he is that – was seated on another hard, upright chair but was neither blindfolded nor tied. His eyes were tight but missed nothing, his thin mouth no more than a line in a face more carved than creased. Aged but ageless. Jade cold, blank, unblinking. He watched. Once, a lifetime ago, he won a game of Mah-jong.

Beside him, sentinels standing on either side, were two men. He of the soft hands was smaller and pudgier but no kinder than his iron-fisted companion. Dressed alike in dark suits, white shirts, dark ties and immaculate black shoes, they too were impassive. They had a job to do. Andy was a task.

A slight nod from the man seated on the chair to the smaller henchman and the silence imploded into guttural Glaswegian.

"Just a few questions, Mr Barrett." Mr Barrett? Now Andy was terrified. "Protectin' our interests. I'm sure ye understand. My name's Lee and it's to me you'll report if we decide to do business. As ye're aware we're lookin' to invest in this area and your services were suggested to us. Ye dinna need to know who. Before we can agree on any terms however, we'd like to know why ye raised the profile of our product in such an, er, unusual way."

Andy knew everything depended on the right response. He might be a scruffy bastard but he wasn't a fool. The blindfold helped him concentrate.

"The Tiger Bites?"

"Aye."

"To sell them."

There was brief pause; Andy felt the question in the air before the elderly man, who never removed his gaze from the skinny prisoner, nodded to Lee to proceed.

"Explain, please."

One chance to get it right. Andy played it confident, cocky.

"Publicity. Now every kid in the country wants them. I can't keep up with the demand. You supply. I sell. Easy."

Had he done enough?

The gimlet-eyed old man's face never changed. The mouth line fixed like a palisade below the sharp nose and hairless upper lip, the eyelids low over the expressionless pupils. Everything waited. Andy did not realise he was holding his breath. Nothing moved, not even the wind.

An almost imperceptible nod from the elderly one and the decision was made. Lee took his cue and spoke.

"Do as we agree, Mr Barrett, and ye'll be well treated. But we wouldna want any disobedience or tricks. Ye work for us. D'ye understand?"

Oh aye, he understood. Perfectly.

In another building on the opposite side of the city, D.I. Catherine Scott was also sitting on a narrow, hard chair, struggling to accommodate her wide spread buttocks. Not tied or blindfolded but equally trapped by protocol and rank and the Chief Superintendent, who was in full spate.

"The rise is shocking. A disaster. Drug abuse in our area has almost doubled since this time last year. Tiger Bites seem to be the recreational drug of choice. All the users seem to be after them. The effects are deeply disturbing." He eyed his D.I. "For everyone" he added. Nice dramatic pause, Catherine was thinking. Very effective. The media handling course had been money well spent. No problem getting that through the auditor but when she wanted more resources, well ...

"Yes." She had to agree. "It's mostly young users, experimenting, lots for the first time. Like our Trick or Treat victims."

"That's what worries me the most. Where're they getting them from?"

Catherine did not know. No one knew. Her hand went to her face and she rubbed her forehead like Aladdin with a piebald lamp, hoping for a genie to appear and solve all her problems. The Chief Super was momentarily distracted – could she feel the difference in colour on her face or was it all smooth? Then he was embarrassed but she did not seem to have noticed. If she did, she never showed it.

"We're watching all the known sources but so far, nothing. I suspect there's a new supply chain with new outlets."

"Links with the county line?"

"Not that we know of."

"So, new kids on the block?"

"Yes. But not children. Not amateurs. This is a professional operation. Well hidden. No one knows anything; we're asking everywhere."

"We have to find them, Catherine." You mean I do, she thought glumly but knew he was right. Again. Damn it. "Top priority. Everything else comes second. You're the one with the degree. You find the answer."

The old chip on his pipped shoulder. Sometimes she wished she had never graduated. So much for new policing; the old guard who had worked their way up through the ranks never let them forget their 'educational advantages'.

"Well? What are you waiting for?"

Released, she would carry the chains with her. She heaved herself out of the chair and stumped towards the closed door. An extra-long walk with the girls and no chocolate today she vowed.

Chapter Twelve

Four Days Later: Friday morning.

Head Girl Clare was with Head of School: Sir Peter Henshawe, the just call me Peter but never forget how important I am Chair of the Wyeminster Infirmary Trust Board. Patrician, mid 60s, professional politician who had lost his seat when the city veered unexpectedly to the left eight years ago and, even more unexpectedly, had stayed that way. He still did not quite believe that he would not regain his seat but, life goes on, he was a trooper and would continue to serve in any way he could. Chair of the Trust of his local hospital was part of that service to the community, worthy, high profile and coincidentally, extremely lucrative, not that that was his motivation of course. Lady Henshawe felt differently, spent the money for both of them and her husband affected not to notice.

With Clare, sitting behind her desk but slightly to one side so as to demonstrate suitable deference to her hallowed companion, was Hugo Chadwyck, the Investigating Officer appointed by the Trust to deal with the allegation of failing to follow medical protocol made against Tommy Yeo. Debbie had been forthright and adamant; she had evidence to support her allegation. She had an eye witness. The hospital had no choice but to take action. Hugo was shuffling a bulky file of loosely tied documents and reports as he sat next to Clare, using her desk as his own. She minded that he shoved her family photo and pens to one side and pushed her desktop back to make more room for himself but that was Hugo. He was pompous and smug, but undeniably sharp witted and incisive. Ha! That was the word alright! She suppressed a smile. Hugo was a 'resting' breast surgeon with the kind of private practice wannabe cosmetic surgeons could only dream about. There was almost no-one in the public eye with enhanced breasts that he had not lifted, shaped, enlarged and nippled. No wonder he wore bespoke double-breasted suits. Somewhere under that smug, buttoned up, Windsor-knotted exterior there lurked a sense of humour but he kept it locked away, for private consumption only. Clare knew that Sir Peter did not like Hugo – no one did really, but it was difficult to know exactly why. Perhaps it was jealousy? He wore success like exclusive aftershave – pervasive, cloying but impossible to identify.

Tommy was in the centre of the room, sitting angularly and straight on a supposedly comfortable chair on which Sir Peter had invited him to sit. Obviously, Tommy had accepted, which was all part of the plan. Now Sir Peter could stand over the accused. Not too close – no invasion of his space. That was not necessary; the upright postured height of the Chair of the Trust was more than enough to create dignity and authority.

"As Chairman of the Wyeminster Royal Infirmary Trust I have no alternative but to suspend you until the allegation made against you has been fully investigated. It is a serious breach of medical ethics not to comply with the decision of the Multi-Disciplinary Team."

"I've done nothin' wrong." Tommy's coarse Glaswegian attempted to undermine Sir Peter's received pronunciation and poise, but failed, and died.

"Then you have nothing to fear." Conciliatory. Reasonable. Dangerous. "Hugo Chadwyck," here Sir Peter indicated the man sitting next to Clare without so much as looking at him, "whom I'm sure you know by repute, has been appointed as the Investigating Officer in this case." Hugo looked serious and disappointed that such a situation had ever arisen. Clare looked at her finger nails. Sir Peter continued to stare fixedly at Tommy.

"You have legal representation?"

"Aye." He had the best, but they weren't to know that.

Hugo spoke, as had been agreed beforehand.

"It is my task to establish the truth, Mr Yeo. No more, no less. You may rely on me to conduct an impeccable and thorough investigation."

Sir Peter nodded approvingly; Clare sneaked a glance at Tommy. He was rigid with suppressed fury, lips pursed as if about to spit. Instead, he spoke.

"This is a set up, and I know exactly who's behind it." Bullet-words ricocheting around the room. Clare wanted to duck for cover, Hugo flinched but Sir Peter remained vertical, stiff, unphased in the face of the enemy.

"You will be escorted from the premises, immediately, Tommy." Clare wanted him to know she cared but was powerless. "Procedure" she added, almost apologetically. "Nothing personal."

Tommy ignored her. She leant over Hugo and pressed the intercom on her desk. Immediately there was a knock on the door which opened and admitted two hospital security men who had clearly been on standby outside, awaiting her signal. Tommy stood up, turned on his heel and left the office ahead of them. They followed, slightly abashed, wholly redundant and struggling to keep up with him.

Tommy did not go home but instead, steered the black Discovery towards the home of his parents. It was not a family house of memories and childhood, growing up and teenage angst. He had been brought up in Glasgow in a house far less grand. Not quite the Gorbals granite tenement that people assumed all Glaswegians crawled out of – his parents had lived in a respectable terrace near the city centre. Granite and grey like all the others but spacious, comfortable, increasingly affluent and most of all, theirs. When his father had arrived in Scotland from Singapore, he had had nothing, apparently, but Tommy could recall only comfort and security. Whatever had happened before his longed-for arrival in the world was the unknown and never discussed. They spoke Cantonese as a family and maintained the customs of his ancestors but only to a point; real life was modern, the here, the now. Profit was made in the present, not the past.

The car halted outside the impenetrable double gates set in the high wall that ran the uneven circumference of the property. Not big enough for an estate but imposing, substantial and very solid. Two worlds, within and without the wall; the gates a border crossing point manned by CCTV and remote control. There was absolutely no way of opening the gates except from inside. Tommy had rung ahead and was expected. He waited no more than a few seconds before they silently split apart and glided into obscurity, just long enough for him to select drive and gently ease the mechanimal into the pea-gravelled pen. He brought it to rest behind the blacked-out vehicle that had recently conveyed Andy to his appointment then back to Wyeminster, still blindfolded, and spewed him out onto the pavement outside the Nine Gates of Heaven restaurant where his journey had begun. Andy had only a red silk scarf, creased from being knotted too tightly and a single use telephone number committed to memory to show for his travels. Pay as you go phones would be provided, he had been told, once he had called the given number at the appointed time. From then all instructions would be one way; he would simply do as notified.

Tommy cut the engine and left the key in the central console for someone else to park. It would also be washed and valeted, not that it needed it, but nevertheless, it would happen. It always did. His parents' world was ordered, predictable, spotless. One of the high double doors opened to admit him and he stepped into the dim hallway to be greeted by an ivory figurine, Wallis Simpson gaunt, clad in heavy navy-blue silk; always silk. His mother. Even Tommy had no idea how old she was. Her face had always been serenely smooth, her lips carmine, her precise eyebrows dark and pencil slender. She exuded elegance, made high street clothes designer, eschewed ornamentation, very rarely spoke and was omnipotent. She haunted his dreams, chose his wife, moulded his life after her own ambitions. He adored her; she terrified him.

One alabaster cheek was presented as a head on a plate to be kissed and then, their reunion completed, she turned and indicated that he should follow. They crossed the cavernous parquet floor in solemn procession, she leading, cat quiet, and he in submissive pursuit. The rugs on the floor, the lacquer ware and the carved hardwood chairs designed to be admired not occupied were as familiar to him as his own body and yet he felt like a stranger; ever the guest; the school boy heading towards the head's study; the prisoner awaiting an appearance in the dock. None of his qualifications, medical expertise, clinical experience and kudos counted for anything when he was in his parents' house. At a second set of double doors, equally high, heavy and impregnable his mother stopped and opening one only, stood back for him to enter. By the time he had crossed the threshold she had vanished, wraithlike and he was locked in. This was the ante chamber, the waiting room, a 4-D prelude draped in cream brocade with a polished wooden floor upon which every footstep clamoured. Through the curtains he heard the clack of the tiles from the Mah-jong table and knew that his interruption was unwelcome. Worse than that, it was impolite and his father would be embarrassed by the intrusion.

As a condemned man he surreptitiously edged towards the curtained opening where he stood, an awkward youth once more. AT first, he was ignored and the game continued as if his presence was undetected but Tommy knew his father better than that. Mr Yeo smelt out weakness; he missed nothing, observed everything and remembered it all. Lizard-still unless provoked when he would twist and dart away, he tasted people's innermost thoughts as a forked tongue reading the air. The smallest of the four men playing the game at the square table in the centre of the room he was also the most powerful. An insignificant nod from him and the game was immediately paused. Tommy bowed slightly in his direction and followed a respectful distance behind the players as they rose from their seats and followed their leader into a room beyond. There they stood at the round mahogany table, north, south, east and west. Guardians of the world. Their downturned palms, ring fingers and thumbs linked, other fingers soaring free as the Heilokbaat brotherhood makes holy communion is private. Only when Mr Yeo sat and the others followed did Tommy dare approach.

The spokesman was Lee, the same suited, shiny-shoed interviewer of Andy Barrett. Through his Cantonese the Glaswegian accent was subdued but no less abrasive. Tommy felt it scratch and sting as Lee spoke.

"Are these accusations true? Your answer is important for the honour of the family."

"No." Unequivocal. Suppressed passion in Tommy's voice. "They're false."

Heavy silence descended like mustard gas in a trench and settled itself on the ground. Waiting.

"Explain, please." Lee, the suited dummy, speaking for his master, the puppeteer.

"They were wrong. The decision the Multi-Disciplinary Team made was the wrong one. The patient deserved a second chance and that's what I gave him. I know what I did was right. This is a witch hunt. Debbie Crawley's incompetent and uses diversion tactics against me to conceal her deficiencies."

"Debbie Crawley is your colleague? Your superior?" Her name sounded bizarre amidst the click snap of the Cantonese but Tommy did not notice. He was on the line.

"Not officially. Self-appointed on grounds of long service."

Lee was reading the old man's face, preparing to speak his words.

"A long serving colleague should be respected. Especially a woman."

"Ordinarily yes, I agree. But this woman does not deserve respect. And does not have it" he added hastily, "from anyone."

The silence shifted slightly and circled around their ankles.

Mr Yeo's face was impassive save his eyebrows which had ascended towards his distant thinning hairline. Lee continued.

"It is men that should battle, women that should nurture."

"That is as it should be." Tommy knew what had to be said. "But this woman cares only for her cat. She nurtures no-one. Not a husband, or children; not even her patients. That," he paused, "is why I did not follow the directive of the Multi-Disciplinary Team. The MDT is a team of leaders in their clinical field from the whole hospital. She has presumed to appoint herself as their representative and to speak for them. I have no doubt that, given the facts, they would have respected my decision." Another pause. Should he add more? Or would he talk himself through the sale? He chose silence.

Throughout the entire interview the father had been scrutinising his only son, his name bearer, the family line incarnate. Now he turned his head towards Lee and, almost imperceptibly, nodded. Once only before he returned his cool, thin-eyed gaze to his beloved.

“We must not be dishonoured.”

Judgement. Lee’s words echoed around the room, stirring up the sedentary silence into whirlpools of agitated sound that embraced the Mah-jong table in the adjacent room then floated into the ante chamber beyond. The words whispered their way through the keyholes in the double doors and came to rest outside, where Mrs Yeo was standing. Monumental marble, cold. She heard. Slowly her face began to crack and splinter. She smiled.

Chapter Thirteen

The Beginning of December

Christmas was everywhere; tinsel-bright. Nigel tried to pretend it was not happening, that the invitation to conspicuous excess did not include him. He studied his Hush Puppies even more closely as he ambled reluctantly around the supermarket and avoided the high street. At the hospital he adroitly side-stepped any attempt at jollification or enjoyment: no, not for him thank you - mince pies gave him acid reflux and he never drank on duty. Not in his position. Debbie secretly yearned for all the trappings – twinkly lights round windows, blue lit plastic icicles hanging from gutters and porches, a themed tree in the plate glass window beaconing and winking to its compatriots across the street in a secret language of light. Most of all she would have liked to celebrate with Nigel. A cosy, tasteful Christmas. Smoked salmon on blinis with something cold and bubbly on his arrival, the opening of a sophisticated gift that he had modestly presented to her, exquisitely wrapped, then their Christmas lunch. Lunch. Absolutely not dinner. Everyone knew that dinner was eaten in the evening. They would have venison or something gamey, sprouts with bacon and chestnuts, roast parsnips and potatoes, all in small but delicious quantities; she would be the perfect hostess, he the ideal guest. She might even wear a dress. It was a pleasant dream and occupied much of her private time. Miss Muffat would be included of course: a new collar, something jaunty, festive, maybe even a hint of diamante on black velvet. Very Audrey Hepburn.

Lizzie loved Christmas. This year would be the best ever. Andy was a new man; she barely recognised him. This new business, whatever it was, had really motivated him. Not only did he have money now but he got up in the morning, had bought some new clothes, regularly brushed his hair and even wore deodorant. He had cigarettes enough for them both and had talked about them getting mirror tattoos. She was in heaven. If she could have erased Rohan Patel from her life it would have been perfect.

And now here she was, in Wyeminster High Street, outside a jewellers' shop, waiting for her man. Andy had told her he would meet her at 11.30 - sharp. It was her day off and she was excited. Did this mean they were getting engaged? He had not actually proposed, gone down on one knee or even talked about getting married but that was Andy. Individual. Did things his own way. That's why she loved him. They were together forever; who needed a ring or a piece of paper he always said. Right of course, but still, it'd be nice. One furtive glance at her watch, a cheap Casio bought from Argos when she started work as a student nurse and now so dated it had apparently become a collector's item, and she registered that it was nearly noon. Her stomach cramped. She buried herself further into her parka and tried to disappear. The faux fur trim on the hood fell forward over her face and hid the howl of dismay in her eyes.

“Sorry. Held up.”

“Andy!” She tried to keep the relief out of her voice. Did not want him to think she had doubted him.

“Come’n then.”

“Where’re we going? In here?” With a shrug of her head inside the capacious hood she indicated the shop behind them, the Siren diamonds, glittering precious metal; shiny, irresistible.

“Nah. Better. Gotta a plan.” He turned and walked away and she followed, just behind him. Uncertain but devoted. A little way down from the fashionable end of the high street he turned into a narrow alley between two charity shops and grabbed her hand. She was ecstatic. Clamped onto his fingers she willingly allowed herself to be guided out of the alley into a side street inhabited by a dry-cleaners, a cut-price card shop, a pretentious, hopelessly overpriced art shop and a pawnbroker´s.

“Here.”

“Here?”

“Yeah. Come on. It’s all sorted.”

The clamped hand was led into the chipped yellow doorway under the three golden balls and Lizzie found herself walking past Uncle’s ‘we promise to pay a fair price’ grilled window to a scruffy chair in the back of the shop beside a glass counter under which lay several trays of someone else’s rings. Just as the cramp in her stomach was reasserting itself Andy surprised her.

“Choice of two. You decide.”

She had to speak. Quietly, an anxious whisper.

“Are you sure? Can we afford it?”

“Yeah. Told you, didn’t I? That Fentanyl was the last time. I’m clean now. Gotta job. I wanna treat you.”

“Oh Andy!” Almost incoherent with love and relief. But there was still so much she did not know.

“You gotta job?”

“Don’t sound so surprised.”

“I’m not.” Said a little too hastily for absolute conviction but he did not notice. “What job?” Said with innocent curiosity, a ‘just out of interest’ type of enquiry.

“Market research. For a local business. Canvassing opinion, what people think of them, that sort of thing. Sort of undercover. So that people don’t know they’re being asked.”

“What local business?”

“Can’t say but people eat Chinese food there. Know what I mean?”

“Wow.” She really was impressed. “So, you find out what people want and tell the … business … and then they do what you suggest?”

"Yeah. Somethin' like that."

"So, you're a sort of consultant?"

"One way of looking at it. Yeah. A consultant. Not one of your medics though!" It was jest and she laughed, mostly with relief and optimism.

"Come on. Time to choose."

Uncle was unexpected. Late twenties, sharply dressed in a suit with thin lapels and narrow trousers with an open necked white shirt, groomed, stubbled and scented, Rolexed and very smiley.

"Hi! You must be Lizzie. Congratulations! Andy has told me all about you. All good! Hahahahaha. Two beautiful rings to choose from. Always let the lady make the final decision, eh, Andy?" As he spoke without pause for breath, he was spreading out a black velvet cloth on the counter upon which he immediately placed two rings.

"There!" A magician who has just produced rabbits from nowhere, he stood back with a flourish and smirked at his clients.

She was entranced. They were so beautiful. Stunning. And Andy had done all this. For her. She squeezed his hand with all the love she could cram into one set of fingers. Her man.

Both men waited, Uncle patiently with a fixed smile, Andy less so but even he knew that this was Lizzie's moment. It was an impossible choice. One ring was an even yellow gold band, inset with a line of square cut coloured gems – colour and understated quantity. Modern, spare and subtle. She loved it. The other was white gold with three diamonds bulging out of its shank, a magnet for light that it seemed to absorb and regurgitate twice as brightly. The room glowed around it. Lizzie was mesmerised. She more than loved it; it was beyond dreaming. Almost too heavy for her anorexic bony finger when she put it on, the ring glittered at her, illuminating her love and her life.

"This one." Transfixed. "Oh Andy. It's beautiful."

"It's yours."

She was an engaged woman.

***

An important appointment – a commitment. It was on the diary in the kitchen, the hard copy confirmation of the high-tech smart phone Catherine carried with her at all times. The girls needed their annual boosters so she would get the vet to check them over at the same time. Euclid's breath smelt so there might be something wrong with her teeth. Decay was dangerous; had to be excised at source. Catherine had phoned the vets a few days ago to make an appointment at what she assumed would be a quieter time of his day; she did not have time to hang around in waiting rooms. Her life had been consumed by the Tiger Bites case and the Chief Super was on her back like a heavy, hot coat, too tight for comfort, constraining her movements so that she could not even lift her arms above her head, even to surrender. But the girls were her world. Euclid and Pi, two feisty Jack Russells, as far removed from their calculating namesakes as salt from sugar. If Catherine had hoped that such cerebral names would influence their demeanour, she was sadly mistaken. The girls were exuberant to the point of wildness; yappy, energetic and relentless. Pi was moderately less lively but life to Euclid was a rat that needed pursuing, pinning down, then violently shaking until either she was exhausted or it was dead. Usually the latter. Although the elder by two years, Pi followed Euclid in all things except into cold water. They slept on Catherine's bed, in a specially commissioned double dog basket made by a local craftswoman, on the sofas – living room and conservatory, on the spare bed and in 13.5 tog duvet comfort in the boot of her VW estate. Disciplined, stone-rigid at work, unemotional and measured, Catherine wore her heart at the end of two tangled leads that tugged relentlessly, never did as they were told and always panted. The girls went with her everywhere. Literally. They snored untidily in her office on a large bean bag and accompanied her to calls, crime scenes, arrests, raids, searches and team meetings. Catherine without her girls was a phenomenon. As she was good – occasionally excellent – at her job, the Chief Superintendent tolerated what he had once overheard referred to in the station canteen as piebald policing; all three were white with patches.

Catherine swerved her car a little too fast into the vets' small car park. She was taking time out of her day but hell, she put in so much extra no-one could argue, not even the Chief Super. Better not to take too long though. The car stopped with a slight jerk and the girls were thrown against the rear of the back seat. One of them yelped.

"Sorry girls!"

Good, not many cars. It was quiet. Hopefully the appointment would be on time but you never knew what with emergencies and the like, and that was fine; Catherine witnessed carnage and cruelty on a daily basis but could not bear to see an animal suffer.

"C'mon girls. Don't pull." They ignored her until she opened the door to the surgery and the smell of vet stopped them. In their tracks.

"C'mon! Catherine was almost laughing now that she was dragging them behind her into the abhorred antiseptic prison where their claws clacked insecurely on slippery floors and they would have to be lifted up onto one of those cold, shiny metal tables to be prodded and mauled by strangers. The receptionist asked them to take a seat and Catherine sat down opposite an untidy grey woman clasping a cat basket on her lap. She was whispering to the basket and seemed agitated, fluttery and nervy. By now the girls had resigned themselves to their medical fate and were taking a more enthusiastic interest in their new companion, the inhabitant of the creaky wicker receptacle on Debbie Crawley's hairy lap.

"Girls! Behave! Sit!" Then, "Be quiet!" With a combination of tone and biceps Catherine manoeuvred the dogs into some semblance of good behaviour, gripped their collars to maintain order and smiled apologetically at the woman.

"Sorry!

The woman looked up for the first time. She seemed haunted. Thin. Her hair was dripping out of an elastic band over her ears and face and her sleeves, Catherine noticed, were laced with cat hairs.

"Perhaps they're nervous" she said. Catherine was astonished. Close your eyes and listen to her voice and she was a Madonna, an angel, a femme fatale. "Miss Muffat hates the vet" the woman continued. An earnest glance at the basket in her knuckly grip explained that this was her cat which was squinting spitefully at the dogs. More or less the same size, she would be more than a match for them, together or apart.

Referring to her girls, Catherine exaggerated her regret. "I wish! They're always this badly behaved I'm afraid." It was not really an apology; Catherine was actually rather proud of her girls' energetic approach to life but she was mindful of dog owners' codes of behaviour. Like the parents of badly-behaved small children – sound rueful but let them do it anyway.

"Nothing wrong I hope?" The woman seemed genuinely concerned.

"No, just their annual injections. And you?"

"Miss Muffat has been a little under the weather so I want her checked out before Christmas. All the excitement you know. She's a Blue Persian." This was delivered not so much as a description as a diagnosis. "Yes," the beautiful voice continued, "she's delicate. Very sensitive to atmosphere. It's the pedigree. The breed. Renowned for it."

"Really." Catherine was wondering quite how to respond further when Euclid could bear it no longer. She erupted into a white and tan missile of Exocet proportions as she torpedoed towards the cat basket. Catherine found herself on her knees at Debbie's feet. Miss Muffat had been heaved into the air in her basket and was tottering unevenly within it, mewing plaintively. Debbie was standing and staring at the heap of woman and dog draped over her scuffed shoes.

"Sorry!" Catherine gasped out real remorse this time, yanked the dog's collar and fell over onto the unforgiving floor. Pi at the end of her lead had had no choice but to participate in the melee and was skidding her way across to join them. To Catherine's relief and Miss Muffat's disgust, Debbie started to laugh. The sound rang around the room, melodic and graceful, casting its light over the prone Catherine and even the dour receptionist.

"I'm Catherine. Pleased to meet you."

Catherine gathered herself up and sat down, pinioning the girls with stranglehold leads while the cat basket was returned to Debbie's bony lap. She draped herself over her cub like a mother tiger, murmuring consoling sweet nothings to the impervious Miss Muffat.

"Eunice and Pip" the receptionist announced from behind her computer screen. You can go through now. Door three."

Catherine rolled her eyes. "Euclid and Pi" she said, for the millionth time. Debbie was impressed, in spite of herself.

"What unusual names. Erudite."

Catherine's smile had real warmth.

"Thank you. Yes. I'm a mathematician by training. Nice to meet you."

What a brave woman, Debbie thought when they had gone and waited for her summons. No make-up at all. Vitiligo was so ugly, so disfiguring.

Chapter Fourteen

The Following Morning

Lizzie's shift could not come soon enough; never had a day off seemed so long. Or so short. Andy had left her to make her own way home after the visit to the pawnbroker´s – business to attend to he had said and who was she to argue, even on such a day? He was a marketing consultant and with that came responsibilities; serious obligations. Mesmerised by the fire on her finger its light led her through the luminous Christmas streets. It felt as if she was part of another world – the radiant world of the soon to be married woman. For so long condemned to stand on its borders looking in, she was now to be admitted, to join the hallowed beloved, the attached, the never alone. Andy would forever be Her Man. The thrill she felt sizzled as much as her joy in the ring itself. She would have to try and remove the nicotine stains on her ring finger though, then hold her cigarettes in her other hand. Might even get her nails done.

She arrived early the next day, gloveless despite the morning chill, and upbeat. No furtive cigarette behind the hedge to ignite the shift today – she wanted to be seen. It took a nanosecond. The 'she's got a ring on her finger' alert went out as soon as she waved to the receptionist before changeover. It was managed superbly; a nonchalant wave under the grotty overhead NHS strip light to interact with the diamonds and the deed was done. Maureen would tell everyone; she was famous for it. Lizzie had chosen her herald well and Maureen was on top form. Especially as this was unforeseen and unexpected. Real news! Such excitement. Lizzie's chances of marriage had never been rated higher than 100 to 1; those who knew Andy (and those who did not) had all written him off as a potential husband. By the time Lizzie arrived in the Emergency Department everyone was looking for her left hand.

"My God! It's huge!" Sesi was undeniably astonished; she was running-busy but had diverted from Acute Care to triage for a glimpse of what she heard described as mega-bling. Maureen was prone to embroider but not on this occasion. The ring was beyond vulgar, flamboyant to the point of self-defined good taste. But Sesi had met Andy. How the hell could he afford such a bauble? Shaking her head in bemused disbelief she ran on to the blood and carnage of the Acute ward and left Lizzie in the centre of an admiring group of nurses, auxiliaries, hygiene maintenance staff, admin staff, porters, passers-by and patients. She could hear the oohs and aahs behind her all the way down the corridor and almost collided with Rohan padding plumply towards her.

"What's the fuss?"

"Lizzie's engaged. Massive rocks." Her words floated behind her; Sesi was gone before they had settled on Rohan and soaked in.

“What?” Now he could see for himself. Lizzie was the eye of the admiration storm, almost hidden behind the screen of exclamations and congratulations circling her like crows on carrion. Women especially, all affecting to be delighted but resenting the ostentation and size of the ornament, were following her every move: seagulls around a fishing vessel, ready to swoop and dive. As soon as Lizzie was out of hearing they would be discussing the showy gewgaw and speculating about the wedding. By lunchtime Lizzie’s wedding dress, reception, first dance music, honeymoon, impending motherhood and occasionally her fiancé would have been discussed, dissected and derided in minute detail.

Lizzie must have sensed Rohan approaching because she looked up out of her throng of admirers. Well, nothing for it. She could not avoid him. It had to be done, and done now. Nothing for her to feel guilty about anyway; Rohan knew it was all a game and she had done it for Andy. Her husband to be. That alone was enough to make her face any number of Rohan Patels.

“Do you like it?” She had lifted her hand above the circle of heads for Rohan, hovering on the border, to see more clearly. The diamonds leered at him.

“Very nice, Lizzie. From your boyfriend?”

Now Lizzie leered. Mocked. Offended by his insinuation. Just what did he think she was?

"Of course! Who else?" Rohan did not reply but it did not matter; his silence was lost in the competitive oohing and aahing of the rest of the audience. He tried again.

"So now you are an engaged lady?" As if to confirm what he already knew but perhaps to make a point? He emphasised the word 'lady' in such a way as to sound sarcastic. She chose not to understand.

"'Fraid so."

"No hope for anyone else then? Even if they were on a promise?"

Lizzie hit him between the eyes. Blatant. Defiant.

"No hope at all. Rohan. No hope at all." She ignored his puppy dog eyes and her smile kicked him in the abdomen. He wanted to retch. He tried to smile back as she returned her attention to her retinue and they all moved in a clump towards the reception area, where new admirers were to be found. Rohan felt outraged. Repudiated. Rejected. The risks he had taken for her! Fentanyl was the class A drug of choice, worth a fortune on the street; everyone wanted it and he, he! had risked his job, reputation, everything for her. She had promised! He might have become a thief but he would never have reneged on a promise like that. How dare she? His stomach heaved; lurched towards his throat. He just made it to the toilet.

Only some time later would Rohan hate her, but he kept smiling. Revenge was a dish best served icy cold. He would wait.

Lizzie was early but Debbie was about to be uncharacteristically late. She, who prided herself on her punctuality and reliability, was about to become one of those flighty types who could not be depended on and always blamed their car or public transport for what could only ever be described as their own failure. Leave earlier, get the car serviced but don't blame anyone but yourself for being late. She had said it a thousand times; people should take a leaf out of her book. It was their duty, their responsibility to arrive at work on time. She led by example.

This morning was the exact replica of every other morning and at 7.15, precisely, she was bidding a fond farewell to the imperious Miss Muffat, installed on her chair in the living room as a furry monarch in a dimly lit throne room.

"Shall I leave a light on for you, my poppet? Yes, I think I shall. Such dark mornings. Never mind. Soon be Christmas and Mummy will be home with her darling Missy Muffat." Here the darling was snuggled and kissed and Debbie became still more hairy. "There!" A depressed beige-shaded lamp was switched on and peered desperately into the gloom, blowing its feeble light like a dandelion clock into the air into which it promptly disappeared. Miss Muffat shook herself free of the polyester embrace and settled down into obdurate slumber. Debbie reluctantly stood up, picked up her carrier bag and keys and headed for the front door. She never bothered with a handbag – her cloth carrier, souvenir of a Colonoscopy conference in the noughties at which she had been an invited delegate was so much more practical. Light to carry, big enough for all her needs – hanky, small bottle of water, purse, phone, reading glasses, occasionally a shopping list. The bag was marvellous really: no need for additional bags in the supermarket and it even went through the washing machine. She picked up her grey polyester headscarf and twisted it loosely around her neck then removed the good, dark grey, wool coat from its hook on the wall and pleated it over her arm as she unbolted and unlocked the door. Nigel had once commented on her security measures which had touched her, deeply. So nice to know he cared about her safety and a woman living on her own could never be too careful, especially when she had a cat to protect.

It was a cold, gunmetal grey morning, not quite dark but not light either. A sort of diurnal no man's land, trying to make up its mind whether it was sun up or sun down. Morning twilight. A dress rehearsal for the shortest day soon to come. Her brown 1.4 VW Golf was on the drive, barely visible against the murky backdrop but, as ever, pristine. Hard to believe it was ten years old but she had had it from new and, as her father always said, if you look after a car properly it will look after you. Debbie shivered in the chill and briefly regretted that she had not put on the coat over her arm but it was such a short distance to the car which would soon warm up. The comforting ping of the remote locking system opening itself up and she had opened the driver door. The tang of the citrus air freshener hanging from the rear-view mirror, her leather driving gloves in that convenient little cubby hole in the central console, the settee cushion on the back seat and the trusty box of tissues on the rear parcel shelf – all part of the familiar morning routine.

But something did not feel quite right. Key in the ignition she was about to start the engine but stopped. To think. Had she forgotten something? She examined the contents of the passenger seat beside her. Reading glasses? She had used them for the newspaper yesterday evening; she liked to do what she could of the cryptic crossword even though some of the clues were obscure to the point of stupidity and it was no wonder that she never finished it. No, everything was there. She pulled on her gloves and flexed her fingers inside them as her father had taught her. So much better for a grip on the steering wheel as well as an echo of the day trips they had enjoyed together after her mother died. Perhaps it was Miss Muffat? Had she left her enough water and food for the day? She was sure she had, but should she go and check, just in case? Glancing at her watch she saw that time was against her and it would not do to be late. No, Miss Muffat was fine. Debbie started the engine, depressed the clutch and put the car into reverse gear. She released the handbrake and let the car start to roll down the slightly inclined drive towards the road. It felt sluggish, heavy, unwieldy, the steering wheel would not move, felt somehow fixed. Why? Something was wrong. Changing to neutral and yanking up the hand brake she opened her door and stepped out. Standing back from it, she studied her car. And was horrified. Shocked. Bewildered. Every tyre was flat. The rims were resting on the drive, shielded from it by only a flaccid ribbon of black rubber which spread out below them like an ink stain.

It was noisy in the corridor and Clare could hardly hear. Hospital primetime: changeover at 8.00 a.m., was an inviolable hour. That was when night became day, regardless of what was happening in the outside world. Surgery day cases started earlier; the day ward reception area was already full of nil-by-mouth patients, clutching their dressing gowns and slippers, awaiting their summons to the knife. No one called their Chief Executive much before changeover unless it was personal – it was the best time to talk to her – or urgent. She saw that the caller was Debbie and was surprised.

Struggling to hear what she was saying, dodging the stream of humanity flowing down the main corridor, nodding preoccupied greetings to those she recognised, with one finger in her ear so as to hear (not much better) while she balanced her briefcase under her telephone arm, she discovered to her chagrin that she was unreasonably annoyed.

“Can’t you get a taxi? We’ll send one for you if you like. If you’re not here it’s going to cause chaos. All your patients and Tommy’s will have to be cancelled and rescheduled. Couldn’t you come in once the car has been towed?” Clearly not. Her eyes rolled involuntarily upwards and she grimaced, but still somehow nodded greetings to oncoming staff as they diverted past her as a stone in a stream.

“Well. We’ll just have to manage won’t we. Keep me informed, Debbie.” She ended the call abruptly. Furious.

“Bloody hell.” She stopped being sociable, put her head down and marched towards her office, stabbing the speed dial for the Medical Director as she went.

Chapter Fifteen

The Same Day

Wyeminster Police Station was made of Cotswold stone, quaint, of architectural significance and totally unfit for purpose. Restricted by space, budget and imagination, the interior had been modernised and updated so often it felt like the Tardis. No one quite knew where they would land next in terms of innovation and improvement but one thing was assured, it would not be suitable, big enough or technologically reliable. In theory Catherine had a small office on the second floor adjacent to the larger open plan work space of her team. She was, in fact, merely partitioned off from them by chipboard through which all her conversations and the snores of the girls could be heard with a clarity unobtainable on many of the landlines in the building. But her team were used to it and while a new, spacious, well-lit bespoke building was something only dreams were made of, they had grown so accustomed to the cables draped across the floor like ivy frightened of heights, the clutter, the arcane coffee machine, the gurgle of the nearly always empty water cooler, the incongruity of high-tech policing within Victorian Gothic walls laced with gargoyles and arched windows.

Catherine had not been the first to arrive that morning. This Tiger Bites case had overwhelmed everything else and, not just because kids were involved, everyone wanted it resolved. She could hear the murmur of the team members outside her door as they geared up for another frustrating day – coffee, the briefest of updates on their social lives, love lives, marital problems, last night's telly then the sound of concentration as they settled themselves in front of computer screens and buried themselves in data and documents. She finished the sudoku puzzle she set herself to complete every morning; a catalyst for creative logical, sequential thought. Catherine liked definitions and lines, formulaic patterns and answers. Essentially box-like, in body and mind, she also rejoiced in the ability to think outside the grid which made her agonisingly uncomfortable company in anything social but the girls never noticed so who cared?

She looked at her watch – peculiarly frivolous and expensively delicate for such a sturdy no-nonsense wrist. Time for the morning briefing.

"Stay!" Neither of the girls had the least inclination to follow anyway so simply continued snoring but Catherine seemed gratified by their obedience so was smiling, almost, when she stood herself in front of the whiteboard in the centre of the room. It was the focal point of the investigation, hearth and home, scribbled with coloured marks and badly wiped smears from previous attempts to unravel the case. What they really needed was an interactive whiteboard but that would come with the new custom-built police station sometime in the foreseen never.

"Right. Where are we? I've got nothing new so let's hear what you have to say. Mike, you recap for us. Maybe hearing it from someone else will help us think; see things differently."

"Yes, Ma'am." Mike sprang eagerly out of his battered swivel chair. He was always enthusiastic; it was exhausting. How he found the time and energy to run across fells and up mountains mystified Catherine. He also sang in a choir and was a leading light in the Wyeminster Gilbert and Sullivan Society. Nauseating really, she thought, but she still bought tickets to his events which she never attended. Mid 50s going on 30 she thought. Fair play to him though, exuberance was in short supply as a rule and he had kept them going on more than one occasion.

"Well, we know the victims" here he pointed to the names Joshua Critchley and Taya Addo written on the whiteboard, "and we know when and how they got the drugs but so far we don't know anything about the supplier. Donald Trump." They all studied the picture of the American president stuck up on the board with a red line scrawled across his throat. Might be better if the Chief Super doesn't see that thought Catherine. Mike continued.

"There has been a substantial rise in identified cases of Tiger Bites substance abuse so we know that the distribution network is effective and increasing. Users are mostly young – teenagers – buying at the school gates and in clubs, usually at weekends." There was a silence. "And that's where we are." Another brief pause. "Oh, but we do know that the two kids have recovered and are OK so that's good news."

The silence was deafening.

"Anyone got anything to add?" Catherine already knew the answer but it was worth a try. She surveyed the blank faces, all keen to have something to contribute but all barren. No help at all.

"Or ask?" She added hopefully.

D.C. Nicole Marechal raised her hand. The new kid on the block, anxious to please, even more anxious to impress. Not only the newest member of the team but probably the youngest – she certainly looked it.

"DC Marechal? Nicole?" Catherine was surprised. This had better not be a waste of time.

"What about the man in the mask?"

"What about him?"

"There's no trace of him anywhere?"

"Back in the White House. After a brief sojourn in our historic city for a spot of trick or treating the illustrious president of the United States has now, according to news reports, returned to his home in Washington." Nicole blushed. Catherine was irritated. "If there was a man disguised as Donald Trump, dead or alive, still roaming the streets of Wyeminster don't you think even we would have picked him up by now?"

No one looked anywhere but the floor, or at the ceiling, or at a sudden blemish on a hand that had materialised from nowhere. Nicole burned. Mike sought to clean some of the smears off the whiteboard with his shirt cuff. Catherine was unrepentant and nothing if not determined.

"Anything else? Anyone?"

"What about the increase in petty theft and vandalism? We had a report about randomly slashed car tyres only this morning. All four tyres, nice quiet street in one of the villages, no sign of disturbance, noise, nothing." It was a sensible question; Mike had saved the day and Catherine forgot her annoyance with the rookie D.C. in order to reply.

"Probably no connection. Just the usual brand of local hooliganism from our discontented youth who have nothing else to do. One of the villages you say? Not the city? I'd be more interested if it was in Wyeminster itself, but keep an eye on it, Mike. And all of you. With Christmas fast upon us I want this case sorted. Or none of us is going to be either festive or on holiday. Not to mention the kids at risk." The smell of despondency hung in the air. Catherine relented, just a little, just enough to give them her brand of pep talk.

"Think of it as algebra. Use the knowledge of where and when to find the value of x, ie. the supplier, and then it will all fall into place. And get on with it."

***

Lizzie was still getting accustomed to the demands of senior nursing while wearing a carbon explosion on her ring finger. Reluctantly she dimmed its glory in sterile sticky tape when on duty and accepted that she would have to remove it to wear the statutory latex gloves. Perhaps she could put it on a chain around her neck so that it was still visible, but what if she bent over and caught it on something – or someone? It might get damaged. No, better to take it off and put it in her pocket. Precious pocket which she patted countless times an hour as if to console the ring for its absence from public gaze. Maureen the receptionist, she of the irrepressible tongue, had told her to wash it in gin if it got dirty or bloodied. Lizzie was weighing up the merits of supermarket gin versus the more expensive brands as she wandered into the waiting area in pursuit of her next patient when she noticed an agitated middle-aged woman leaning into the window of the reception area.

"Taya Addo. I'm her foster mother, Annie Ghebo. She's on your system already. She was only discharged a little while ago. Opioid poisoning. The Tiger Bites girl." The woman was speaking very loudly and painstakingly as if talking to a child or a foreign language student taking dictation. A wan, limpid Taya was slumping next to Ella on one of the unforgiving plastic chairs, as vividly bright as she was pale. Ella had her arm around her as much to maintain her upright as to provide comfort.

"Taya!"

"Hi Lizzie."

It was impossible to resist.

"Look!" Lizzie's left hand flashed forward, fingers wiggling as if drying nail varnish. Taya blinked. Ella was stunned.

"Wow. Congratulations. Is it real?"

"Yeah. Diamonds." The ring was thrust forward for closer inspection and admiration. Taya focused carefully on the glitter at the end of her nose. Ella stared in aggressive disbelief. It was only then that Lizzie saw the girl rather than the opportunity and felt the heat of her breath on her nicotine-yellow finger ends.

"You OK, Taya?"

"Of course she's not okay." Ella was livid. "She wouldn't be here if she was, would she?"

"What's the matter?"

Fortunately, Taya answered before Ella could detonate.

"Bit hot."

"Anything else?"

"Bit headachy. And tired."

"Come with me." Ella immediately forgave Lizzie and helped Taya to stand. Annie abandoned the reception desk and sprinted after them into the assessment area.

"High temperature and rapid pulse. Says she's tired and has a headache which has got steadily worse all day. Her foster parents were concerned so brought her in about an hour ago. One of them was so concerned she didn't go into work today." Lizzie was describing Taya's symptoms and Sesi was listening intently. "Her pelvic area and abdomen are very tender to the touch."

"Bloods?"

"Done as soon as she came in."

"Hm. We need the results but if it's what I think, she may have perforations in her bowel. Not surprising after what she's been through. Better find a bed for her and I'll contact the Colorectal consultant. If I'm right it may mean surgery." She was speed dialling the lab for the results of the blood tests as she spoke.

"Are you certain?" Debbie did not want to appear sceptical but she was a senior consultant and Sesi still had much to learn. "Oh. Well, if her bloods are abnormal and there are raised inflammatory markers then yes, obviously she is urgent. But we simply don't have the capacity at the moment." Debbie was trying very hard to be patient. "We're understaffed and our lists are completely full. And yes, I am very well aware that this is a high-profile case but I don't know what you expect me to do about it." Her lips folded in on themselves under her thin nose with repressed fury. “You’ve spoken to the Medical Director?” The cat hairs on her sleeves bristled; her lank hair tried to shrug itself free of its elastic band to protest; her outrage overflowed into the mobile phone to soak Sesi on the other end, but she stood firm, shook off the deluge and stayed dry. Debbie had to capitulate.

“Well, obviously, she has to be operated on. As soon as possible. It will have to be a sub total colectomy for perforations like that… I’ll do it tonight. Out of hours so that we can clear the lists… Not much choice is there? You’re lucky that I’m on call.” Incandescent but icily polite. Professional. Cornered. Calm. But Sesi had made an enemy.

***

Miss Muffat never minded being home alone. It did not bother her if the thin grey one was there or not. Cuddles were an occupational hazard to be tolerated, not least because they were invariably the prelude to comestibles and treats. Besides, being the centre of attention was always so gratifying. Darkness was immaterial as long as she was warm. Consequently, she hardly noticed the two black-clad, balaclavaed men who crept silently into the house by the back door as she reclined on her dusky throne. Their slim torchlight barely disturbed the darkness once they had closed the curtains and they seemed to know their way about, so what was it to her? The one in the kitchen made the same sort of metallic bumping noises as the thin grey one but with none of her flat, slappy footsteps. The one upstairs had seemed to float his way upwards, soundlessly lithe and swift. Miss Muffat stretched out her front legs and languidly flexed her claws before settling herself ever more comfortably and falling into an untroubled slumber. She did not hear the men as they let themselves out of the front door and blended into the night.

***

Debbie preferred theatre number two but three was the only one available so here she was, standing at the table leading a full team opposite Abebi Agbaje, her assistant surgeon. The Consultant Anaesthetist was new to her, a recent addition to the hospital and it would be interesting to discuss him with Lesley after the event. He seemed capable enough; quiet and cooperative, acknowledging her superiority in the room even though it was within his power to call a halt to proceedings at any time if he felt the patient was at risk. This was the Anaesthetist's trump card, rarely played but hanging over every Consultant Surgeon like a sword, in and out of the operating theatre. Her team were unused to working with her, a mish mash of those who happened to be on call or were available. No agency nurses thank goodness, that would have been just a step too far for something as delicate as this. Let them loose on the wards by all means but Debbie liked to know that those she was commanding had knowledge and experience of Wyeminster procedures. Her role was difficult enough without having to nursemaid supposedly qualified staff; they were there to support her, not the other way around.

Things were not going well. Incision, opening up and establishing access had been routine. Taya's abdomen was now exposed and retracted, a wide, open eye pinned apart by metal clips, staring and unseeing, mushy and red. Debbie was watching Abebi's hands rummaging inside the orifice, fudging the issue. They had hardly begun the difficult part of the procedure; all he had to do was wash out the colon and suck out the contamination. He was clumsy and hesitant and it was extremely annoying, but how was he to learn if he did not do it himself? Did she have to do everything? Against the background hum of monitors and the breath of the ventilator, the mannerly clatter of instruments against metal trays and the lip-smacking slurp of suction, there was tension.

"Suck... More Suck. Suck. I said suck!" Her voice was now shrill and ugly; getting ever louder. "Of for goodness sake! Just suck it."

Abebi was sweating, freely, his sterile mask becoming damp and dark over his nose and mouth as he breathed heavily and continued to fumble inside Taya. He blinked the sweat from his sable eyes and wished someone would wipe his brow but no one moved. No one dared. Miss Crawley was so intractable. Initiative was insubordination in her book and no one wanted her input on their reports, not if they wanted to progress in the medical world. He wanted to sigh, but instead focused his energy on a renewed attempt to extract the pus at his finger-tips.

“That’ll do. I’ll take over.” As Debbie probed her way into the peritoneum there was a hiss of released gas. “To be expected” she announced. “Typical of colonic perforation.” So Sesi’s initial diagnosis had been correct; the knowledge made Debbie grimace.

“I’m going to mobilise the right colon without…” here she peered irritably into the aperture, “damaging the duodenum or cutting the right ureter, which is all too easy to do.” She said this more for her own edification having done so on too many past occasions. It would be awkward if she had to call in a urologist to put in a stent from below; there was no one immediately available and, as the upstart Sesi had reminded her, this was such a high-profile case. The team watched closely as she started to open the lesser sac by clipping and dividing the vessels. Only startled eyes under flying eyebrows expressed their consternation when she got lost. The eyebrows disappeared into hairlines when she quietly abandoned the right colon to move onto the left, taking care, again, not to cut the left ureter. By now she too was sweating, beads of moisture ornamenting her sallow brow and trickling down the crevices alongside the angular nose down into her mask. No one offered assistance. It would only be misinterpreted. She was still rummaging in the Taya’s abdomen however, approaching the sharp colonic bend close to the spleen – the splenic flexure. Cutting this out was always notoriously tricky and everyone knew it; the spleen was perilously close nearby and if damaged in the process, the result would be catastrophic bleeding. There had been an occasion a year or so ago when she had attempted the procedure but compromised the spleen. The subsequent bleeding had caused her to panic and freeze; she had had to hand the procedure over to Juan who had been in theatre with her and who had discreetly assumed control of the situation. Since then she preferred to operate with him than without.

Debbie focussed her attention on her latex covered hands as she removed them from Taya and held them slightly aloft, as if invoking the Gods to bless her endeavours. She was oblivious to the anxiety of her team, watching her, waiting for her next move. Abebi was sweating again, mostly from apprehension. Somehow, he knew what was coming. Whatever happened, it would never be her fault.

"I am concerned, Mr Agbaje. And surprised. I am sorry to have to say this to someone with your qualifications and experience but," now she looked directly at him, hands still raised in supplication. "You do not inspire confidence as an assistant surgeon." He flinched. "It is unfortunate that this has had to happen at this time of night when no one more capable is readily available." A slight pause. "And this is such a sensitive case," she added reproachfully, as if that was also his fault.

The audible gasp in the room was partially subsumed in the inhalation of the ventilator. Oblivious to the disquiet, Debbie summoned the runner.

"Juan Morales lives locally. Call him at home. Say Miss Crawley wants him in theatre, urgently. He's to come at once." Then to the stunned Consultant Anaesthetist sitting at Taya's head,

"Stabilise her until he arrives. I'm stepping out for a minute." And she was gone, not even a rogue cat hair in her wake.

A moment of profound silence embraced the leaderless operating theatre and then the outrage erupted. Only Abebi and the Consultant Anaesthetist said nothing, both too shocked to speak. They recognised the reality of Miss Crawley's decision. To allow a junior, however capable, to participate in an operation the lead surgeon had to be confident in their own ability to repair any inadvertent damage that could occur. They had to be able to deal with any situation that might arise. Experience and a cool head under pressure were prerequisite and Debbie clearly did not have faith enough in herself and her expertise to proceed. Abebi was the scapegoat; his reputation had been sacrificed for the greater good of Debbie Crawley. He knew it. That hurt more even than his public humiliation. It was unfair. Unjustified. And there was nothing he could do about it.

Juan was equally unhappy. His plans for the evening had been aborted almost at the point of conception. He had dressed carefully – bespoke black tie, soft but crisp, white wing-collar shirt, professionally laundered and pressed. Immaculate. As he drove his classic E-type through the dark streets towards the infirmary he tugged the bow tie undone. Damn. It had taken him almost ten minutes of tying and retying it to achieve symmetry and perfection and now, it was all wasted effort because Debbie was in another surgical lather. Really, the woman was a liability. How did she get away with it? She had not even had the courtesy to phone him herself but had sent some hapless runner to do the deed on her behalf. As he swung the car into the car park entrance, swiped his pass and waited for the barrier to rise he thought ruefully of the evening that would now never be. Poker, an excellent meal, seduction and pleasure. Abandoned for scrubs, faeces and a hairy colleague. He put the memory of the just poured glass of chilled Chablis sitting on his dining room table to one side and parked the car.

They had been operating now for about two hours and Juan was leading, Debbie standing opposite, supervising. Abebi stood to one side of Juan, observant and mortified. Miss Crawley had not spoken a single word to him since her return to theatre but Mr Morales had been friendly enough; perhaps he did not know what had happened? He would find out soon enough though, as would the rest of the hospital. There would be little else discussed the next day, especially as the runner despatched to fetch Juan had already WhatsApped a large section of the admin and nursing staff with a particularly salacious account of what had happened. It would be common knowledge by the next morning's changeover and ancient history by lunchtime. Everyone but Senior Management would know all about it.

"As we are not doing this by keyhole," Juan looked at Debbie as he spoke, "I'm taking particular care with the sutures. We don't want to have to come back." Abebi nodded heartily.

"The small bowel – look, Abebi – is strategically positioned for the ileostomy. Nice and discreet for a young lady."

"Will it be permanent?"

Debbie answered the redundant assistant surgeon without so much as looking at him.

"We'll decide later, depending on how she gets on. Thank you, Mr Morales. That, Mr Agbaje, is how it should be done." What was left of Abebi's shredded self-esteem trembled and fluttered to the floor where it would be sluiced away by the early morning cleaning crew.

"I'll take over now and tie up the ends." On cue, Juan stood back as Debbie bent over to concentrate, close and complete. She did not see the exchange of glances that flew between the team standing around her, dipping only to include the seated Consultant Anaesthetist who, perhaps for the first time in his illustrious career, had found complete understanding with a surgical team. Anaesthetists were a breed apart

– the clever ones, aloof, detached, independent. It was a new experience for him to be bonded by outrage to the rest of the surgical fraternity. Impossible not to want to know more; he would talk to his anaesthetic colleagues. The short, fat more Welsh-than- the-Welsh one, Lesley something. Always talking but saying nothing. She'd be bound to know and only too glad to tell anyone willing to listen.

Chapter Sixteen

What Happened Next

It was very late – or was it very early? Juan was not sure until he glanced at the dashboard and saw that it was indeed the next day and very early indeed. He slid the car as quietly as all its horsepower and throttle permitted into the bay outside his house. The street was motionless; not even a blink from the stark-eyed lights of the overhead lamps gazing at the cars below them, rigid sentries until daylight relieved them from duty. The house was Victorian and immaculate; period perfect, double fronted with a sombre black door under an arched fanlight. Inconspicuous affluence; self-contented, self-contained, smug. It smirked superiority. Apart from Juan, no one from the infirmary had ever ascended its smooth stone steps and crossed its brass-edged threshold. The Connemara marble black and white tiled hall floor might just have been visible to uninvited callers when the door was opened but no hand-made leather soled shoes other than Juan's had ever graced its chilly perfection.

He liked being an enigma. His wealth was mysterious, unaccounted for, apparently limitless. Speculation had been epidemic when he had arrived in Wyeminster ten years ago and was still a perennial topic of conversation, rearing its familiar head whenever he appeared in a new-old car, always classic, always British racing green. Although he downplayed his prosperity, the idea of compromising taste and style was insupportable so he carried with him an air of understated prosperity. Sophisticated chic, not shabby; tailored, charming in an old-fashioned gentlemanly way that offended no one, not even ardent feminists who found his manners engaging; ingratiating rather than offensive. Juan could get away with murder.

As he unlocked the front door and opened it sufficiently only to edge round and disappear into the dark interior, he was preoccupied. It had been a long night but there was still time enough to salvage something of his original plans. In the dining room the glass of Chablis was now dejectedly tepid, but still full. The second glass on the table was empty and the open bottle half full beside it. Walking straight past he entered the dimly lit kitchen, all stainless steel and barren granite worktops and opened the double doored fridge. The exploding funnel of light blazed over his chiselled Mediterranean features, casting the dark stubble into shadow below the high cheekbones and heavy eyebrows. Juan's Spanish antecedents made manifest, once an Adonis but now older, a little plumper and a great deal wiser. It was not that he had anything to hide, except perhaps that unfortunate incident with the Geography teacher when at school but he had been a minor and no charges had been brought. Since then he had learned the value of discretion. The profit he made from gambling and his private life, especially affairs of the heart and more often, of the body, were kept completely, utterly clandestine.

He reached for another bottle of Chablis but changed his mind. Why not? The Dom Perignon was cradled as carefully as a newborn under his arm as pressed the handless cupboard door which obligingly swung open, enabling him to pick up two clean glasses (crystal but not cut glass: so dated) with his other hand. Then, with weasel agility he bent down into the fridge and from a bowl of fruit, sucked an apple into his soft mouth where he held it, undamaged and juicy. Balancing champagne, crystal and Cox's Orange Pippin he swiftly ascended the carpeted stairs.

***

Winter, deceptively amiable in tinsel and LED lights, was increasing the pressure on the sun's throat and the days were noticeably shorter. In Debbie's house it made little difference. Miss Muffat occupied a twilight realm in shades of brown, dusty and dim. Even when her mistress would arrive home, evening or morning, the stale sepia interior remained much the same. A forty-watt world, interminable, unchanging, more hirsute even than Debbie herself. In her kitchen gasps of sunshine had managed to sieve through slim gaps in the yellowed Venetian blinds which were permanently half closed and never altered. The once white cord holding them in situ had not been used for so long that it had cemented itself with dust and hair into a Gordian knot and the imprisoned blinds had gradually fossilised into brittle plastic bars across the window, sealing in the dark. The impudence of the penetrating sun tantalised the gloom with bright fingers but strayed no further than the window sill and once stainless, steel sink. When her father died and left her the value of a similar house in a similar city in the next county, Debbie had briefly contemplated installing a new kitchen. But then common sense and Nigel had prevailed; waste of money; nothing wrong with the current one; keep the money in the bank; don't invest in stocks and shares but choose something dependable. Less return, but less risk and inflation would never be as bad as it had been in the 70s and 80s would it? So, the kitchen had stayed but she had splashed out on a microwave which sat, white and alien on the beige worktop and glared with hostile modernity at the rest of the room.

This morning however, the microwave had been galvanised into outraged action. It stared at the timer on the cooker opposite which was flashing and ringing. Damn thing had had the temerity to turn itself on at 8.00 am precisely and would not stop its infernal noise. On and on it went, remorseless, tinny and intrusive. The whole kitchen had been set on edge; the noise ricocheted around it, bouncing off the surfaces to rebound against others, abrasive and grating. Fracturing the silence, tormenting solitude, the repetitive clanging contrasted sharply with the most recent additions to the room: two silent, smooth white stones, no bigger than a baby's fist curled in sleep. They sat placidly on the window sill in full view of the appalled microwave and the shouting cooker. On the wall the clock was dead, its hands forever pinned at 6.00.

Upstairs, in perfect harmony, the digital alarm clock beside Debbie's single bed was ringing in similar fashion, 8.00 flashing in vulgar, insistent red. Miss Muffat, now cossetted by pillows and duvet, took absolutely no notice. No more did Debbie as she parked the brown Golf on the drive when she finally arrived home after such an arduous night. Really, the responsibilities of senior consultancy were sometimes just too onerous. She would say something at the next management meeting; it was unacceptable to have to operate with insufficiently experienced colleagues, regardless of their paper qualifications. In the case of Mr Agbaje she had wondered, not for the first time, whether or not it was wise to employ medical staff from other countries. They had different standards of training. Of course, she could not comment, but it was noticeable how many of them struggled to adapt to the standards demanded by the NHS. Naturally she could only speak from her own experience and would not dream of criticising, but this was not the first time and sadly, she feared it might not be the last. Was it just her? When no one responded, as she knew would be the case, she would know that she was totally vindicated. Someone had to say these things, no matter how unpleasant or politically incorrect. Never shirk your responsibility, Deborah! She could hear Father saying it now.

The road was quiet. Before the school run and after the main exodus of those heading off to work, Debbie rejoiced briefly in the unobtrusive exclusivity of the street and locked the car then, like Nigel the beloved, checked the driver door to make sure it was secure and headed towards the front door. It was chilly so she had put on her coat. The cloth carrier bag sagged despairingly over her shoulder, limp, defenceless while she rummaged in it for her house keys, much as she had rummaged inside Taya. Keys found, she inserted them in the lock, opened the door and entered. Through the dirty frosted glass of the closed door her thin shape fissured and faded as she disappeared into the unlit hallway.

***

Unlike the cash starved police station, Wyeminster Grammar School was a concrete and glass tribute to the foresight and generosity of a city council that manifestly valued the education of it young people, and their voting parents. The only part of the original nineteenth century building that remained was the tree shadowed, oak panelled hall – now a reception room – and a cloister-like long corridor lined with Rolls of Honour, preserved, polished and read only by potential parents on Open Days and anxious offspring sitting entrance exams. The school had an 'excellent reputation' and was the school of choice for aspiring parents and grandparents from a large catchment area and beyond. Competition for places was ferocious, not just because of the promise of academic success but the social cachet of being able to modestly broadcast that one had a son/daughter/grandchild/miscellaneous relative at The Grammar School. And of course, there were no fees to pay. The mark up on the cost of their exclusive blazers sent the only local retailer skiing in Colorado (no language barrier) every winter, but back well in time for Entrance Exam Results Day in early March when there was always a rush on supplies. A private education at public expense. Perfect. The elaborate wrought iron school gates guarding the well-trodden path to the old hall were kept shut and locked. Access to the school was now further down the same road away via a wide drive with electronic barriers and electric gates activated by swipe cards, monitored by CCTV, open, well-lit and public. The only way in and out; secure, efficient. No other means of access or escape from a campus surrounded by high steel fencing. No chance of a Dunblane or Columbine here, thank you very much. Now a sprawling mass of 'innovative forums of learning' according to the succession of architects tendering for contracts, the school had grown hugely. Its pupil intake had been steadily increased so although exam success was still required to enter its hallowed portals, standards had quietly dropped. But no one seemed to have noticed; safety in numbers.

This morning, as Debbie was arriving home, the scholars of Wyeminster were making their way towards their esteemed temple of learning. The entrance gate was a mass of heaving humanity punctuated by cars, laced together by the threads of bicycles, skateboards and scooters. A huge living corset, seething and squeezed with all shapes and sizes of youth shifting together. The single exception was the tall, skeletal male who was walking away from it all towards the reclusive old gates, without so much as a backward glance. He knew he would be followed. All he had to do was wait.

***

Catherine was not waiting for anyone, not even Euclid and Pi who were being particularly uncooperative.

"I know it's cold and dark but what can I do about it? Now do you want a walk or not?" Murderous looks from both by way of an answer and a stubborn refusal to move.

"Alright. We'll go straight to work. Fine by me. Come on." She patted the pocket of her all weather, guaranteed 100% showerproof quilted jacket. So practical. "Damn. No keys. Wait there."

Euclid and Pi exchanged glances and sat down. Yes! Catherine wound their already tangled leads around the driver wing mirror of her car and headed towards the front door of her sturdy detached (only just) four-bedroom, fireplace optional, new build, one of five, set back from the road in a pea gravelled crescent. Exclusive and new, functional, reliable and predictable. Exactly what she wanted although the integral garage had had to be converted into a utility room for the girls' paraphernalia. How had they accumulated so much?

"Wait there while I get the keys. Won't be a sec." For very probably the last time that morning, they did as they were told. On her way out of the house, slamming the door behind her with car keys and purse in hand the girls heard the familiar summons of Catherine's mobile phone. Instinctively they settled down to wait.

"Nicole. Good morning. When? ... Broken in? Anything taken? ... Have the report on my desk when I arrive. I'll be there in about thirty minutes, traffic permitting. Just back from walking the girls." She frowned at the dogs, as if defying them to contradict her and rang off and opened the rear door of the car, lifting it up ready for the dogs to jump into the morass of leads, tartan rugs, bowls, crumbs, half-eaten hide chewies, umbrella, dog hairs, mud, wellies and spare socks. Unravelling them from their leads which she kept in her hand she began the loading process.

"Pi, in! Oh! You are! Good girl. Come on, Euclid. Mummy'll lift you."

The girls swayed and rocked as Catherine swung the car out of the drive and accelerated towards the office.

***

"She wants the report on her desk by the time she arrives! What does she think I am?"

"Wonder woman?" Mike suggested. Nicole was not amused.

"It's not funny, Mike. She'll be here in any minute and it's not like I've got anything else to do." The untidy pile of papers and files on her desk needing attention stared at her reproachfully; how much longer would they have to sit and wait? "Is she always like this?"

"Pretty much."

"Is she autistic or something?"

"What, as well as the vitiligo?"

Nicole was embarrassed. She had avoided the subject of Catherine's appearance and as far as she could see, so did everyone else. It felt uncomfortable to hear it spoken of so baldly. Mike clocked her discomfort and continued.

"We're all on the Spectrum somewhere, but she wouldn't ask you to do something she wouldn't do herself, I'll give her that. She's a mardy cow, except with dogs." He looked at his colleague, marginally more sympathetically this time.

"Wouldn't you be if you looked like that?"

Nicole was even more embarrassed. Now he would think she was a heartless bitch. Why did she always say the wrong thing? Mike took pity on her.

You'll get used to it. You're new and she doesn't like change that she isn't in charge of. Everything has to be systematic and tidy" Then, as an afterthought, "Yeah. Autistic in a way I s'pose. But maybe more OCD than actually autistic."

"How does she cope with a job like this? When you have no idea what'll happen next and everything changes all the time?"

"Ironically that's what makes get results. She sorts things out, puts them in order. She thinks in lines and numbers. Patterns. Doesn't do random." Nicole was staring at him like a rabbit in headlights, the vehicle bearing down on her. Mike laughed.

"Don't worry! She's better when you get to know her. Well, as much as anyone ever does. Keeps herself to herself does our Catherine."

"You don't call her Catherine?" Nicole was shocked.

"God, no. It's Ma'am. Always. Rank is order." Mike glanced at the time on his computer screen. "Hadn't you better get on with that report? Do a good job and she'll be easier to deal with. Might even get to like you."

Nicole had already opened a new window on her desktop and started the report, tap tapping the keyboard as fast as only a generation brought up to text and type instead of writing by hand could.

"What's with all the diamonds?" she asked after a few minutes, without looking up from the screen.

"What, Catherine's? No idea. Someone asked her once and she said that they were hard earned. Royal connections, whatever that means. But that's probably just a story. Who knows?"

"What's her house like?"

"Couldn't tell you. Never been there. No one has. She doesn't do socialising, not with work anyway."

A panting and snuffling from the end of the room heralded the arrival of Catherine herself, announced by her canine vanguard which led the way straining at their leads like Phaeton's horses.

"Morning troops. What's all this medical mystery then?"

"Morning, Ma'am." Mike spoke; Nicole kept her head down. "Miss Crawley from Wyeminster Infirmary reported a break in at her house this morning. Nothing taken, no damage but she's completely hysterical. Strange goings on apparently. Says she's being stalked and targeted."

"What do uniform say?"

"Nothing much. Had a look around but didn't find anything. No signs of a break in, no obvious damage, but her bedside alarm had been set off. They calmed her down and took notes. Nicole's got the report for you." Nicole looked up from her labours to add,

"And the timer on the oven. That was set off too." Catherine looked at her as if seeing her for the first time.

"Didn't she have her tyres slashed, this Miss Crawley? A few days ago?"

"Yes, Ma'am." Nicole tried to sound deferential as well as self-assured. Catherine appeared to ignore her.

"She might be overreacting. Odd though. Isn't she a consultant at the hospital? Some sort of surgeon? Wouldn't she be more rational than that?"

Nicole was about to speak but Mike's eyebrows rose and signalled danger. She kept quiet. Catherine was thinking.

"I'll take a look at the report first. As soon as you like please, Nicole."

"Email or hard copy?"

Catherine looked surprised and not displeased. "Hard copy. Sod the waste of paper. Hate reading things on a screen. Give me a book every time." She disappeared into her office to the sound of the printer chugging out the document; the girls were ready for a biscuit, bed and a comfortable sleep. Catherine might have to leave her sudoku until later. She resented a change in her morning routine but needs must.

"Nicole!" Catherine's pinto face appeared in the doorway.

"Yes Ma'am?"

"Find out where she got her tyres fixed. See if they can tell us anything."

Mike winked at his colleague.

"She's thawing."

***

It had been a long night but Juan looked immaculate. Late nights, early mornings and lack of sleep never seemed to affect him as they did others. Urbane, designer shaved – close but not baby faced, twinkle eyed and ever charming, he wandered into the Emergency Department as if were an art café and he wanted nothing but an espresso and a quiet moment to enjoy the pictures. With him was a tall, impossibly slim woman; very young, very pretty but very uncomfortable. They were arm in arm, she leaning on him. He sauntered, she shuffled.

Lizzie was on duty and surprised to see them.

"Hello Mr Morales. Didn't expect to see you this morning."

"Good morning, Lizzie." He made as if to kiss her hand – the one without the ring to avoid scratches or damage from those vulgar rocks – but did not release his hold on the young lady who looked as if she was about to collapse.

"A slight change of plan. This young lady requires immediate medical assistance."

"What's the problem?"

The young lady's mouth was locked shut, tight and thin. She glared at Lizzie, then at Juan whose benignity bathed them all in its rosy glow as he replied with absolute composure,

"An inadvertent rectal foreign body, I fear. It might require surgical removal." Juan smiled, the young lady scowled and Lizzie failed not to look amused. "Utterly shameless" she told everyone afterwards. "You'd have thought he was buying a bus ticket." They knew that wasn't true; Juan would never go anywhere by bus.

“Right.” Lizzie pulled her face together. “Have a seat while I take some details, Miss ...?”

Miss ...? said nothing; Juan spoke for her.

“Miss Lisowski. Katya L I S O W S K I.” He spelled it out so that there was no margin for error. Still nonplussed, Lizzie wrote the name down in block capitals and held it out for inspection so that Juan could approve her handiwork, an obedient pupil seeking teacher’s approval. He nodded assent. Katya meanwhile had discovered her voice and was eyeing the hard, plastic chairs in the reception area with distaste.

“I’d rather stand, thanks.”

“Perhaps you’d like to lie down?” Lizzie was concerned. The poor girl looked really pained. Katya threw her a grateful glance, retreated back into silence and nodded. Talking hurt. Everything hurt. It had seemed a good idea at the time. Bloody Juan Morales. Who said older men were more to be trusted? Accompanied by her cheerful accomplice in crime she followed Lizzie to a cubicle in the assessment area and planted herself with excruciating care on the narrow bed within it. As she grimaced, Juan gave her a cherubic smile and Lizzie closed the curtains on them as she resisted the inclination to snort with laughter.

“What’s so funny?” Busy as she was, Sesi could not walk past without knowing. Lizzie’s face was twisted with the agony of suppressed mirth. Not daring to speak she gestured that Sesi follow her into an empty consulting room and slammed the door shut behind them. Then she set herself free and howled her glee out loud.

"Lizzie! What? What is it?" Sesi was also laughing although she had no idea about what; Lizzie's hilarity was contagious. "Tell me!"

Swallowing her gasps and snorts, Lizzie explained. Sesi's disbelief was almost more than Lizzie's mirth could bear so she stayed in the consulting room for a few moments while Sesi, the Consultant once more, straightened her face and went to talk to the patient. By the time Lizzie the Staff Nurse re-emerged she was sufficiently in control to stand and earwig the rest of the concealed conversation.

"An apple?" Sesi was magnificent. No reaction whatsoever. Just another normal day in A&E.

"I'll just take a quick look... Can you turn on your side for me? That's it. Try and relax, Katya. What a pretty name. Unusual."

"Ow!"

"Sorry. Cold hands."

Silence. Lizzie knew she must not make a sound. Hers would be death by suffocation brought about by stifled laughter if she did not pull herself together. She headed back to the waiting area with the happy expectation of a hilarious coffee break to come, patient waiting times permitting.

Juan and Sesi were conferring outside the curtain.

"Quick trip to theatre and general anaesthetic to remove it. Do you want to assist, Juan?"

Even in scrubs Juan somehow managed to look sophisticated and designer. Designer scrubs! Sesi smiled at the concept. Bet his crocs are the real thing, not like my Primarnis she mused. Hey ho. Katya was unconscious on the table – merciful release from her embarrassment, but Juan was unabashed. Weirdly paternal in his concern for Katya but endlessly sanguine, charming and pleasant. No wonder people talked and now, Sesi had to admit that she would be one of them. She prided herself on her professionalism but really, Juan was something else. Admirable in a way, but not enviable. Not for her anyway.

She and Juan were scrutinising Katya's rear end. Still pert and perky but cool to the touch and drugged into oblivion. The foreign body was well lodged, quite at home and reluctant to move. Fortunately, it was quite small; a Bramley or even a generous Granny Smith might have been more problematic.

"I think the best way would be to … ", Sesi paused. Thinking on her feet. Then, to the theatre runner,

"Can you contact the canteen and get me two dessert spoons please?"

The runner's eyebrows soared upwards, collided with her hairline and stayed there. Her eyes were well-sucked gobstoppers, white and just starting to show their aniseed centres.

"Dessert spoons?"

"Yes. Clean. Not serving spoons. Too big."

Gobstopper eyes set off for the canteen.

"Have you known Katya long?" Time for some pleasant chat with Juan before the spoons arrived. Sesi really was curious to know. Don't sound too eager she thought or he won't tell.

"Not really. Early days. She's a dental nurse. We met when I lost a crown."

The idea of Juan having anything less than perfect teeth was a novel one and Sesi could not think of a reply. She was saved by the arrival of the spoons.

"Give them a wipe" she told the runner. "No need to sterilise, not for where they're going."

Wiped to a shine by gobstopper eyes, they were then presented to Sesi as sceptre and orb to a monarch.

Wielding them like forceps she manoeuvred them deftly into Katya's nether region and extracted the apple. Still intact. A little squashed, showing some signs of bruising but perfectly edible if thoroughly washed.

"There!" Sesi held it up in triumph.

Juan smiled, just.

Chapter Seventeen

Later the Same Day

Lesley and Nigel had come to the rescue, abandoned the sick and turned up at Debbie's house as soon as they could after they heard about the break in. It had been decided, mostly by Lesley, that Debbie needed more security so Lesley, who had been loudly describing the calamity throughout the hospital from the moment the news had broken, had phoned a local firm recommended by one of the admin staff in Colorectal. They were at Debbie's now. The noise of drilling, hammering, tapping and intrusion was escalating and overwhelming but they had been prompt, the quote had been reasonable, they came by personal recommendation so the decision had been made and the work begun. It would be finished by the end of the day, without fail, they had the personal reassurance of the managing director of the company who had taken a particular interest in the job. As he had said,

"We owe so much to the staff of the infirmary. The least we can do is keep them safe." His accent was hard to place – certainly not local or even British, but how nice to be appreciated. And the cost was so reasonable; it really did look as if they were getting a preferential rate. Lesley was inordinately pleased with herself, fluffed out like an overfed Robin pecking and picking at the workmen, eyeing them beadily from corners and crevices before flitting back to the safety of the living room where Debbie sat, traumatised and silent, with Miss Muffat on her knee. Nigel was sitting with them sipping a mug of coffee. Debbie's was untouched. Miss Muffat watched every move Nigel made, ready to pounce.

Catherine had to ring the doorbell several times before anyone heard it. People were obviously there – she could see their shapes morphing shadowily through the frosted glass (which was undamaged she noticed, and the lock unforced). Eventually the door was hesitantly opened by a small man of Asian appearance wearing jeans and a black sweatshirt. He had an electric drill in one hand and seemed uncomfortable. Immediately behind was a tubby woman, no taller than the workman who retreated deferentially behind the door which he still held open.

"Yes?" Suspicious, Welsh, hostile.

"Police. D.I Scott." Catherine towered over both of them as she held up her ID card. "Miss Crawley?"

Lesley warmed up, microwaved rice pudding, lumpy but no longer congealed.

"Yes. I mean no, not me. She's in the living room. Come in."

The small man shut the door quietly behind the two women then resumed the cacophony of his drilling. Lesley led Catherine into the gloomy hall and her past: a childhood set against a backdrop of avocado and brown, cheese plants, conflict between warring wallpaper and violent carpets, dimly lit bickering parents. The living room was no better but on entering it, she was astonished.

"Miss Crawley?" It was the woman from the vet's waiting room. Now that she had not expected.

"Yes?" Tight, pale, even more thin and grey. Debbie did not recognise Catherine.

"D I Scott. Wyeminster Police. Catherine. We've met before." No, not even a glimmer of recollection. "In the vet's waiting room? My dogs? And this must be your cat. Miss Muffat isn't it?"

Debbie's trance lifted.

"Oh! Yes. I remember. Miss Muffat's check-up."

"Was the vet happy with her?"

"Very. She's in fine form. Marvellous example of her type apparently." Maternal pride, animation and response. Catherine was relieved.

"I'm here about your break in. Would you mind if I took a look around and then we had a chat?"

Debbie had no objection but clung to Miss Muffat. Nigel sipped his coffee. Lesley stepped in.

"I'll show you round. Lesley Thomas. Consultant anaesthetist. Friend of Debbie's. Miss Crawley, that is. Alright Debbie?" Without waiting for an answer, she was leading Catherine towards the kitchen. "This way.

We haven't touched anything, obviously so you'll find everything as it was. The police who came were most insistent that nothing should be moved or interfered with and were very helpful I must say. Poor Debbie – Miss Crawley - was in a terrible state. You've met her before you say? At the vet's? She adores her cat – Miss Muffat. We've arranged, well, I have with her agreement, for security cameras and an alarm to be installed but the workmen know nothing is to be interfered with relating to the break in so nothing will be compromised but the most important thing is to keep Debbie safe, don't you agree? And give her peace of mind, nothing matters more than peace of mind does it? Especially in your own home."

Catherine barely listened and did not answer, not wanting to feed the flood. She wouldn't be heard anyway.

"Those are the stones?"

"Yes. Just as we found them, well, as Debbie did." Lesley was being helpful. "The cooker timer was on-started at 8.00 apparently, according to the setting."

Catherine surveyed the room. Beige, tired, innocent. All in order. A faint musty smell, stray cat hairs. Miss Crawley did not seem to be much of a cook much but clearly Miss Muffat was well fed; her full bowls were on the floor, over filled and barely touched.

"What about the clock?"

Lesley looked up at the wall for the first time.

“Oh. I don’t know. It seems to have stopped. I’ll ask Debbie.” And she was gone, like a clockwork toy rolling on wheels too small for its speed; she might have fallen forward and rolled over at any moment. Catherine took advantage of the sudden quiet. The stones seemed innocuous enough – small, white, unblemished, smooth. The sort of thing to pick up off a beach and keep in your pocket to rub at times of stress – worry stones. But why white? The digital timer on the cooker might just have been caused by an electrical fault but combined with the stopped clock – coincidence? – and the stones, it was more interesting. An enigma. And she did not believe in coincidence. Then Lesley returned, panting with excited eagerness. Nigel was in tow.

“Debbie says the clock was working fine yesterday when she looked at it. She remembers because she always checks the time for feeding Miss Muffat and getting to work. She’s never late, is she Nigel? So, the clock must have been working and she says she put a new battery only last month.”

Nigel nodded but said nothing. Like Catherine he was inspecting the room. He walked over to the window sill and studied the stones carefully.

“Do they mean anything to you Mr…?” Catherine liked to know with whom she was dealing. Lesley the hostess leapt in to make the introduction.

“Doctor. Nigel Alsop. Consultant Radiologist. We all work together at the infirmary – senior staff, obviously.

Nigel and Debbie are dear friends." Lesley was not entirely sure about the exact nature of Debbie's relationship with Nigel and felt inordinately pleased with herself for describing it so succinctly.

"Hmm. Quite aesthetic really." Dr Alsop had spoken.

"Nigel!" Lesley was outraged. "Is that all you can say? It's not the stones, it's how they got there that's the problem. It's terrifying." She started an involuntary humming, something holy, Baptist, Welsh, tuneless but comforting.

"Perhaps better to keep your voice down?" suggested Catherine, too late, as Debbie stood in the doorway clasping Miss Muffat like manually controlled pain relief.

"Don't say that! I can't bear to think about it. The fact that someone has been in my house, touching my things. I feel invaded. Contaminated. Violated. And what about Miss Muffat? Anything might have happened to her!" Here she clutched the cat so hard that her tail went rigid as she struggled to breath and wriggle free.

"She looks alright to me." Nigel had spoken, oddly deep toned against Debbie's increasing shrillness. Miss Muffat glared at her rival. What did he know?

"But she might have been hurt. And what if I had been here? I might have been attacked. Raped. Killed. Or worse."

Lesley broke off her humming to offer comfort.

"You weren't here though, Debbie., so no harm done. And all this," she indicated the intermittent noise of the security system and CCTV cameras being installed in rest of the house, "will keep you and Miss Muffat safe."

"How will the cat get into the garden?" Nigel always referred to Miss Muffat as 'the cat'. He spat out the words like an angry tom.

"She's a house cat really, Nigel, as you know." Debbie was calming down; talking about Miss Muffat was therapeutic. "But she does like to go out sometimes so there's an electronic cat flap in the back door which I had put in last year. She's got a transponder on her collar to activate it. Look." Miss Muffat squirmed as Debbie twisted her collar round for communal inspection and glared at Nigel, as if was responsible for her discomfort. It had to be his fault somehow. Catherine was about to speak when Lesley voiced her thoughts for her.

"Should she go outside?"

Debbie was stricken.

"How can I stop her? She's always done it. That would be too cruel. And she only goes into the garden; she can't get out."

Nigel stepped into the breach.

"No one can get in. That's what matters."

The throb of drilling was suddenly replaced by the jaunty ringing of the landline in the hall. Catherine had been witnessing the dynamic of the group, cat included, with undisguised fascination. Now she was watching Debbie's reaction to the sound of the telephone. The woman had gone absolutely white under the grey, lank hair; as white as the stones on the window sill. Her eyes had widened with fear and fixed themselves on middle space.

"Shall I get that?" Lesley, the ever helpful.

"Leave it!" Debbie's voice was low, menacing and distorted. They stared at her.

"But it might be important?" Lesley offered. The phone continued to ring.

"They ring off as soon as I answer. Every time." Debbie was catatonic with fear, lined, old and vulnerable.

"Has this happened often?" Catherine the D I, asking questions. If she had hoped to restore calm and measured thinking, she was wrong.

"Yes. All the time. Number always withheld. Someone is out to get me." Debbie began to cry.

Chapter Eighteen

Down

Clare was not having a good day. To start with, her Colorectal Department was two consultants down. Debbie was at home, having the vapours by canteen accounts, accompanied by one consultant anaesthetist and Wyeminster's most senior radiologist. Cancellations had thrown the appointments system and the day's lists into meltdown, the infirmary was grinding exceeding slow and very creaky and all of this she knew, was going to cost her money. Specialist locums would have to be brought in at short notice, an expensive member of senior staff would almost certainly be put on sick leave, there was the Tommy Yeo case eating its head off in legal costs, she never had enough nurses, overtime was out of control, not to mention the migraine-inducing levels of day to day running costs. She wondered, again, if the heating could be turned down. Even just one degree would translate into precious cash. She sighed and reached into a top drawer for paracetamol – supermarket bought, pills not capsules, cheaper, discreet and no one's business but her own. Ironic really, she grimaced. Surrounded by bloody drugs and I buy my own with the groceries. She was going to need them. Hugo Chadwyck was with her and they were discussing Debbie. The headache was inevitable.

Hugo's preliminary report about Tommy Yeo was spread out before them on Clare's desk, brazen white, in black Times New Roman. Pink highlighted passages winked at Clare, occasionally accentuated with lime green. You could tell Hugo was a cosmetic surgeon Clare grimaced again, what was wrong with a red pen? Ah well, better get on with it.

"I've asked Juan Morales to join us, Hugo. He'll be here shortly. He knows Miss Crawley and Mr Yeo, has worked with both so knows them professionally, as well as the dynamics of the department. I think his observations might be helpful."

Hugo looked serious and as crestfallen as his jaunty tie and the matching silk handkerchief coyly peeping from his top pocket would allow.

"Is that a problem?"

"Juan is part of the problem."

"What do you mean?"

"Only on a cost basis, not personally. Within the department he is well liked and the patients love him." Hugo rifled through the report and found the lime green comment he wanted. "He's 'the glue that holds it together' one of the junior Colorectal staff has said about him."

"Only on a cost basis?" Clare was always very interested in money. She had to be; her emphasis on the word 'only' was scathing. Even Hugo noticed. Then,

"Juan is part of the problem? What problem? I thought this was about Tommy Yeo?"

Hugo regretted what he had said. He paused, mentally phrasing his next comment. Clare could not wait.

"Just give me the bottom line, Hugo and I'll read the full report later. Is Tommy Yeo guilty?"

"Certainly not where Mr Mitcheldean is concerned. It's not Tommy Yeo who's your problem."

"I don't understand."

Poor cow, Hugo thought. She really doesn't. She's not going to like this one little bit.

"Your senior female colorectal surgeon is the real issue."

"Debbie Crawley?" Clare was incredulous; not a good look.

"It seems she has a habit of doing 'urgent' follow up colonoscopies out of hours and finding nothing worse than a hernia. Costing you a fortune. Have you any idea how much money your Colorectal colleagues are costing the infirmary?"

"Colleagues?" She hissed the plural s which floated out into the room like a wet fart.

"Juan as well."

"Go on."

"This is the problem I referred to. Colorectal are haemorrhaging money – no pun intended." He smiled obsequiously. Clare felt slightly nauseous and swallowed down rising bile.

"They have been creating 'necessary' expensive, overtime obligations and surgery that have to be paid for. However, their motives are different. Juan is a popular surgeon; people specifically ask for him to operate on them so overtime is necessary to accommodate his lists which are always longer than anybody else's. He does seem to make a habit of finding elusive polyps at colonoscopy that others would dismiss as normal because what does a polypectomy make him in terms of financial gain?"

Clare's creased flying eyebrows provided the answer. Hugo turned the knife a little more and the pain increased.

"So, to fit in all his surgery he invariably has to work overtime. But," here he looked straight at Clare, "it is arguable on clinical grounds that he is just being thorough and there is no doubt that he provides excellent patient satisfaction."

"And Debbie Crawley?"

"There are concerning reports about her surgical skills, or lack of them. You know she has never trained to do keyhole surgery?"

Clare did not.

"Go on."

"Tommy Yeo does – did - all of that for her, as well as the more complicated procedures."

"What about the Lavery case?"

"Yeo definitely disobeyed the Multi-Disciplinary Team directive but, controversially, he may have been right on clinical grounds. The very positive outcome of his surgical intervention suggests that the MDT made the wrong call."

Clare reached for the paracetamol. She punched two out of their silver packaging with undisguised aggression, swallowed them without water. Hardly noticed the bitterness on her tongue.

"Debbie is a senior member of that team. Doesn't she chair the MDT?"

"I don't think so but I don't know. Beyond my remit of course. However," he could not resist the temptation to overstep the report boundary mark, "she is certainly keen on expressing her views and I suspect they are not entirely up to date."

There was a chirpy knuckle rap, rap, rap at door. Who other than Juan? Even his door knocking had panache and dash. Clare mouthed 'Juan' at Hugo and called out.

"Come in."

Juan sauntered over the threshold, graciously nodded by way of greeting and settled himself in one of the more comfortable chairs in the room. He shifted a little for greater comfort, crossed his legs, smiled even more graciously and offered his services.

“How may I help?”

Hugo was impressed; Juan’s timing was dramatic and impeccable; he must try it himself. Clare was not. Just Juan being Juan. She abruptly introduced them to each other and cut to the chase.

“We have been discussing the Colorectal department, Juan, in the light of Hugo’s investigation and would like to have a more personal account of it from you in your capacity as an associate specialist; a comparatively objective point of view. We will be talking to others, of course.” That gracious nod of assent, but also an air of enquiry. Clare got it. “About Debbie Crawley” she added, though not as an afterthought.

“The truth?”

Clare and Hugo tried not to exchange glances but surprise bettered them and they gave in, their eyebrows raised in unison and Clare answered for them both.

“The truth.”

“Off the record?”

“Off the record.”

“Nice lady. Half baked. Surgical nightmare. Malicious in her approach to colleagues if she thinks they are a threat. Selective, subjective reporting and documentation.”

If eyebrows could fly, Hugo's and Clare's would have been circling the room on thermals of hot horror. Juan shrugged nonchalantly but not apologetically.

"Well, you did ask. And yes, I can substantiate."

Clare collected her eyebrows from the ceiling.

"Surgical nightmare?"

"Tommy Yeo does all the complex procedures – she schedules it that way. When she operates, I'm always there to assist – because she does all the scheduling - and I do all the tricky bits for her. She doesn't even remove large polyps at colonoscopy. Have you never wondered why she doesn't have medical students in with her?"

"I thought she was too tied up with clinical governance, paperwork and the Multi-Disciplinary to teach."

"Smoke screen."

Not spiteful or vindictive by nature, Juan was somewhat shocked to find that he was rather enjoying himself. He had not realised quite how resentful he had become he mused, as he watched consternation reforming Clare and Hugo's features. Now the latter entered the fray. Having observed that Juan had the decided advantage he decided to weigh in on his side, advancing from the flank. Not his battle anyway; this was Clare's conflict. He was just the mercenary.

"She certainly files lots of incident forms, mostly about Tommy Yeo."

Clare sensed his desertion.

"How did I not know this?"

"Because she is in charge of clinical governance. Everything everyone does at work is documented, except her." Juan felt almost sorry for his CEO. No one likes to be made a fool of.

"But everyone speaks so highly of her."

"You've clearly never spoken to the junior staff or some of her surgical colleagues."

There was a desperation in Clare's voice now which she did not even bother to disguise.

"What are we going to do?" Juan and Hugo had both had the same immediate thought – 'We? Since when was it our problem?' Clare was distraught.

"We can't lose two senior colorectal surgeons. The department will collapse completely. It's already at breaking point."

Hugo took up the gauntlet. He did not intend to increase Clare's misery but, really, he had to know.

"Half baked?"

"Off the record?" Juan had to be sure. Hugo nodded, not as graciously as he had seen Juan, but not a bad imitation. He would practise later in front of the bathroom mirror. Reassured, Juan delivered the death blows.

"Paranoid. Insecure. Fruit loop."

Silence. Time stopped. Clare gasped, the only sound of life in the room. Juan watched, Hugo pondered for a moment, frowning, then murmured to Clare,

"There might be a way round it." He was not a world renowned private cosmetic surgeon for nothing.

As Juan was leaving Clare and Hugo to their machinations, Catherine was sitting in her office trying to make sense of the Tiger Bites case. There had to be a pattern somewhere but she was damned if she could see it. Like her sudoku puzzles, there was a mind behind it an she had only to work out the thought sequence and, theoretically, it would fall into place. Then they had to substantiate it but at the moment, there was no logic there at all apart from the most basic law of economics: supply and demand. One fed the other. A vicious downward spiral but extremely lucrative for the supplier. Then there were these other, frankly, odd events/occurrences/messages – what did one call them? – relating to a surgeon at the local hospital. It did not make sense. There was a polite tap at her door and she could see Nicole hovering outside. Really, if it was important enough to interrupt her, why didn't the girl just come in and say it?

“Yes. What is it? Come in, girl, I can’t hear you out there.”

“Sorry to bother you, Ma’am.”

“What is it?”

Nicole shrivelled and spoke.

“The slashed tyres, Ma’am.”

“Yes?”

“It might be nothing.”

“I’ll decide that. And if it is, I’ll tell you. What about them?”

“The garage remembered them because each tyre had four clean knife cuts, all the same length, in the same pattern on each tyre.”

Nicole had Catherine’s attention. Even Euclid and Pi, cocooned in their beds on the floor opposite the desk where Catherine could keep an eye on them seemed to take notice. They stopped snoring and were motionless. Catherine’s uneven face creased into variegated striations as she concentrated, fixed on Nicole.

“Interesting. Thank you.” So, not nothing then. Nicole exhaled with relief and scarpered. Catherine was still fixed on the place where her rookie DC had been standing. Always a pattern. She just had to find it.

Chapter Nineteen

Forward

Taya had been moved from Intensive care into the high dependency ward and from there, into Women's Surgical, again. Used now to the hospital routine and cognisant of the company she could expect there, she was more confident, especially as she was recovering well. Armed with her mobile phone, on silent but constantly vibrating with exuberant texts, emojis and exclamation marks, she could participate in her real life even though displaced into a world of old age, catheters, poly cotton nightdresses and complaints. Even though she had had to abandon pyjamas for the time being to accommodate staples and dressings, Taya had made it clear to Ella and Annie that she was not going to be reduced to the level of a smock nightdress in a sickly pastel shade of anything, especially yellow. They had risen to the challenge. Ella had gone on a mission to Primark and found two fluorescent knee length shifts, one in green the other in pink with wholly unsuitable logos on the front which the other ladies did not understand and which made the medical students smirk. Taya sat in her bed or, more often now, in the chair beside it, like a vibrant beacon guiding ships in the fog and mediocrity of the rest of the ward. When Lizzie popped in to say hello as she was heading to the canteen for a slug of hot caffeine that was not machine made, she was bedazzled. Her ring was overwhelmed, almost colourless by comparison.

"Wow! Look at you!"

Taya tore herself away from her phone.

"Lizzie!"

"How're you feeling?"

"Great. Much better. Soon be outta here."

"Looks like you've settled in ok."

"Yeah." Her phone buzzed.

"Your friends?"

"Yeah. Kezia and Courtney. The mates I was with at Halloween. They're supposed to be in PE but they skived off."

"And you wonder why your foster mums don't like them?" Lizzie felt like an older sister, not that she knew what that was.

"Kezia and Courtney aren't bad. Everyone hates PE. They never skive off real lessons, not ones that matter." Lizzie was laughing now. She had done exactly the same. "My foster parents are alright though." Taya was loyal and she liked Lizzie, whose good opinion mattered. "I like Ella best. She's a teaching assistant at my school so you won't tell her about the PE?" Lizzie nodded and Taya chatted on, pleased to be able to have a verbal conversation instead of a written one, no matter how badly spelled. "My friends think it's cool they're gay."

"What happened to your parents?"

"Dad gambled and got massively into debt so my step mum went off with my little sister. Social services took me."

"What about your mum?"

"Dunno. She left me and dad years ago, before I can really remember. I don't mind but I miss my sister. She was cute. I used to look after her, baby sit and that. You got any sisters?"

"No. Just me. That's why I'm glad I've got Andy. He's my fiancé."

Taya sighed. "Yeah. You're so lucky. Can I see your ring again?" Lizzie held out her hand and Taya, fluorescent and lurid, gushed over the diamonds that refracted the light from her pink nightshirt and broke it into pieces over Lizzie's skinny finger, a rosy pencil of stained glass. Taya bent devotedly over Lizzie's hand,

"You're a sister nurse, Lizzie. We could be like sisters." Small voiced, beseeching, uncertain. She did not look up but let the words find their own way home.

"I'm not cute. And you're a bit too old to need a babysitter." Lizzie paused. "But yeah, why not? It might be fun. You'll have to do as you're told though!"

"I will." A strange proposal, unexpected, spontaneous, over a ring but not about it, an agreement and an understanding. Taya was thrilled; Lizzie was surprised but not sorry. She started in role immediately.

"No more Tiger Bites, okay Taya? You've been really ill."

"Yeah, I know. Mr Morales told me. Dunno what happened to me but I know I shouldn't have done it. Everyone else who takes them just seems to feel amazing."

"They're dangerous and highly addictive. You weren't the only one to have an adverse reaction, remember."

"Was he alright, that lad?"

"Yes. But that's not the point. No more, Taya. Promise?"

"Promise." She meant it. "Won't be easy though. Everyone's at it."

***

Once Juan had left, Clare felt free to slump in her chair.

"I had no idea."

"She's been at the WRI a long time – most of her career. Something of an institution here I believe?"

Clare nodded.

"There's something else."

"What? More?"

Even pompous and pretentious Hugo Chadwyck was capable of real sympathy and at this moment, Clare had it all.

"I mentioned the numerous incident forms about Tommy Yeo? Unfortunately, there are others who have come in for criticism."

"Go on." Too late to turn back now; get it all out. Clare liked to know exactly what she was dealing with. How much worse could it be?

"Almost all those, the vast majority, on whom Debbie Crawley delivers the incident forms tend to be, er ..." Hugo stalled. How the hell was he going to put this?

"What?"

"Non-white."

Not like Clare, who was ashen. For a second Hugo thought she would faint but he had underestimated her.

"Shit." Then,

"I need evidence."

"Of course." He reached for a pile of documents and took the first one from the top of the heap. "This is the most recent – two days ago, about Dr Abebi Agbaje, who was her assistant surgeon on the occasion in question, fourth year surgical, excellent record apart from her complaint. Apparently, the procedure had to be halted because he lacked the appropriate skills to be able to assist properly."

"How is that relevant to the race issue that you seem to be implying?" Clare was getting back in harness. Retaliating.

"Miss Crawley objects to the quality of training he has obviously received in his native country. Says it is," here he consulted the paper in his hand, "clearly below the clinical and surgical standards required by the NHS."

"He's from West Africa?"

"No. Dorking." ... "Surrey."

"Which med school?"

"Warwick. Graduated not quite with distinction but almost."

It was too soon for more paracetamol but Clare was tempted. Hugo had not finished.

"Tommy Yeo trained in Glasgow, where he was born and brought up, I believe."

"Yes, Hugo. I know. Thank you." She stared aggressively at him; sympathy for her withered and died. "The question is, how is this to be dealt with? You said there might be a way round it." She had distanced herself from the problem Hugo noted, speaking in the third person except where it related directly to him. Clever. Easier to be ruthless. He hinted at salvation.

"You're part of a new senior management team I understand?"

"Yes, Chair. Appointed last year."

"And you are clearly scrutinising hospital practices and personnel with a view to making further financial savings?"

"Yes. Without compromising standards, of course."

Hugo was on safer ground now, simply reporting and recommending, no sympathy required.

"Debbie Crawley obviously feels extremely threatened, maybe inadequate. It's a shame. She's a clever woman who has been systematically deflecting attention from herself onto others for some considerable time."

"Diversion tactics."

"Exactly."

"And Juan has been covering for her in theatre?"

"He said as much himself."

The paracetamol winked alluringly at Clare. She ignored them, thinking ahead. Problem solving.

"If only we could reinstate Tommy Yeo."

"Until he has been cleared of risking patient safety by transgressing medical protocols, he absolutely must remain on suspension."

"It all depends on Juan, then?"

"Yes. It all comes down to Juan."

Who was being discussed.

Sesi, Lizzie and Abebi were in the pub; not gossip central, the one closest to the hospital but an older establishment on the edge of the city with claims to historic interest and craft beer. It also had slot machines and a wide screen TV which graced the panelled walls, wooden floors and converted treadle sewing machine tables with a certain modern luminosity and a great deal of background noise. However, there was a real fire, with logs and ash and wood smoke which attracted punters like a Promethean magnet. Lizzie had walked across town to meet Sesi there, who had Abebi in tow. Since the debacle with Debbie Crawley the assistant surgeon had achieved a certain unsought notoriety and a great deal of sympathy – a sort of downtrodden local hero of the underdog variety and he was in high demand for anecdotal evidence about his experience.

"Pint for you Abebi, don't know what but it's supposed to be authentic, cider for you, Lizzie and mine's the white wine." Sesi deposited the drinks with expertise, acquired as an upper sixth covering the graveyard weekend/public holiday shifts at a working men's club in Droitwich. Lizzie's tattoos were being itemised, described and admired by Abebi who was fascinated by the salamander which could be made to writhe and undulate when Lizzie flexed her muscles and braced her thin arm. Sesi had seen and heard it all before. Time for a subject change.

"Here's to our new consultant!" She raised her glass.

"Only a locum and not substantive, but enough of a consultant to make all our lives easier. Cheers!" Heartfelt relief as Abebi's pint clashed with Sesi's wine glass and then Lizzie's glowing pale cider. His "Anyone's better than Deborah Creepy bloody Crawley" was even more heartfelt.

"I bet Juan's pleased. It'll suit his image" was Lizzie's contribution. "It's not like he needs the money though. He's loaded. Where does it all come from? Not the hospital that's for sure."

The speculation about Juan's finances was once more the on-trend topic of speculation, especially since his promotion. It was only a matter of time before his car changed.

"Search me. He's forever talking about his business interests, whatever that means." Sesi took another sip of wine as if supping from the fount of knowledge, to no avail. "And he's always on the phone but you never know who he's talking to."

Lizzie was more practical. "What do we call him? Juan or Mr Morales?"

"Mr Cox!" Sesi spoke then screamed with laughter. Lizzie swallowed her cider which went down the wrong way and she began to choke, but not before she managed to splutter out an alcoholic "Rector!"

"What?" Abebi briefly wondered whether Lizzie would recover or he would have to do an emergency tracheotomy – he had a biro in a pocket, somewhere, but it was much more intriguing to find out just what they the hell they were talking about. He did not have a clue.

“You haven’t heard?” Sesi’s laughter was now mixed with incredulity, and even more raucous. People were beginning to look at them, smiling involuntarily, listening, caught up in the encroaching hysteria.

It was difficult but between them, sharing sentences and gasps of life-giving air that they hiccupped and howled, Sesi and Lizzie managed to speak.

“Juan brought his latest squeeze into E.R with an apple up her arse.”

“A Cox’s Orange Pippin!”

“Which Sesi removed with...”

“a pair of dessert spoons”

“from the canteen.”

“An apple?” Abebi could not believe it.

“I’m more of Huawei girl myself!” Sesi screamed again.

Now neither she or Lizzie could talk, or sit upright or stop laughing and Abebi had joined in, along with those nearest them who had overheard and who began relaying the information round the pub until the whole place was in a frenzy which would be perpetuated outside the building and beyond. Thus began a legend.

Chapter Twenty

The Following Morning

It was raining hard; cold needles floating on the wind, clattering against glass before breaking into soft wrecks to trickle dismally down to earth. An unbroken claustrophobic grey sky squeezing the life out of the world which cried but stood steady. Debbie's house was its usual dimly lit jaundiced self, yellow behind dirty windows framed by peeling paint which seemed to be weeping in sympathy with the weather. Unusually however, above the noise of the rain and wind could be heard the sound of Debbie, the tones of her voice distorted by increasing hysteria and desperation. She had lost Miss Muffat. Could not find her anywhere. Had searched the whole house, including the spare bedrooms and heavy oak wardrobe containing Father's clothes. She had simply disappeared. Perhaps she had gone outside? Into the garden? But it was raining, and Miss Muffat hated getting wet. Besides, it was breakfast time and Miss Muffat never missed her breakfast; she and Debbie always ate together; Debbie made sure of it. She had white toast and a cup of coffee while Miss Muffat picked at her wet food then had a scattering of semi-skimmed milk in her special bowl. Semi-skimmed for them both; they watched their cholesterol together.

There was no indication that the cat flap had been used – no sign of wet hair or moisture and Miss Muffat had been on the bed last night so it seemed unlikely that she had gone out. But you never knew. So, Debbie opened the back door and peered out, calling, calling, calling. She pattered across the scrawny lawn, inspected the depressed flower beds decaying along the fence bottom and found nothing. Not a sign. She could not get out, so she must have gone in. She had to be inside.

It was not until later, when Debbie opened the front door that she found her. Miss Muffat was on the doormat. Dead. Slashed with deep, precise, clean cuts. Her intestines sat in a neat pile beside her.

When Catherine arrived at the house a uniformed police officer was standing beside the plastic sheet covering the remains of the cat. The sheet was large enough to cover the claret soaked doormat and doorstep, down which blood had dripped once the mat could contain it no longer. It had stopped running when Miss Muffat finally died. Death had been recent; slightly sheltered from the rain the blood was congealing but not dried and there was no smell, yet.

"She must have been killed here, outside her own front door by the look of the blood. Not elsewhere and then moved." Catherine was shocked and spoke under her breath. It was an act of barbarism and daring. Medieval. A small crowd had gathered in the street outside Debbie's house, filming themselves and the plastic bundle. The police officer stood upright and erect and pretended not to notice as he resigned himself to getting wetter and wetter. No sheltering in this doorway.

"Placed where she was bound to find her." Catherine stepped back to assess the scene, oblivious to the rain. It seemed sacrilegious somehow to ring the doorbell and calmly step over the corpse of Miss Muffat to enter by the front door. Fortunately, Lesley the ever helpful had spotted the detective's arrival through the grimy picture window upon which she tapped, importantly, to attract her attention.

"Round the back" she mouthed through the rain streaked rivulets and gesticulated wildly; a rotund clockwork doll popping out from below a clock as it struck the hour, all jerks, arm waving and nodding.

The back door was open when Catherine reached it, manned by the redoubtable Lesley.

"Come in. Debbie's in the living room. She's in a terrible state. Can't speak for crying and shock. I came as soon as I heard; she rang the police and they obviously asked who they should contact and she must have said me. Not sure why she didn't ask for Nigel – Dr Alsop – but perhaps she did and he couldn't make it or he might even be on his way. This way, that's it." She shut the door behind Catherine. "Terrible weather. How could anyone do such a thing? To a cat? And so close to Christmas. I just don't know how Debbie – Miss Crawley – will cope. Miss Muffat means – meant – everything to her. They were inseparable." At this point she was obliged to breathe. Catherine seized the opportunity.

“Is the cat exactly as she found it?”

“Yes. Absolutely. Just as she found it. Her. Oh dear.” Lesley paused, but not for long. “She was too shocked to move anything. Terrified. Traumatised. Well, you would be, wouldn’t you?” Catherine wondered, not for the first time, how good an anaesthetist Lesley was. Presumably she was not so talkative in an operating theatre.

In the kitchen the clock had been removed leaving a grubby ring on the wall where it had resided for so many years. Inside the ring it was pale yellow, a watery sun now in a mustard sky. The cooker timer was switched off and the stones had gone from the window sill, bagged up as evidence in Wyeminster Police station. What had seemed officious and an overreaction to the hard pressed, understaffed forensic team now looked far more significant. The murder of a family pet was heinous enough, but what it signalled in terms of threat and danger to human life was far more serious. Starting block for a psychopath.

Taking a pair of latex gloves from her fleece pocket Catherine filled them with her hands as she walked through the house, along the mouldering hall to the front door which she opened from the inside. Again, so sign of forced entry, no damage; not even a minute disturbance of the grime on the frosted glass from fingers or hands. Had Miss Muffat got out and been killed, or had she been taken out? The CCTV camera footage would be useful; she would get Nicole onto that straight away. The girl seemed to be thorough and conscientious which rendered her a little less annoying. Bending down in the doorway, Catherine gently lifted the plastic sheet away from the body but held it up over the corpse to prevent prying eyes, mobile phones and selfies with a stiff. In the back of her car the girls had seen her and started barking. She ignored them.

Miss Muffat lay on her side, stiffening. Legs splayed and broken. Her eyes were dull, her belly a gaping hole, cleanly split, neat edged and deep. Her intestines, pale sausage skins, flaccid and lifeless were joined to her by a gossamer thin sheet of flat yellow fat lined in an eerie, silver treelike pattern of once vibrant and pulsatile vessels, now empty and listless. It was too early for any foul odour but they were beginning to seep the fluid of death. On the plastic sheet the rain continued to fall. Noisy. Relentless. Crocodile tears.

In the kitchen she removed the gloves, peeling them off inside out and discarded them in an ancient pedal bin beside the kitchen unit. At the sink she washed her hands in running water from the cold tap, repeatedly scraping her fingers, her thumbs, palms and the backs of her hands with her short square nails. The abrasive chill of the water and friction suppressed the inclination to cry. Suppose it had been one of her girls? She rinsed her hands one last time and studied the place on the window sill where the stones had sat until

Lesley's hymn-humming, irritating beyond endurance, arrived in the kitchen and obliged her to turn around.

"I'd like to talk to Miss Crawley. D'you think she is calm enough to answer a few questions?" The humming stopped. No more Rock of Ages for the moment, at least. Catherine sighed with relief, annoyance and the effort of maintaining self-control.

"Oh no. Nothing like." Lesley answered self-importantly - the medical expert. "She couldn't possibly answer questions at the moment. She's in a state of shock and may need a sedative."

"We'll take care of the cat..." Catherine began when there was a shriek.

"No! Don't take Miss Muffat! I won't let you. This is her home. This is where she lives. I won't let you take her away." Debbie had come into the room, a banshee of grief.

"She mustn't see her. Can you ...?" Catherine appealed to Lesley who nodded, resisted the urge to hum and infinitely gently guided Debbie out of the kitchen and back into the living room, where she shut the door.

Andy had wheels. He had swept into the drop off area of the infirmary in a cloud of emissions, cyclonic, black, shiny, loud and fast. Screeching and squealing to a halt he had lowered the driver window – briefly, the rain was pissing down – to announce his arrival to Lizzie who was expecting her betrothed to be on foot when he had said he would meet her as she came off duty, not in a souped up black steed with red trims.

"0 to 60 in 6 seconds! Get in, quick." And he had pressed the button to close the window, as smoothly and silently as the music from his iPod plugged into the sound system was loud and throbbing. Lizzie got in and turned down the volume so that she could speak. Andy immediately turned it up again from a device on the steering wheel as he spun the wheels then launched the car into the road and accelerated towards the lights, a couple of hundred yards away. Lizzie found herself thrown against the back of her seat as she fumbled with her seat belt buckle. Andy had not bothered with his, which bothered her but she said nothing. Let him have his moment. Which she would share.

"Wow!" She had to shout to be heard. "It's amazing!"

"Yeah." They were waiting at the lights now, Andy beating the steering wheel along with the Foo Fighters and revving the engine. "It's only second-hand but it's low mileage and it's got all the gizmos. And it's fast. Shit off a shovel."

"Where did you get it?" Lizzie tried not to gasp as she was flung across two lanes and swept into another halt at the next set of lights.

"Comes with the job! I need to be mobile, go places, meet people." He was crouched over the steering wheel, the first to be off at the lights so that he could cut ahead into the single lane up the hill and show Wyeminster some style.

"They paid for it?" Her gut reaction; she had said it before she could stop herself and now, he would be narky with her. Damn. But she was unaccustomed to

Andy having money. However, she had misjudged him. The car seemed to have softened him and he was pleased with himself.

"This is just the start, Lizzie. Good times. You stick with me, babe."

"Where're we going?"

"Taking my girl for a spin." And so up the hill to the mini roundabout and over they spun, then out into the suburbs and on into the countryside in the dark VW Golf, double exhaust, red trim, imitation leather seats and turbo, all sound and fury signifying nothing. Lizzie sat back. Andy was in control and happy so she was content and maybe he was right. Good times indeed. She really had to learn to be less negative, more trusting, nicer. She sighed at the remembrance of her own shortcomings.

"You alright, babe?"

"Yeah. Just happy." Andy grinned. What he wanted to hear. He became quite chatty.

"Tommy Yeo still suspended?"

Lizzie was touched. So, he did listen to what she told him about work and what happened at the infirmary. She felt such a heel for ever doubting him.

"Yeah."

"Any sign of him coming back?"

"Not that I know of. These things take ages and no one tells the likes of me anything. We're just the workers."

"You don't say nothing against him, right?"

"Course not!"

Andy nodded in satisfaction. Lizzie noticed and was pleased.

"What about the old cow with the cat?"

"Miss Crawley?"

"That her name?"

"How'd you know she has a cat?"

"God, Lizzie. You've told me enough. Always covered in cat hair isn't she?"

"Yeah! They stick to her polyester clothes like shit to a blanket. By the end of the week she looks like a rug." They both howled with laughter, as one, a proper couple. Lizzie felt as if she had come home.

Chapter Twenty-One

The Next Day

It was still raining. Antediluvian. Inside Catherine's office the girls were warm in their bed while their mistress stood before her team in their large room with a board marker in her left hand, lid off, poised for action. Behind her she had divided the whiteboard into two exact halves with a perfectly straight line. On one side she had written 'Tiger Bites' and on the other, the number '16', under which there were images of the disembowelled cat taken from a variety of angles. Nicole and Mike were surprised but chose not to show it; Nicole was learning fast and Mike had no idea what was happening. But Catherine usually had a logical explanation so no doubt he would know soon enough. If the other members of the department were surprised they also kept it to themselves, heads safely below the parapet.

"Well? Any ideas?"

Clearly not. Catherine had guessed as much – counted on it. Now she had the floor.

"The cat has sixteen symmetrical cuts across its body and has been disembowelled. All the cuts are the same length and depth. This is calculated."

"Like the tyres." Nicole had interrupted. Catherine however, was not displeased.

"Exactly!" She jabbed the board marker towards Nicole for emphasis before she continued. "Then there are these." She pointed to the two white stones on the table beside her, wrapped in a clear plastic evidence bag but perfectly visible, innocuous and inoffensive. "Not to mention the time on the clock, the cooker timer and the bedside alarm."

"Well?" "Anyone?" The girls snored; no-one spoke. "I'll go on then, shall I?" Catherine was enjoying herself. She turned to the board and wrote a sequence of numbers on it, saying them aloud as she formed the figures.

"16, 16, 2, 8 and 6." Someone spoke up.

"2 plus 6 plus 8 equals 16".

"Yes, Mike." Finally. "The number 16 seems to be significant. But why? And why Miss Crawley? And what, if any, is the connection with Tiger Bites? Why do I have a feeling that they're connected?"

Then Catherine astonished them.

"Because I really don't know, but gut instinct tells me they're connected, somehow, and we need to find out why, even if it is just to prove me wrong. Now don't tell me that you wouldn't like to prove me wrong?" An uncomfortable silence and then an anonymous snigger winged its way up from below the parapet.

"Thought so. Right. Mike, after briefing check out if Miss Crawley has any enemies, disgruntled patients, that sort of thing. The rest of you, think 'links'. What could possibly connect the two cases? It's too much of a coincidence that they're simultaneous. This is Wyeminster, not Bristol or London or Glasgow. There's nothing on the CCTV from Miss Crawley's house, which is odd in itself and I've got the techies looking into that. So, open floor. Let's hear your ideas, whatever they are." This was one of Catherine's favourite brainstorming techniques. She knew that 'brainstorming' was a banned word as non p.c. in case it gave offence to epileptics so had opted for open floor as an alternative, but they all knew what she meant.

"Anything and everything. Nicole, you start."

"Tigers are big cats. Same family."

"Yes. Someone else."

"There are drugs at the hospital, where Miss Crawley works."

"Yes. Different drugs but we'll pay them a call. We need to talk to them about Miss Crawley so we'll make the infirmary a priority."

"What else?"

Voices and ideas began to be heard from around the room, blocking out the sound of snoring dogs and rain trying to break in through the windows.

"They're all even numbers, multiples of two."

"Twos are pairs."

"Knives were used for the tyres and the cat."

"Were they the same knives?"

"What about the anonymous phone calls? How many were there? Were they made in multiples of 2?"

"What time were they made?"

A sudden interruption of a rude ping on Catherine's phone to announce a text was followed by a shower of pings, buzzes and ring tones on all the other mobiles in the room. Creative thinking abandoned, everyone consulted their messages. Then the landlines began calling. Catherine took the floor.

"Incident at Wyeminster Grammar School. Let's go."

The paramedics were there first and the ambulances close behind. The entrance to the school had become a confusion of flashing blue lights, sirens shrilling near and getting closer, green clad people lugging medical equipment out of vehicles into the school buildings as hordes of students and staff were being evacuated out onto a playing field. There they stood in dishevelled serried rows in the pouring rain, answering to their names, clutching each other, huddling under hoods, clip files held over heads and for a lucky few, umbrellas.

Inside the long central corridor, the main school artery linking learning to administration a small group had gathered outside the entrance to the boys' toilets. A young man lay on the floor bathed in red, smelling of iron and fear. Around him knelt two men in green and one in a dark suit; three wise men trying to revive the dying. Around their knees a skirt of blood was silently spreading, a life flowing unchecked onto vinyl, soaking into cloth, drenching hope, staining flesh and memory. Three other boys were nearby, all wearing blood stained school uniform like young hunters at the scene of their first kill. Initiated. Two were slumped on the floor, pale, lifeless but alive, unfocussed but conscious, wearing pin point pupils in their open unseeing eyes and spaced out expressions. The third was standing, pinioned against the wall against which his outstretched wet arms and body left an image of a crucifixion in someone else's blood. At his feet lay a Butterfly knife, sullied and red.

When Catherine appeared in the corridor framed by Nicole and Mike, four further paramedics had taken their places beside the lifeless living boys and were in the process of removing them to ambulances which then took off in a blast of sound and light towards Wyeminster Infirmary. Pinned to the wall by Ella, Taya's foster mother and another member of staff, the assailant looked lost, helpless and frightened. He was as much being supported as restrained.

"What's happened?" Catherine was the first to speak. The man in the dark suit kneeling in the pool of blood looked up at her to reply.

"A knife fight. Over drugs apparently."

"Is he...?" They had to know; Catherine had to ask.

One of the paramedics shook his head while his colleague answered.

"I'm sorry. There's nothing we could do."

***

She was being carpeted. No other word for it. The summons had come by phone from the Chief Superintendent's secretary which was bad enough, but on arrival she had been made to wait for five minutes before invited to enter after knocking, was not offered a seat and abruptly instructed to shut the door behind her. At least there was no third-party witness; that happened the second time.

"We're following a couple of lines of enquiry, Sir." It sounded feeble and Catherine knew it.

"So, nothing, in other words?" The Chief Superintendent was nothing if not direct. "Three kids. Two critically ill and now one dead. A drug related knife fight inside – inside! - a local school – a Grammar School - and you have nothing apart from a man in a Donald Trump mask and a couple of lines of enquiry? What the hell am I to say to the Press and the people of his city? To the parents of the dead boy? To everyone else's parents?" He paused, for emphasis and to regroup his phrases. Catherine stayed mute. When in doubt, say nothing.

"We've become a national statistic, Catherine. Drugs on the streets, at the school gates, fatal stabbings, kids at risk, anxious parents. Here. In Wyeminster. We're all on the line - and don't even mention police cutbacks and limited resources because there's nothing I don't know about that. And frankly, at this precise moment, I don't care. Deal with it. I want a result and I want it now. And if you can't deliver, I'll find someone who can. Do I make myself clear?"

Abundantly. Her pale variegated face said it. She nodded and turned to leave.

"And keep those bloody dogs out of my station."

Chapter Twenty-Two

The Next Day

The Nine Gates of Heaven looked very different at the back. Industrial green and blue wheelie bins proclaimed the dented, unpainted, metallic back door. Sodden cardboard, cigarette ends, scraps of food and dog faeces ornamented the ground at the feet of the two men standing there, barely visible in the dark alley where even the bin men trod with care. Behind the door the kitchen was noisy with chopping, chatting, laughing: heavy duty preparation before service started. In the alley the only sound came from Lee, hushed and icy. Andy would have preferred it if he was shouting.

“The dead boy was one o’ yours?”

Andy nodded miserably. No point in lying. Lee always knew.

“Yeah. Supplying.”

“The boy with the knife was also one o’ yours?”

Andy nodded again, head bent, avoiding eye contact.

“Fightin’ over territory?

Andy stared at a pile of dog poo, runny with rain and unsuccessfully trying to disintegrate on the cracked tarmac beneath them. He did not even bother to nod.

"You'd two suppliers in the same place?"

"Thought it'd make them sell more. Competition, y'know?"

Lee's silence suggested that he did know, far better than Andy ever would, but that it was of absolutely no interest to him.

"This is very disappointing, Mr Barrett. You've created a problem - a very serious problem. Operations have had to be suspended for the time being. You'll say nothing. To anyone. You'll wait until you're told what to do next. We'll contact you. No attempt must be made to contact us. D'you understand?"

Another Andy nod, eyes fixed on the desolate dog turd.

"I need to hear you say it."

"Nothing. Won't say nothing."

"Give me yer phone."

Andy pulled it from his back pocket and handed over the unregistered pay-as-you-go. Immediately he was given another: the school bully being humiliated by the schoolmaster who once stood in his place. As Lee disappeared through the back door, Andy and the dog turd continued to remain motionless in the alley.

It was equally cheerless in Clare's office but drier. Safer underfoot too - no dogs allowed. She and Hugo had coffee and were discussing the Colorectal Department, again.

"No decision on Tommy Yeo yet I suppose?" Clare tried not to let the hope in her voice lift her spirits.

"Sorry. We're still waiting. The General Medical Council work in their own time."

"You've...?"

"Yes, of course I've followed it up. I think it just makes them go them more slowly."

"We could really do with him back in post. Debbie Crawley is giving cause for concern."

"How so?" Hugo sounded surprised. He had thought she was already concern enough.

"Erratic behaviour. Lack of focus. Things are slipping – paperwork, scheduling, attention to detail. All the things she seemed so good at. People are starting to complain. Patients are even asking to be assigned to other consultants."

"Which you don't have." Clare sipped her cooling coffee and swallowed her irritation. Hugo pretended not to notice and slid the conversation sideways.

"Is this ... falling off ... just work related?"

Claire looked up from her coffee with interest. What was he implying?

"There's this thing with her cat."

"What thing?"

Hugo failed to hide his surprise. Had she really not heard? He explained. Clare's coffee went cold.

"But it's just a cat! Horrible of course, cruel and shocking, but not the end of the world. Distressing for her, yes, for anyone, but surely not enough to unhinge her? Life goes on. This is a hospital; she has a job to do. Responsibilities."

"I believe she was very attached to it. And the circumstances are disturbing. The police are investigating, apparently."

"Then she has nothing to worry about. Couldn't we get her another one?"

Hugo understood now why she was the CEO. He moved the subject on. "The situation has to be dealt with. Juan Morales will just have to keep an even closer eye on her. I'll get on to the GMC again and see if they can be persuaded to make a decision about Tommy. Maybe if I stress the detrimental effect of their delay on patients, they'll get their act together. Otherwise they'll be investigating both our senior colorectal surgeons. Debbie Crawley's an accident waiting to happen."

***

A vigil was being held at the Community College. As soon as darkness had descended the candles had been lit and lined up along the outer security fence, now adorned with tangible grief. Balloons had been tied to the sharp vertical struts and school scarves lovingly folded around them as mothers wrap up their children to protect them from the cold. There were flowers everywhere – on the pavement, at the foot of the fence and then piled on top of one another as if trying to climb over it into the school grounds. Many of the slim bouquets in cheap cellophane had cards and notes attached, written in childish hands, strewn with kisses, damp, soiled and sad in the weeping rain. There was even a teddy bear slumped with the weight of the water it had absorbed hanging from the floral wall, dripping miserably onto the cascade below. In the middle of the sorrow was a picture of the dead boy, Jason Pierce, grinning out of his school uniform, tie straightened for the camera but top shirt button undone behind the knot – got to make some sort of statement as a teenager. The school photograph rested on an easel borrowed from the art department made funereal by a covering of black cloth against which Jason rested his head. His was the only smile.

Taya, Kezia and Courtney were part of the crowd lining the flickering candlelit pavement and spilling out onto the road in rows of wet grief. Underneath the make-up and the attitude they were small girls again, too young to understand, shocked by the finality of death. They stood together, arms entwined.

"I never thought I'd come outta hospital to this." For the first time Taya has begun to realise what death meant and how close she had come to it. Until now it had been just a word in other people's mouths, a diagnosis, a possibility but not a reality.

"Jase was OK, y'know? He didn't deserve to die." Courtney cannot make any more sense of it than Taya. Kezia was angry.

"Bloody Tiger Bites. You been dead lucky, Taya." She gasped. "Oh my God. I just said dead."

Everything had changed, even the language they would use in the future.

From behind the expanding line of mourners Catherine has been watching: who arrives, who leaves, who stays. Eavesdropping. Listening to what was said, who said it and to whom. Patrolling unnoticed in the darkness she was still searching and finding nothing. She stayed until the candles had burned themselves out and the only person left was Jason, smiling out for all eternity from the sodden black frame of the artist's easel.

Chapter Twenty-Three

The Next Day, All Day

"Sorry girls. Not today. You've got to stay here." Euclid and Pi assailed Catherine with their most accusatory axe murderer glowers but submitted, turned away from the front door and headed upstairs for the comfort of her bed and the king size duvet. They had ways of making their displeasure felt.

What had been a long night for her was going to turn into an even longer, lonely day. Catherine was tired beyond sleep so no point in even trying; better to go straight to the station and interview Tyler Morgan, the lad charged with stabbing Jason. Not that there was much doubt about it, but legal protocol mattered, especially where minors were involved and they would all be at pains to couch their language and accusations in principled doubt, especially when they were being recorded and there was a solicitor present. It was hard not to feel sorry for the lad but they had a job to do, parents to placate, not to mention a Chief Superintendent who was watching his chances of an MBE (at least) being sluiced away with the blood from the post mortem on the ill-fated Jason.

The lad sat with his solicitor opposite Mike and Catherine in the stale, windowless interview room. His parents had wanted to be with him but he had refused. The seriousness of his alleged crime dictated that he was put in a high-security unit, even for interview. A uniformed officer was positioned by the door in the event of an attempted escape. It was absurd and they all knew it but there Tyler sat, a teenager-child in adult's clothes from the remand centre. The grey tracksuit trousers he wore kept slipping down and he had repeatedly hitched them up as he had scuffed his way into the room. Necessity not Grunge; low slung jeans were a lifestyle choice which did not apply to a remand centre uniform. One-way glass gave the impression of a window on the far wall but no one was deceived. Eyes everywhere and no way out except through the closed door. Artificial light only; the real world a prison sentence away. It was on occasions like this that Catherine's vitiligo gave her an unexpected advantage. Interviewees were discombobulated by her appearance; it disarmed them and more often than not, they felt sorry for her, which made them more cooperative. The staring, the surprise and then the formalities over, Catherine began.

"How old are you, Tyler?"

"Fifteen."

"The same age as Jason?"

"Yeah."

"You were in the same year at school?"

"Yeah."

"But different forms?"

"Yeah."

"Were you friends?"

"No."

"But you knew him?"

"Yeah."

Break him in gently. Easy questions. Nothing leading, just simple yes or no responses. Solicitor obviously happy with that. Slowly, slowly. Poor kid.

"You've never been in trouble with the police before?"

Slight pause.

"No... Not really."

"What does that mean?"

"My client has received unwritten police warnings on two previous occasions, one for suspected shop lifting - never proved - and the other for unruly behaviour. He has never been formally charged with any offence and has no police record." Catherine replied not to the solicitor who had just spoken but directly to Tyler.

"That's good, Tyler. Helpful. It helps us to get to know you."

Look him in the eye. Engage. Help him help us. Me.

"So, it was an argument about territory?"

"Yeah. He was on my patch."

"Jason was?"

"Yeah."

The solicitor looked as if he was about to intervene but Tyler ignored him. What had happened was not his fault and he wanted Catherine to know.

"He was nicking my customers, taking my sales. It's not what we agreed."

"And you got into a fight about it?"

"I didn't mean to hurt him. Just warn him, y'know? But he came at me and I panicked. It was self-defence."

He's been watching too many TV cop shows Catherine thought, but it was a valid point and clearly the solicitor was going to run with it. Tyler would probably get off with it too, and after the amount of time he would spend on remand before the case came to trial his sentence would be a token, if imposed at all. But that was not what she was interested in. He and Jason were collateral damage – tragic, harsh fall out.

"What were you selling, Tyler?"

"You already know that."

"Please just let me know for the record. It's not going to make any difference to the charges against you but we need to find out who put you up to this."

Tyler and the solicitor exchanged glances. A nod from the latter and the former answered.

"Them Tiger Bites that everyone's taking. The orange ones."

"Thank you, Tyler. And was Jason selling the same thing?"

"Yeah. On my patch. I never went on his." Hot indignation; tear-filled eyes.

"Who put you up to it, Tyler?" Keep using his name; personalise the interview; win his trust. "Who were you working for?"

Behind the one-way glass Nicole, the Chief Superintendent and a large chunk of the investigative team jointly held their breaths. Movement stopped, the opaque glass opened its eyes wide as if to wrench the information from the unseeing Tyler who tensed and gazed at this woman with the funny face.

"He said his name was Donald, but I don't think that's true."

"Why not?"

"'Cos someone Jason knows.." he hesitated, briefly appalled, then carried on. "...knew, said his name was Andy."

"Second name?"

"Dunno."

"Could you describe him?"

"Yeah. Easy."

"Good. Thank you, Tyler. We'll get a photofit organised immediately and see if we can identify him that way. You'd know him if you saw him again?"

“Oh, yeah. No sweat.” Catherine was making a note on the pad on the desk when the moment arrived.

“I know what motor he drives if that helps.”

***

“Back up?”

“Meeting us there. Can’t we go any faster? How the hell did you pass the police pursuit driving test, Mike?”

“Didn’t kill anyone” Mike muttered to himself but put his foot down nevertheless. Wyeminster was in shock – never seen anything like it. If roofs could turn and windows blink the streets would have twisted necks and open mouths. The mid-morning coffee hour was now blue lit, a pack of howling sirens as the convoy of police vehicles plunged themselves through the city towards the Victorian terrace housing Andy and Lizzie. Once Tyler had given them details of the car, it was easy to trace the owner. Catherine stood back while the men in bullet proof vests hammered on the front door and then they all waited for a response. Which never came. Nothing.

“Try again.” The door vibrated slightly but did not open.

“Break it down.”

Now it did move; cracked, splintered, yielded with a loud wooden cry of protest and they poured in, fanning out over the small interior with barely enough room to avoid bumping into each other. Catherine followed the heavy mob in. It was obvious that no one was at home and that they were unexpected.

She knew she was obsessed to the point of autism with order but Catherine was disgusted. How could people live like this? The ingrained dirt which appeared even worse because someone had clearly tried to dust and clean, occasionally, but not in corners or under things or above body height. Some of the surfaces were sticky and was that a sofa? Its depressed avian inhabitants peered out from behind beer cans, stained cushions and food stains pleading for mercy – release. Even just an open window and some fresh air. The curtains were drawn but cheap and unlined so half-light coated the room in a dim shroud like dust sheets. On the carpet were more beer cans – Special Brew mainly and the accumulated detritus of weeks of meals on knees, cigarettes stubbed out on any available surfaces, mainly plates bearing traces of ancient meals or empty pizza boxes.

"Turn it over. Everywhere. And think! Where would you hide things?"

The Chief Super had given her carte blanche on this one – signed every warrant she wanted and would have had them printed for her if she had asked. She experienced a brief moment of jubilation when he had told her to do whatever she thought necessary and he would back her all the way, but this had almost as quickly disappeared on the realisation that she would have to get results. No such thing as a free search warrant, especially with sides of armed back up.

The house was being taken apart at the seams; unpicked and deconstructed like an old coat, once substantial and proud but now moth eaten, shapeless and threadbare on the elbows. It gave in easily, anxious to please, owing its current occupants nothing but resentment for neglect and ill treatment. Its nicotine breath was cold and heavy with dust as carpets were pulled back, floor boards wrenched apart, cupboards ransacked and pillaged. Furniture collapsed as gloved hands groped and probed, the sofa died another death, clothes and linen were flung like waste paper into heaps and left where they fell. In the main bedroom Catherine noted the nurse's uniforms she found flung by the searchers onto the floor outside the wardrobe. They were clean and on coat hangers, which was more than could be said for anything else that had been in there. She heard Mike speak from behind her as she stood in the bedroom.

"Nothing, Ma'am."

"There must be." But where? "What about the loft? The roof?" She looked up at the ceiling above her as she spoke.

"We've checked the loft space; there's nothing."

"Well look again. Check all the ceilings. Look for any sign of redecoration – shouldn't be hard to spot in a house like this. New paint, uneven surface, any type of disturbance that might have been covered over. Check the floors again and the stairs. Behind all the skirting boards. I don't care if you have to pull the radiators off the walls to look inside them or empty the boiler. Or the water tank if there is one." Inevitably this led to the suggestion that Mike was dreading.

"What about the drains? Pipes, sewage? We'll dig up the street if we have to."

"Yes, Ma'am." He descended the stairs with the heavy news as Catherine remained at the top, surveying the ceilings and running her hands over the walls as if inspecting one of the girls for ticks or mites.

"Ma'am! In here!" It was Nicole, shouting up from below, her voice echoing up the now uncarpeted stairs. "In the bathroom!"

Catherine's bulk hammered down the exposed wood and flung itself with astonishing agility into the kitchen, hurdled over the piles of utensils and paraphernalia strewn on the floor and arrived panting at the entrance to the bathroom which was housed in a one storey extension that had been tacked onto the kitchen. Originally an outside privy, the DIY explosion of the 1970s had converted it into an integral bathroom with all the benefits of modern living except central heating. The Dimplex wall heater was long deceased so the room was cold and permanently damp, heated only by steam from hot water poured into bath and sink. Not often enough, was Catherine's thought, judging by the personal hygiene of its occasional occupants. She carefully avoided the toilet bowl and resisted the temptation to look into it. Close behind came Mike hoping against hope that this meant that the drains would be left intact but fearing the worst. Nicole was perched on the side of the avocado coloured bath, balanced precariously and holding onto the shower rail that ran above it. At the tap end was a calcified shower attachment that hung snakelike from a clasp on the tiles about three feet above the taps – just a little too short for an effective spray of water for anyone of a reasonable height. The room was damp and musty; black spots of mould stained the yellowing ceiling. The shower curtain was brittle, stained and rusty brown at the bottom after years of exposure to sitting water and lack of ventilation. There was a window but because it was on the ground floor at the unseen back of the house it had been screwed down for security and had not been opened within living memory.

Nicole had secured her feet now and was reaching up to the wall behind the shower attachment. In the far corner right up against the ceiling was a once white air vent, wide enough only for a hand to enter and clearly not fit for purpose. It was filthy. In the dusty light of the small room it was barely discernible but Nicole was examining it with interest.

"I think someone's tried to open it. There're marks on the sides and the screws are missing."

"Can you pull it out? How is it attached to the wall?" Eagerness in Catherine's voice. If only she was smaller ... but Nicole would have to do.

"No. It's stuck."

"Without screws?" Impatience overwhelmed enthusiasm which was rapidly becoming frustration. "Pull it. Harder. Come on girl, put some effort into it."

Nicole's annoyance translated itself into physical force and she yanked so hard at the air vent that the slats in the middle buckled and snapped into her hands so that she fell backwards off the bath onto the floor and crumpled over Catherine's feet.

"Sorry Ma'am."

"You okay, Nicole?" Mike asked from behind his boss's square backside.

"Yeah."

"Good. Get back up. There's something up there." It was Catherine who spoke. She had not even moved her feet never mind looked at her DC who was now wiping the grime from her streaky face with even streakier hands and now looked uncannily like a darker version of her superior. Whose gaze was fixed on the place where the vent had been. The edges of it were still firmly fixed to the wall but in the space once covered by the slats was something soft and fleshy, alien, and certainly not air. Nicole clambered back onto the side of the bath balancing with the aid of Catherine this time, who offered her arm for assistance and held it steady as the girl leaned up and over to grab hold of the whatever was in the vent. Sod health, safety and risk assessment. Just get it.

"Wait!"

"What Ma'am?"

"Gloves! Here."

Nicole swore mentally. She should have been wearing latex gloves before she even climbed up on the side of the bath the first time. Another bloody rookie error. She slid her hands into them one at a time then, flushed with embarrassment, resumed her search. Whatever it was in the vent hole was wedged tight, immoveable, jammed in and never meant to be dislodged. But that was before it encountered Nicole, who was mortified and who had something to prove, and was going to get the bloody thing out if it was the last thing she did, which she thought it might be in her capacity as a DC working for Catherine Scott.

It gave way with a gasp and a suck. Nicole found herself lying in the hideous avocado bath surrounded by clumps of coagulated dust, insect corpses, cement dust and a corner of the ceiling. In her hand was the empty head of Donald Trump with a cut throat.

***

Daylight was fading, Christmas was approaching, there would be an overnight frost and more rain was forecast for later in the week with possible snow showers. Debbie had turned up the heating in the house so that Miss Muffat would not get cold. She was such a sensitive cat. The food in her bowl on the kitchen floor was untouched and the level of the water the same as yesterday which was a concern. Perhaps she was ill? Debbie fretted loudly as she pottered about the house, an opened tin of cat food in one hand and a packet of Dreamies in the other. Anything to tempt Miss Muffat out of hiding. She was bound to come out soon either because she was hungry or the house was warm enough for her not to have to nest somewhere. Debbie had rearranged the cushions of the feline chair in the lounge and found a tartan rug - one of Father's that he kept in the car for picnics and cold days just like this one. The rug was neatly arranged on Miss Muffat's seat; all it needed now was the cat herself.

It was very perplexing; where was she? Debbie had been up and down the stairs several times, checked all the cupboards and favoured hidey holes but the beloved one was nowhere to be found. Oh, but of course! How could she have been so foolish? She could almost hear Father's voice calling her a silly-billy. Miss Muffat would be in the garden, making the last of the fading light before settling down for the evening in the cosy living room where they would sit, side by side, not speaking but just enjoying each other's company. Debbie had had an early bath – such a treat when at home with a free evening to look forward to. Rather than get dressed again she had put on winceyette pyjamas and Father's old dressing gown. It was designed for a man, but such excellent quality: wool, full length, a little tickly but that was the price you paid for Merino wool. It was tied with a heavy cord which was echoed by the piping on the pockets, lapels and cuffs. She was also wearing a pair of ancient sheepskin slippers, shapeless, flattened inside but comfortable old friends. They had spread over time and now fell off her feet when she walked so she was obliged to shuffle to keep them on but that suited her rather stiff-legged walk. Father had always told her to pick her feet up when she walked but since his death she had somehow got out of the habit and now trailed the ground rather than stepped over it. You had to walk like that wearing crocs in theatre and on hospital floors so it made little difference to do it everywhere else.

In the kitchen she put down the tin of cat food on the worktop by the sink and went to the back door where she bent down, stiffly, to examine the cat flap. Yes! There were hairs on it. Miss Muffat must have gone out. Straightening herself up, with the packet of Dreamies in one hand, she opened the door with other and stepped out into the scrubby twilight. Lit by thin lines of mustard thick light trying to escape from behind the blind at the kitchen window, Debbie wandered out into the garden to begin her search. She had soon passed well beyond the extent of the light from the window and was to be seen leaning over, peering at the foot of the fence, an ancient garden gnome bent over a pond in a dressing gown and slippers carrying a packet of cat treats instead of a fishing rod and calling aloud.

"Miss Muffat! ... Miss Muffat! ... Where are you? ... Naughty girl! Mummy's looking for you."

She rattled the bag of treats to tempt and allure between each utterance, waiting for a response, but nothing happened. So she wandered further into the garden and the unbroken darkness to continue her search.

***

"No, this does not count as overtime. We've a job to do. If you're home for Christmas that'll be payment enough." Catherine was addressing her team. The day was dying but as far as she was concerned, they were only just beginning. They knew the identity of the Tiger Bites' supplier on the street. It was a break through; momentum was everything.

She was in her usual position in front of the whiteboard but this time she was holding the board marker with vigour. She spoke as she wrote, turning occasionally to engage with her audience.

"Andrew Barrett. Known as Andy. Age 30. Small time supplier and known user of soft drugs: weed, that kind of thing. No convictions for anything more than shop lifting and possession, always below chargeable offence levels. We know from Tyler Morgan – the lad who stabbed Jason Pierce at the school – that Barrett's been running a small-scale local network employing schoolkids to sell Tiger Bites to their friends and contacts, in and out of school. He's a nasty piece of work but not the main event. Not clever enough. Certainly not clever enough to set up something like this on his own."

Here she drew a heavy line across the board from Andy's name to a question mark on the other side of the board. She vehemently punched the dot under the hook of the question mark as she continued speaking.

"He's only the middle man. We still don't know who's bringing in these drugs, or where they're coming from. We've found the bottom end of the supply chain. Now we've got to track it back to its source."

"Has he said anything?" Nicole was keen: over compensating for her lack of gloves and capitalising on finding Donald Trump.

"Nothing. Too frightened. He's terrified of what his 'employer' will do to him if he squeals. He won't talk. Not under any circumstances."

Nicole pressed home her advantage. "But he's definitely our 'trick or treat' man?" she asked.

"Yes. But therein lies the problem. The mask's not enough. Without a direct connection to the drugs we've got nothing but circumstantial evidence and that won't hold up in court. The CPS won't touch the case without proof positive." She paused. They knew what was coming next. "So that's what we've got to find."

Catherine looked around the room, her gaze flitting over every member of the team to include them in the task.

"Where are they? If we don't find him in possession of Tiger Bites, we've got no real case. There was nothing, absolutely nothing in the house although thanks to DC Marechal, we found the mask." Nicole tried not to glow and kept her glance on her hands which she noticed still had dirty fingernails. There was a limit to what could be achieved in the Ladies at the station after doing battle with a clogged-up air vent. It turned out that that it had been superglued to the wall after the screws had been removed when the mask as inserted in the holed. The edges of the vent cover were on the wall still.

“What about his car?” Mike wanted to know.

“Being taken apart as we speak.”

“His partner, girlfriend, whatever, Elizabeth Gilbert. She’s on the tenancy lease with him. She works at Wyeminster Infirmary.” Mike had a copy of the lease in front of him which the landlord had been only too happy to provide. He had seen the state of the house even before the police had taken it apart; his insurance wouldn’t cover him for repairs and redecoration unless he could prove every effort to evict his tenants.

“She does.” Catherine agreed with some satisfaction. “Known as Lizzie. A staff nurse in the Emergency department.” She drew another line from Andy’s name off at a tangent at the end of which wrote Lizzie’s name, then had great pleasure in swinging a line across the board from there to Debbie Crawley and the photo of Miss Muffat.

“A link! Tenuous, but a link nevertheless.” The air was full of her unspoken “I told you so”. Mike sighed; now she would be even more insufferable. However, they were not there yet and Catherine knew it.

"Our priority is this Tiger Bites case." She had returned the pen to Andy's side of the board and she was aggressively underlining his name. "The Chief Super is under pressure so I'm under even more. Which means that you lot are going to be very busy... The girls won't be allowed back in the station until we get a result." A brief silence to enable them to absorb the enormity of the situation.

"I want to know everything there is to know about Andy Barrett. What is it that he's too scared to tell us? Mike, follow up the search on his car. And check out this Elizabeth – Lizzie – Gilbert. Nicole, with me. We need to pay a visit to A&E."

Chapter Twenty-Four

That Night

It was dark. In the sky the orange glow from the city leaking upwards into the unseen was briefly evident between incoming rain clouds and obscurity. It was cold but clear; a band of high pressure sitting defiantly over Wyeminster until elbowed aside by the low on its way in from the Atlantic north. The High Street shops were closed, some shuttered, others with their glass windows screened behind close iron grids; all locked. Their bright come-hither Christmas window displays incongruously festive and jolly in the quiet, forlorn street, like stills from a cartoon waiting for someone to press the resume button. In the shadows there was a slight movement and an urban fox, thoroughly at home in the abandoned city sauntered out onto the pavement before crossing the road towards the waste bins behind the shops. A regular route, familiar territory; no hurry; all night to wander, sniff, discover and devour. However, he had been spotted.

"Miss Muffat! There you are! Come here, darling. Mummy's got treats for you!"

The fox picked up speed and noiselessly disappeared, startled by the intrusion. Debbie, clad in her father's dressing gown and sloppy slippers hove into view at the other side of the street. Previously unseen, part of the cityscape, a figure frozen in space and time, she appeared from nowhere and suddenly picked up clumsy speed to pursue the animal. The car could not avoid her. The driver tried, swerving violently to the side but caught her by the hip, twisted her off the ground into the air where she hung for a fraction of a second before she crumpled onto the road. Apart from the squeal of brakes it was remarkably silent – a soft bump, a moment and then a clump as the car reasserted itself on the street and pulled up, engine muttering, Debbie made no sound but the Dreamies left her hand and flew through the night sky after the fox as if to continue the chase unaided.

Two men opened the front doors of the car and ran simultaneously to the lumpy body behind them where they stopped and stood. Awestruck. The driver was immaculately suited, shiny shoed, visibly appalled. The other was in casual clothes, chinos not jeans, tailored shirt and designer sweater, preppy and expensive, soft shoed, dressed for comfort and lamp lit interiors not the garish reflected light of shop windows and deserted city streets. Both stared at Debbie in her father's dressing gown, tightly corded, feet buckled and legs askew. Her face was half hidden by her lank hair, still trying to escape from its elastic band and by the fact that her features had come to rest awkwardly against the unrelenting tarmac of the road against which the face had remoulded itself to fit. Her nose was bleeding, her eyes were closed. The second man knelt down to her level. His cuff-linked arm reached out to check the pulse at her neck, he surveyed her position and angled limbs. Then he pulled a mobile out of his pocket and punched in the emergency number, spoke tersely, gave away nothing but their location, requested an ambulance and rang off. They then ran back to the car where the open doors swallowed them up, sealed them in and drove them away from the scene.

From above one of the shop windows a curtain twitched. A narrow line of inner light beside the window frame and part of an unknown face watched what was happening below. The light vanished as the curtain closed and the car drove off.

On the emergency switchboard the handler was in a quandary. To believe or not to believe? No details, just a location and an urgent request for an ambulance in a Scottish accent so thick it couldn't be real. No identification, didn't stay on the line long enough to answer required questions for an assessment of the situation, no contact details – number withheld. It had to be another bloody hoax – didn't it? How the hell was he to know? It was a relief when the second call came in from an eye witness who wanted to remain anonymous but yes, there was a body in the street. It had been a hit and run and they not only needed to get an ambulance there as soon as possible but also the police. No, they weren't sure if it was a man or a woman but whatever it was, it seemed to be unconscious. The body certainly was not moving and yes, there was blood. So, could they please hurry?

On the outskirts of Wyeminster the black car pulled up outside the large electric gates and waited for them to open which they did, too slowly. The car had bolted through the widening gap before the gates even reached their destination and by the time they were closed, the car had pulled up outside the large house into which both men had evaporated.

Inside, dim, subdued, with lighting from low lamps plotting their path across the wooden floor, shiny shoes and loafers strode into the inner chambers, past the suspended game of Mah-jong, straight through to the large polished table at which sat Mr Yeo. Paterfamilias. So small, so scrawny, silent but ineffable. For the first time in living memory, his wife was there, sitting beside him. No greeting. No sign of recognition. The suited man stood back as Tommy took a seat some distance from his parents but in full view of their combined gaze. Then, when invited, Lee joined them.

***

So far, touch wood, the evening was quiet. There were a few people in the E.R waiting area, none in apparent agony or distress. The arrival earlier of a small boy who had had an argument with his sister on the other side of a heavy door which had resulted in a broken nose and split eyebrow had been dealt with and peace resumed. An occasional sniffle from behind a curtain in the treatment room paid testament to his stitches and receding pain, but the power of local anaesthetic and a packet of sweets had done much to restore him to health. His parents would have a fine time of it when the anaesthetic wore off, but by then he would be long gone from the infirmary. Sesi wandered into the waiting area debating whether to go for a break now or to make do with the muesli bar she had in her bag. Murphy's law had it that if she left the department something would kick off but if she stayed, all would remain quiet. She opted for the latter and a peaceful life. The late-night receptionist caught her eye – she was holding the phone receiver in one hand and waving at Sesi with the other.

"Everything okay?" Sesi asked as she approached the desk. The receptionist, whose name was Lorna How can I Help You? according to the badge on her shirt but whose mugshot on her lanyard suggested otherwise, hissed at her, one hand over the receiver.

"The police are here, asking questions."

"The police? What about?"

Listening to the voice on the end of the phone while conversing with Sesi was causing Lorna problems. She shrugged her shoulders, rolled her eyes and returned to the voice, leaving Sesi to work it out for herself. However, the conversation was not over. Rohan Patel had been pottering about in the area behind Lorna, had overheard what had been said and wanted to know more. Rohan often pottered about the admin areas of departments, wherever he happened to be working at the time, and no one was ever quite sure what he was doing. No suggestion of anything untoward; he was not like that. But he did often seem to be so much busier than everyone else, in an 'I'm holding this important piece of paper which I have to take somewhere else' sort of way. Good old Rohan, plump, sweaty, cheerful and ever present. A fixture and fitting; part of the infirmary DNA.

"The police? What do they want?" Rohan had emerged from behind Lorna, large, open mouthed, peering over her shoulder like an overfed blue parrot.

"Drugs. Knives. Take your choice." Sesi's flippancy was misplaced. Rohan went white.

"Where are they now?"

Lorna answered.

"They're in with Clare Howard-Jones at the moment."

"In her office?"

"Yes, I think so. Are you alright, Rohan?"

"Fine. Tired. Long day."

"Tell me about it," Sesi added and headed back towards the treatment room to find her muesli bar. Rohan retreated back into the office behind Lorna and shut the door. As soon as he was on his own, he slumped down onto a chair and looked as if he might cry.

Catherine and Nicole were indeed in with the Chief Executive Officer. Clare sat opposite them in her office with a furrowed brow. Her forehead was more lined these days she had noticed.

"I understand the urgency of the situation and its severity, of course," she was saying.

Catherine readied herself. Always an 'of course' before a 'but'.

"But you must see that I cannot allow any interruption in the work and smooth running of my hospital." Clare was glad no one who worked there could hear her describe it as smooth.

"We only want to ask a few questions and interview Miss Elizabeth Gilbert, who is on duty." Slight pause. "I can insist, of course" she added, eyeing Clare who did not notice. "But I would rather not have to. So much better if we can make our essential enquiries with your full cooperation and approval."

"Lizzie Gilbert?" Clare was astonished.

"In connection with her partner. We have no reason to believe that she's done anything wrong."

"Lizzie is an excellent nurse. Reliable, professional and gets on well with everybody. We could do with more like her. People like Lizzie are the backbone of the NHS; we couldn't...

A loud rap at the door cut off her. For the second time in as many minutes she looked astonished.

"Come in!"

Rohan's head entered the room, edging round the door then followed reluctantly by his body, all of it, making itself as small and insignificant as its bulk allowed. Catherine and Nicole were mesmerised. He looked as if was about to pop out of a bottle.

"Can I help? Is there a problem?" Clare was concerned. She knew that by now everyone would know that she was in conference with the police. The hospital gossip network was devastatingly efficient – and insatiable. It had to be something really momentous for her to be interrupted, especially by a Trust Grade anaesthetist whom she recognised by sight and whose name would be on the tip of her tongue given enough time.

"Rohan Patel" he offered apologetically, then launched into a speech he had been rehearsing all the way to the office.

"I'm sorry. I shouldn't have done it. I know that. It was very wrong but it wasn't for me. Not really. I didn't use it. I'm not like that, a user I mean. I've never done it before, ever."

"Mr Patel, please. Slow down. I have no idea what you're talking about."

"The Fentanyl."

"What Fentanyl?"

Now it was Rohan's turn to pause and be surprised. Did she really not know? And if she didn't, then maybe other people didn't either, and it had been a cleverer theft than even he thought. His brief moment of jubilation turned to horror because now they did know, and it was he who had told them. Damn! Well, he would turn this to his advantage. He had to. Lizzie

Gilbert had what was coming to her; this was all her fault. As he relived the humiliation of her rejection of him his throat burned and his breath quickened. Catherine noticed. The man had straightened up where he stood and a look of cunning had come over his face. What was his agenda? Could he be relied upon? Everyone always had an agenda of some sort – twenty years in the nation's constabulary had taught her that. She waited; Rohan's breath steadied and his face assumed a determined, rather self-righteous expression. A penitent, metaphorically on fat knees, about to confess and unburden. And land someone else in it.

Rohan in turn was inspecting the other two women in the room apart from Clare. They must be the police. Funny, he had expected them to be men but no matter, but his offer would be the same. He spoke to the bigger one with the patchy face; she had boss written all over her.

"Give me immunity from prosecution and," turning to Clare, "disciplinary action, and I'll tell you everything."

"There's an everything?" Clare was horrified. Catherine exchanged looks with Nicole as they both had the same thought - was this it? The link?

Lizzie was nowhere to be seen in the Emergency Department when Clare finally escorted Catherine and Nicole there from her office via the strangely empty lift and quiet night time corridors. Visiting time was over.

The infirmary was being settled down to sleep for as long as possible before the interruptions of the night began: a new mother settling a sleepy baby between feeds, snatching rest, hoping for a lengthy reprieve but rarely getting it. They found Sesi in the treatment area as she emerged from a curtained cubicle from behind which rhythmic groaning and wheezing could be heard. Trying hard to pretend it was not happening, Clare accosted her E.R. Consultant. Whose name she did know.

"Hello Sesi. I'm sorry to interrupt but do you know where we can find Lizzie Gilbert?"

Astonishment was catching and now it was Sesi's turn. The sight of a senior manager – 'the' senior manager - on the shop floor at this time of night was unprecedented. It was obviously the police asking questions from earlier that she had with her but wanting to speak to Lizzie? That was bizarre. The only thing that did not faze Sesi was Catherine's face; Sesi was used to reactions to skin colour and never took any notice of other people in the same way as a matter of principle.

"Lizzie? With a patient behind one of these." She indicated the curtain behind her. "She's here somewhere."

On perfect comedic cue, a head appeared from behind cloth on the other side of the room and they all turned to examine it - a surreal 'it's behind you' moment.

Lizzie grinned and her body followed her head from behind the blue and white sprigged material.

"Looking for me?"

Instead of smiling, Clare introduced Catherine.

"Staff Nurse Gilbert, this is Detective Inspector Scott and her colleague who'd like a few words with you."

"With me? Why?" Lizzie was not smiling now but had fallen victim to the epidemic of astonishment sweeping the hospital.

"In my office? Now? Thank you." It was not clear whether Clare was thanking Sesi, Lizzie or the incessant groaning that had underscored the entire conversation but she had already started on her return journey so all of them except Sesi followed.

***

As soon as Tyler had given Catherine a description of Donald Trump's car the search was on. It had been located and impounded almost at once – Wyeminster was not a big place – and now the VW cut a forlorn figure inside a wire cage in the compound of the police garage. It stared blindly out through the bars, headlights dead; resigned. At least it was dry. When the cage was finally opened and a forensic team of masked men in white arrived to dismantle it, panel by screw by bolt, there was nothing to be done except sit still and get on with it. But with what? Mike was getting agitated. The unblinking artificial lights angled onto the vehicle were making his eyes water, the noise of disembowelling and dismembering its body and the lateness of the hour were only adding to his frustration.

"There must be something!" he said for the second time. The forensics ignored him. It was what it was and they were only doing their job. Thank God they did not have to justify their overtime expenses to the Chief Super. Perhaps that was why Mike Padstow was so antsy, or maybe he was missing one of those interminable choir rehearsals he was always banging on about. A single voice emerged from under the car, muffled by mask and chassis,

"Sorry. Nothing."

Mike sniffed, looked at his watch and peered out of the grubby window at his own reflection as the night bounced him back into the room. He looked a mess, needed a shower, something to eat. A change of clothes too. He always wondered why TV police officers had to have a clean shirt – it was the underpants, socks and a deodorant that really mattered. The shirt came last. And that was just the men. He sighed and turned back to the mounting pile of detritus from the car. Red Bull cans, some crushed, some still sticky, chewing gum, several empty cigarette packets, a rainbow of cheap plastic lighters, empty takeout coffee cups, some with lids, sweets and sweet wrappers. They had requested an urgent visitation from the drugs' dog squad but that was taking time so they had started without them. Sniffer dogs needed to rest apparently, which would have been hilarious if it was not so galling. Did they get overtime too? And how was that paid? He pulled himself together; low blood sugar playing tricks with his mind probably. It was only when he was staring wistfully at a packet of sweets on the pile of rubbish in front of him that it happened.

"Where're these from?" he called to one of the forensics.

"Glove compartment."

"Hell! How could we have been so stupid?" He had snatched his mobile from his jacket pocket and was slamming the speed dial even before he finished speaking.

***

Catherine and Nicole were back in the Chief Executive's Office, accompanied now by Lizzie. Clare had taken a seat away from her desk to observe. It had been her suggestion; Lizzie seemed totally disorientated and rather helpless. No longer a capable staff nurse but a rather thin, straggle haired wide-eyed child with inky stains on her arms and, Clare noticed for the first time, on one ankle. The revelations from Rohan Patel, whose name she would never now be able to forget, had been shocking and mortifying. Lizzie was sitting opposite Catherine who had occupied the CEO chair behind Clare's desk. Nicole sat beside her, slightly to one side, taking notes and listening intently, head angled over her right shoulder like a curious robin, all eyes and preparedness.

"It wasn't for me!" Lizzie was bordering on the hysterical and the interview had only just started. The Detective Inspector had emphasised that it was informal, entirely voluntary and that Lizzie was merely helping them with their enquiries by answering a few questions but that was bullshit and they all knew it. Especially Lizzie. As soon as the word Fentanyl had been uttered, she had become flustered to the point of mild panic. Now she was speaking very fast, in a high-pitched tone, leaning forward in her seat, twisting that ludicrous engagement ring round and round her bony finger. She looked as if she might be unscrewing it from its joint.

"I know I shouldn't have done it but I couldn't see the harm. It wasn't going on the street or anything like that. It was for my partner, no one else. It was only left over anyway, going for disposal. No one wanted it." It was not a convincing argument and the more she said, the less she believed it herself. Catherine, as measured and sterile as a steel tray for surgical instruments cut in.

"Fentanyl is a controlled drug and this is a very serious crime. Have you any idea how much it's worth on the street? Even in small quantities?" She did not wait for an answer. Lizzie was beginning to cry and in urgent need of a tissue. She wiped her nose on the back of her engaged hand, taking care not to scratch herself on the diamonds.

"Are you sure that it only happened once? There was no other time?" Catherine pressed the point, speaking slowly and very clearly above the sound of snotty sniffling and wet gulping.

"Yes. Absolutely." Lizzie appeared to be telling the truth which continued to flow. "I tricked Rohan into doing it. I'm so sorry. What'll happen to me?" Lizzie did not know who to look at. So she studied the top of the desk, making no attempt to wipe her eyes or her nose. Clare could not bear it. What if she dripped on the desk? She waved at Catherine and pointed to a drawer, silently mouthing "tissues". The detective took no notice.

"Let's talk about your boyfriend first."

Lizzie abruptly stopped snivelling, wiped her nose first on her hand then on the sleeve of her uniform and faced up to the woman with vitiligo. She realised that she had seen her before – on television when Taya had been on the ward, a lifetime ago. Wasn't she the detective who had made the appeal about those Tiger Bites? Why then was she talking to her about Fentanyl and Andy? It made no sense. Lizzie's puzzlement began to get the better of her tears.

"Andy? He's clean. The Fentanyl was the last time. He's really settled down. He's got a job and we're getting married. Look." She displayed the rock-laden finger of her left hand, still glistening with the mucus from her nose. Catherine cast an expert eye over the ring. More expensive looking than its actual worth thanks to cleverly cut stones but valuable nevertheless. The high shank was unusual; a little dated in style but identifiable. It might be worth checking the lists of stolen jewellery on the computer database. She would get Nicole on to it. Unconsciously she fiddled with one her own diamond earrings – a sizeable stud sheltering behind fair hair. A small fortune in each ear lobe.

"Where does he work?" She stopped fiddling with her earring and leant forward over the desk, resting on her elbows, hands together, index fingers steepled towards her mouth. A supplication – come on Lizzie, tell me, from your mouth to mine.

"The Nine Gates of Heaven restaurant. In town."

"How long has he worked there?"

"Not long. Just started really but it's good money and he's even got a car." Lizzie halted. She had had a sudden terrible thought – had to cut them off at the pass before they went any further. This was why they were interviewing her!

"That's how he could afford this" she said, flashing the rocks at them, "he didn't steal it or anything like that if that's what you're thinking." She sat back, certain she had exonerated Andy. They thought he'd nicked her ring! As if.

Catherine did not care if he had robbed it from a grave or smuggled it out of a diamond mine up his rectum. A quick glance at Nicole before she continued.

"The Chinese restaurant?"

"Yeah. The big one." Lizzie was more composed now, on safer ground.

"Belonging to the Yeo family?"

"Yeah."

"What does Andy do there?"

"He's a sort of consultant – market research, that sort of thing." The pride in Lizzie's voice made Nicole want to weep. Couldn't the silly girl see which way this was going?

There was a brief silence while Catherine studied Lizzie before she angled herself to address Clare across the room.

"You have a consultant here by the name of Yeo, I think. Is that right?"

"Yes." Clare's surprise was tangible.

"Full name?"

"Tommy. Tommy Yeo."

"Tell me about him."

"He's one of our senior consultant surgeons, well qualified, popular with patients, with a sizeable private practice. Unfortunately, he's on suspension at the moment but I am confident that that'll soon be resolved and he'll be back on duty before too long." She gave Lizzie a severe glance and said, "That's confidential of course." The unspoken message being if anyone knows, I'll know how and you're in enough trouble as it is. Lizzie nodded. No-one would hear it from her. Cross my heart and hope to die.

Catherine could not care less and spoke impatiently.

"On suspension? Why?"

Clare sighed. "Not medical negligence or anything like that but for a breach of protocol. He disobeyed a directive from our Multi-Disciplinary team but there were, I understand, extenuating medical circumstances and there has never been any doubt about his competence as a clinician and surgeon."

Catherine wanted to know more. "You haven't said what department he's in."

"Colorectal." Clare replied and then the CEO in her assumed the ignorance of the general public about all things medical and she began to explain what Colorectal meant. Catherine cut her short.

"Yes, I know. Thank you. Nicole, Google the significance of white in Chinese culture."

Astonishment now officially reached pandemic proportions. Everyone stared at Catherine, including Nicole. Had the woman lost her mind as well as her skin pigmentation?

"Go on, what are you waiting for?"

"Yes Ma'am." She bent over her smart phone, keying furiously at a speed known only by the those brought up on keyboards, consoles and VDUs.

At that moment Catherine's own phone rang. She answered; the others listened.

"Mike. I was about to call you. What's happening with the forensics? ... Good. Good work." Nicole looked up from her twitching thumbs to see how her boss looked on the rare occasions when praise was dished out. She looked no different.

"Well?"

"White's the colour of death, Ma'am."

Clare wondered if she had wandered into another dimension.

***

Fortunately for Debbie it was a relatively quiet night and the switchboard operator designated her an emergency so the ambulance reached her within fifteen minutes. It drew up in the quiet street in a flurry of fracturing light, howling its arrival. By now Debbie was not alone. A woman was bent over her with a man behind, on his phone, calling for police and an ambulance. They had been on their way home – took a short cut – just found her. No, she hadn't been moved. Just as they found her. Yes, he had called the police but shouldn't they get her to hospital first? He thought she might be dead? His wife had done a First Aid course at work and couldn't find a pulse. Should they have done CPR? The woman looked up with anguish to agree.

"There's no pulse."

"Alright, love, we'll take it from here. Stand back, that's the way. Thank you." Pushing her aside as politely as possible the paramedic took her place beside the crumpled heap in the old-fashioned dressing gown. Both slippers had come off her feet which were now bare. The toe nails need trimming but were not badly neglected, the toes were well walked on, grubby, flattened underneath, slightly splayed to accommodate emerging bunions. Hard skin, cracked heel, especially on the left: aging, practical feet now scraped and motionless, exposed, naked at the end of thin legs thrust inelegantly from comforting winceyette. Oddly pathetic and vulnerable against the tarmac of the road.

"Any idea who she is?"

No, the couple had never seen her before. Just found her, like they said. Was she dead?

"No, but we need to get her to hospital as soon as we can." Straightened, lifted, braced, strapped rigid in an adult papoose, tied to a drip and oblivious, Miss Crawley, Consultant Surgeon (Colorectal), went off to her place of work in a maelstrom of noise and light to enter not at the main entrance with a lanyard and her trusty carrier bag but via the emergency department double doors, on a squeaky wheeled trolley, with a medical escort.

Sesi was on duty with Analyn from the agency. Her limited language skills made her the last departmental choice in the world for supply cover but she was their only choice. At least she was enthusiastic and turned up. It meant twice as much work because everything she did had to be checked and double checked but they were getting used to her and without Lizzie, who was still apparently holed up with the police and the CEO, Analyn was rapidly becoming indispensable. Rohan was around, somewhere, with his ubiquitous piece of paper. So far, it had been quite quiet if the visiting police were to be discounted. Rohan had gone then reappeared, still holding a piece of paper but looking unusually sombre. He had not even attempted to flirt with Lorna on reception, which was a first. Sesi was relieved in a way to find an emergency on her hands – a semblance of normality; something on which to focus and concentrate; something familiar. One of the paramedics was shouting as they materialised from behind the double doors,

"Female, elderly, unconscious, found in the street. Looks like a lady who lives rough, got a bit pissed and wandered in front of a car. Hit and run though, no sign of the driver at the scene. No id."

"This way!" Sesi called to the paramedics, heading towards Acute Care so that they followed her. Like a baton exchange in a relay race she upped her pace to match theirs as they propelled the trolley in her direction and drew level. She reached out to grasp the metal bar encasing the body to assist and looked at her new patient.

"Bloody hell! It's Creepy Crawley!"

Chapter Twenty-Five

The Next Day

There had been little point in going to bed; it was too late for meaningful sleep and her mind was a grid of confused lines, numbers, incomplete sequences and ideas. The girls were grumpy, under exercised and over fed; they had made a shaggy midden of her bed with half eaten chewies, slobber and what appeared to be at least one dried regurgitated breakfast. The duvet was twisted, the pillows flattened and lumpy, the supposedly fitted bed sheet a travesty of elastic corners and ridged furrows. Impossible to contemplate any type of rest there; she might as well log into the syndicate – just to watch - and try to discipline her thoughts that way. Of course, she knew she shouldn't; the formal warning had been clear and strict but how would anyone know? She owed nothing now and always knew exactly when to stop, but then she was only going to observe, so what was the harm? With a cafetière of coffee beside her she opened up the desk top and clicked on bookmarks, where she found the Poker Parlour. A double click and she was on the log in page. For a moment she hesitated, then yielded. Username The Girls and password the Mathematician entered, she was in and immediately felt the frisson, the flutter of anticipation. Suppressed excitement; a slight tingling between her thighs. God, she had missed this. Who needed sex? So over rated and such a passing pleasure. With gambling there was the thrill of the chase, the anticipation, adept foreplay of mind and body and then a glorious, triumphant climax – with the added possibility of large amounts of cash at the end. It wasn't about the money though. It was about power, winning, being the best. Long after the physical pleasure had dissipated the knowledge of a win remained and had once even made her rich enough to buy diamonds. Ethical diamonds, of course: she had standards. It had been so long since she had played, resisted the temptation, watched the adverts on TV and the internet and always said no. Since the time when the PCC had been involved, she had been promoted, was leading a team of detectives, had an excellent record for solving the unsolvable, pulling in offenders and taking them all the way to conviction. Even the CPS seemed to trust her.

The game was tense, clever and totally absorbing, freeing her mind. Funny how intense concentration and intellectual rigour were so liberating and creative. It made her a better detective. The girls had retired hurt to the bedroom, again, recognising the rapt expression on her face illuminated by reflected light from the screen and the odour of cooling coffee. It would be hours before she moved. Catherine was particularly intrigued by a new player called Hippocrates. Obviously a pseudonym it was an interesting choice of name, suggestive of intellectual tastes and pursuits, a little arrogant perhaps but with a certain medical cachet that intrigued. Hippocrates was also an accomplished player: steady, patient, calculating and experienced. Knew when to take a risk and when not, remembered cards that had gone before and anticipated those to come. It was a challenging game: inspiring even. Time was immaterial and she was surprised when the Today programme digitally burst into action signalling the start of the new day and with it, a substantial financial loss. She was shocked. It felt personal, as if Hippocrates had humiliated her. It would have to be dealt with, but in the meantime, with the emerging dawn came reality: she had two cases to solve and had lost a great deal of money.

"Follow the sequence; find the pattern; crack the code" she said to the water in the shower as she washed away the sour taste of the poker cards with baby shampoo and scent-free, lanolin-free soap, all that her skin would tolerate. "Find the pattern" she reminded herself after spitting toothpaste into the sink with plaque, saliva and coffee. She spat again for good measure, thinking of Hippocrates. Did not bother with a mirror to brush her hair, just ran her fingers through it and left it to dry as she rounded up the girls and headed down to the kitchen, muttering, "But what is the bloody pattern?" At the bottom of the stairs she stumbled over Pi.

"Stupid dog! Get out of the way. Can't you look where you're going?"

Pi sat, unbidden, in an effort to please. Euclid skulked behind her making herself as invisible as possible. Both gazed uncertainly at their owner, heads lowered, eyes wide, upturned, peering out of their sockets. Catherine was filled with remorse. She bent down and caressed both sets of ears in turn.

"Sorry, girls. Mummy's sorry. She didn't mean to shout. Not at you, anyway." They continued their unblinking gaze, tails motionless. Tongue-whipped. Hesitant. Hurt children. Catherine melted.

"Treats for my darling girls? Who'd like a treat?" This was more like it, a language they understood, safe, comforting, edible. Heads went up, tails began to brush the floor; Mummy was forgiven and the incident was forgotten, but not by Catherine, who hated herself. Not as much as she hated the other drivers on the road on her way to the station though. How did such morons pass their tests? They shouldn't be behind the wheels of supermarket trolleys never mind allowed on public roads, permitted to vote or have children. Just give me one person on a mobile phone while driving she prayed as she cursed the speed limit but did not exceed it. Just one. Something, anything to get my teeth into.

She swung too fast into the station car park and swore. Who the hell had had the temerity to park in her spot? She always parked there. Everyone knew she always parked there. Christ! She was furious, tired and demoralised. If she was paler than usual it did not show – one of the few advantages of her skin condition – but the knowledge of losing both the game and money sickened her. Never again. That was the last time. She would delete the website from her computer. At least she had been able to fund the debt which had already been paid – the rules of engagement were very strict like that and besides, it was a matter of honour among players, but her savings had taken a hammering. At least she still had a police pension to look forward to even if the ISA had gone; her mortgage was almost paid off but there would be no more diamonds for a long time. Could be worse she consoled herself as she stumped, girl-free, bad-temperedly upstairs where she bumped into Nicole.

"Morning, Ma'am."

Why was the girl always so bloody chipper?

"Anything to report?" She barged past Nicole into the briefing room.

"A hit and run last night..."

"No concern of ours," Catherine interrupted.

"... involving Deborah Crawley, from Wyeminster Infirmary" Nicole continued as if her DI had never spoken.

"What? The dead cat woman?"

"Yes, the one who had the break in and the white stones left in the kitchen."

"I know exactly who you mean, thank you, DC Marechal. I want all the details on my desk in 5 minutes, after you've got me a cup of coffee. Filter, none of that instant piss." She disappeared behind a slammed office door, only to immediately reappear looking mottled and murderous. “Some bastard has parked in my space. Sort it.”

Fifteen minutes later she was scowling at Mike and Nicole in her office.

“Is that all there is?”

Catherine was holding a coffee in one hand and the report in the other. She was standing up, waving the single sheet of paper at her junior colleagues like a racecourse bookie.

“No witnesses?” “No CCTV?” “What about the person who called 999?”

“Anonymous, Ma’am. Didn’t want to be identified.”

“Weren’t there two calls?”

“Three, but the third came when the ambulance was already on its way.”

“Trace the numbers from the emergency service’s switchboard.”

“The first two numbers were withheld. One from an unregistered pay as you go mobile and the other from a contract mobile, which we’re investigating.” Nicole said.

“Well the callers must have been in the vicinity, seen something, certainly heard something or they wouldn’t have phoned for an ambulance. Get back there and knock on doors, windows, whatever it takes and don’t show your faces until we've got a witness of some sort." She gulped at the coffee. "God. This is awful. Where's it from?"

"The first-floor machine – filter, like you said."

"Next time go out and get proper coffee." Catherine flung the full cup into the waste paper bin at the side of her desk where it slapped a torrent of hot, dark-skinned droplets over the sides of the bin and splashed onto the floor. Nicole flinched.

Catherine resumed her diatribe.

"What else was found at the scene?"

"Nothing. Just her slippers that came off in the collision."

"Slippers?"

"She was in her nightclothes - pyjamas and a dressing gown."

"In the city centre in the middle of winter?"

Mike and Nicole said nothing. Let her vent, get what was bugging her out of her system. Roll with the punches.

"Where's Miss Crawley now?"

"Wyeminster Infirmary. Stable but unconscious."

"We need to talk to her as soon as she comes around. Well, what are you waiting for?"

They scuttled out and Catherine sat down heavily to contemplate her gambling losses, her unresolved cases and the coffee dripping down the sides of the bin to add another stain to the cheap office carpet.

***

The news about Miss Crawley's accident was all over the infirmary by 8.05 the morning it happened. It had been handed out with changeover briefings, patient notes, early morning tea on the wards, the distribution of drugs, the very air circulating in the ventilation system. Sesi had called the Medical Director at home who had called Clare who would call the Chairman of the Trust as soon as she reached her office. Clare's husband, usually a patient man and abnormally long suffering, had been sufficiently provoked by his wife's nocturnal absence and intrusive phone calls to mutter something about her taking up residence in the hospital where he would pay occasional conjugal visits. If she could remember what those were. He stood more chance of sex on men's surgical than at home. Pretending not to have heard him, she had taken the call and immediately picked up her briefcase, blue Mulberry to match her navy flats – her feet still ached from the day before, and let herself out of the house into the dark morning and the car. Debbie was in ICU with a broken leg, facial abrasions, extensive bruising and severe concussion. It was this that was causing most concern.

Nigel had been summoned as soon as she had been assessed and agreed to do the trauma protocol CT scan himself, as well as X-rays. Lesley, who had taken it upon herself to arrive as soon as word of the drama reached her, was now conferring with Sesi in subdued tones a few feet away from Debbie's bed. Not that she could have overheard what they were saying; it just somehow seemed more reverent to speak softly Lesley had said, just in case. However, she, Lesley, wanted to know everything that had been done – she wanted a full report – nothing but the best and most thorough for her dear friend. Sesi chose not to be insulted and resisted the temptation to say that they gave everyone who was admitted the best and the most thorough treatment. She put Lesley's rudeness down to stress and assumed her most measured professional voice,

"As soon as she came in..."

"In a neck brace?" Lesley interrupted. Sesi continued, saintly, as patiently as she could.

"You know, of course, that I cannot divulge any details of her treatment. We need to locate her family and next of kin to consult with them about her condition and what happens next."

Lesley bristled with hostility. A swollen hedgehog, small, round and sharp. Her Welsh accent dropped as her outrage increased, revealing a very English upbringing and education.

"I beg your pardon?"

Sesi placidly replied with a look that had patient confidentiality written all over it. Lesley was spitting livid.

"You do know who I am? I am a senior consultant anaesthetist here and I am also one of Debbie Crawley's closest friends. Probably the closest, with the exception of Nigel Alsop – the most senior consultant radiologist in this hospital. She and I are colleagues – very senior consultants of considerable standing and experience. We go back years. Are you seriously telling me that you cannot tell me about her treatment?"

"We are trying to trace her relatives."

"She has none, not that I know of, and I would know better than anybody. Probably even Dr Alsop. Her mother died years ago, her father more recently. Broke her heart. They were exceptionally close; she adored him. No brothers and sisters just Debbie and her father, and Miss Muffat of course." She stopped and looked tragic. Sesi had to have heard about the terrible death of the cat; Lesley would give her a moment to reflect and repent, maybe even to apologise but certainly to back down. Sesi stood firm.

"Nevertheless, we must make every effort to find her family, however distant. There'll be a contact number on her hospital records that we'll use."

"There's no one. No one. Just me and Nigel. You are being very obstructive, young lady. There's more to being a consultant than just sticking to the small print you know."

Sesi was speechless. Which was a good thing or she might have said something deeply reprehensible. To her relief her mobile pinged a text upon which she immediately focused her attention – anything to avoid spatter from the boiling ball of fat before her.

"It seems that the contact name for Miss Crawley is that of her father. He's dead you say?" Sesi glanced down at the bubbling rotund one.

"Yes. About two years ago. I'm surprised she hasn't updated her records. Most unlike her. She's so meticulous."

"Then in the absence of any family I am at liberty to discuss her treatment with you. On a purely professional basis, of course." Sesi revelled in her pomposity, partly to hide her irritation but more to annoy her colleague. Lesley felt vindicated but peeved, not quite sure who had won the skirmish. She had a feeling it might be Sesi but that could not be possible. The dark-skinned upstart had now assumed the role of an E.R. consultant briefing another medic without so much as a hiccup. Infuriating.

"She came in wearing a neck brace, yes. We checked her pupillary reflex and gave her a 9 on the Glasgow Coma Scale. She was rambling and confused, not opening her eyes and pulling away from painful stimuli. There were abrasions on her right forehead and cheek where she made contact with the road and a fractured right femur from the impact with the car, or whatever hit her. We've put a pneumatic leg splint on to keep it straight until the orthopaedic surgeons get here. She's been intubated and ventilated ..."

"Cannulated for medication?"

"Of course."

"Pain relief?"

"Yes, Fentanyl IV and Suxamethonium to paralyse..."

"Sux yes, obviously and propofol as a sedative?" Lesley the senior anaesthetist was back on home turf now and did not want Sesi, a newly appointed consultant, ever to forget it.

"Yes." It was all Sesi could do to bite her tongue.

"Well, it seems as if you've done a good job, Sesi." Lesley had resumed her pronounced Welsh lilt and said the unfamiliar name with apparent difficulty but they were both consultants, despite the difference in seniority, so first name terms were de rigeur. Lesley knew how to behave. "Now we'll have to see what the day brings and how she gets on. They'll be keeping her in ICU for the time being I expect. I'll make sure they keep me informed of any development and I can monitor her progress."

Sesi was dismissed. She headed back to Emergency and then the prospect of home, bed, and blissful, longed for, well-earned sleep.

***

In her office Catherine was also longing for sleep – any form of oblivion. Outside she could see her team with their heads down, subdued, quiet, manifestly concentrating on computer screens and paperwork, tentatively avoiding each other but mostly keeping out her way. She could not really blame them. Well, there was one thing she had to do and then she could get back to normal, back to work, focus on the Tiger Bites, maybe buy some doughnuts and hand them out at lunchtime. Yes, one of those big boxes of those ruinous Kreme things would sweeten the atmosphere and avoid the need to apologise: too humiliating. A little mollified, she placed her finger on her mouse and spun the cursor on her screen into a Google search. It was a work computer which was risky, but this couldn't wait.

Her contempt for all things computerised was well known. It was attributed to her age but actually it was fear – fear of what she did not understand and had not fully mastered. Although she had become quite an accomplished one finger keyboardist, the peccadilloes of the computer, which always seemed at its most perverse when she was up against deadlines, infuriated, perplexed and grated. Pen and paper every time, especially for reports and form filling. And who said computers saved paper? Everything was printed out and filed as well as stored in non-existent alternative universes. Email was good she had to concede, although she made a point of ignoring as many of them as she could and loved consigning them to that delicious little old-fashioned dustbin at the top of the page: her favourite icon. Weird. All that technology but all understanding of it still based on images of the past – files, bins, brushes, clip boards, scissors and glue. The instant information on databases and the like was useful for grunt work she had to admit, but that was for junior officers. No, Catherine was of the slide rule generation. Nicole would not even know what that was – ironically, would find out on Google. Calculators were the innovation of Catherine's youth. Shame they had not been allowed to use them for O Level but the up side of that was that mental arithmetic was second nature to her. She had known exactly how much money she owed Hippocrates throughout the game which made her dogged stupidity to win it back even more shameful. After permanently signing The Mathematician out of the Poker Parlour and deleting all emails relating to her gambling career, she paused. How else to cover her tracks? Yes! Wipe the browser history. It was that easy and once accomplished, she felt better. Cleansed. Over and done with. Confession, repentance, absolution all from the comfort of her own chair.

The restrained knock on her door was unexpected and she looked up to see Mike hovering on the other side of the door, earnestly studying his feet.

Be friendly, welcoming. "Come in, come in, Mike." His head lifted with his eyebrows and he opened the door, slowly, throwing his hat into the ring as it were.

"Yes, Mike. What can I do for you?" He goggled, briefly, then became animated.

“We’ve found the witness who called the emergency services. She wants to remain anonymous – worried about reprisals, involvement, that sort of thing...”

“Yes. Yes, fine. OK. And?” Catherine really could not help herself. Get to the point man!

“We’ve got a registration number.”

Chapter Twenty-Six

What Followed

Now that Lesley had been recognised as her dear-friend-Debbie's closest connection she took her responsibilities very seriously. Indeed, to the consternation of the nursing staff and irritation of senior colleagues, she was hardly ever out of ICU and there was nothing - but nothing – she did not want to know about her d-f-D's treatment and progress. Nigel too had been acknowledged as an approved contact in lieu of any family Crawley but was more restrained: devotion from a distance, when and as his schedule permitted. Lesley made spectacle enough for both of them. Ever the radiologist, Nigel watched, analysed then acted. In his own quiet way, he had been profoundly distressed by Debbie's demise and was already reading up on Post Traumatic Stress Disorder.

Debbie had regained consciousness and was out of danger. She had been moved from ICU into a side room on Women's Surgical where she continued to make good physical progress. The abrasions on her face would heal without noticeable scarring and her nose, although badly crushed and bruised by the impact with the road, had not been broken. The swelling was receding, her nostrils were clear, breathing was noisy but normal and only its vibrant purple/black/yellow appearance was shocking. However, in the company of one black eye and extensive facial discolouration it looked quite at home – part of a matching set - and did not seem to bother the patient. Confined to bed initially by her broken leg, Debbie lay thin, grey and bruised against the white bed linen. Diminished but increasingly agitated, her state of mind was becoming cause for concern.

It was not unusual in cases such as hers for the patient to have no idea where they were. Debbie's perception of her whereabouts flitted between her bedroom at home and her bedroom as a child, no one quite knew where. She was always looking for something, but the 'what' changed with the 'where'. As a child at home with her parents it was a stuffed toy – the ward sister thought it was a rabbit from the description of the long ears and big feet - which Debbie had lost. She repeatedly tried to get out of bed to search and look for it which created havoc with her broken leg, and when restrained would call out for her father to come and find Cottontail who had run away. When she thought she was in the bedroom in her house near Wyeminster it was Miss Muffat who had vanished, temporarily, only to be found again and greeted with elation and tearful relief. As the cat vanished and reappeared with alarming frequency so Debbie vacillated between wet distress and wet joy with such regularity that the nursing staff began to refer to her condition as cat's in or cat's out. Thus the agitation had started, but now it had begun to take on a more disturbing aspect. She was becoming paranoid.

Everyone was out to get her; to cause her harm. The nurses were spying on her and reporting back to the doctors who were then trying to control her mind with drugs, to confine her to bed, to imprison her. She would sit in bed talking endlessly in a low voice to Miss Muffat, whether she was in or out. Debbie's once lovely voice was no more, but made ugly by gritty suspicion and malice. She sat and picked non-existent cat hairs off her nightdress, the bed clothes, her body and even her hair, long strands of which she pulled around to her face so that she could peer and pluck at them. In an effort to minimise her distress and to make life easier for the nurses who had to wash and brush it, Lesley had suggested cutting her hair to a more manageable length.

"Shoulder length, Debbie. So becoming and chic and easy to manage. It'd really suit you and would be so convenient." The reaction had been terrifying. She had exploded into rage, anguish and persecution.

"No! It's my hair! Leave it alone. Father doesn't let me cut it. You just want to take it away from me but I won't let you. Miss Muffat's told me what you're planning." When Lesley, genuinely distressed, remonstrated and protested she was rewarded with even greater vitriol.

"You hate me. You and all the others who're trying to kill me. But Father won't let you, he's told me. You won't dare do anything when he's here." And she had smiled spitefully to herself, nursing her sense of security like a blanket.

She was convinced that there was a conspiracy to kill her, kept muttering about telephone calls and clocks that stopped and alarms that went off. Small sounds – and sometimes no sound at all – startled her and made her peer suspiciously, narrow-eyed and nervously around the room, up at the ceiling and along the floor where it met the walls. She would try to get out of bed to look for Miss Muffat if she was out, or clutch her tightly to her skinny chest if she was in. Her father had become a constant companion. He was looking for his dressing gown – would get cold without it – what had Deborah done with it? Deborah did not know, could not remember, was perplexed. Wasn't it on the back of the bathroom door like always? The empty window sill was an obsession; she would ask if the windows were locked a hundred times a day and night, which had merged into one and both seemed the same to her. Only when she flat out refused medication and became violent with the nurse on the drug's round was it decided that some sort of action had to be taken. For one so thin and immobile she had shown remarkable strength when she had grabbed the nurse with bony fingers and remorselessly pinched her. Then while clutching at her with one hand she had swiped at her face with the other and left deep scratches from grimy untrimmed nails. The nurse wore the marks for weeks and was given a tetanus injection to be on the safe side. She was also tested for HIV and Hepatitis - routine, but the knowledge of which when she found out shocked Lesley more than anything else that had happened so far. She would never look at Nigel Alsop in quite the same way again. Debbie had by this time, as well as refusing oral medication, pulled out all of her cannulas so administering any form of sedative, pain relief or other drug was virtually impossible.

It was agreed that a psychiatric evaluation should be made on her to determine what should happen next. Physically her progress was good but it was obvious that she could not go home where there was no one to care for her and in her current precarious state of mind, she would be a danger to herself as well as others. The decision was made to section her and move her to an inpatient psychiatric hospital where, under Section 2 of the Mental Health Act 1983 she would be kept, initially, for 28 days for diagnosis and treatment. Hers was clearly a delusional disorder and she was prescribed with chlorpromazine which had to be given intramuscularly amidst great protest by her and considerable physical restraint on behalf of the nursing staff.

Lesley was distraught, vocal and horrified but did not challenge the decision. Neither did Nigel who did not comment but silently returned to his office where he turned off the lights and sat, alone, motionless, for a good twenty minutes. Throughout the hospital there was an air of at first, disbelief, then general sympathy and people stopped referring to her as Creepy. She was Miss Crawley once more and would have been touched had she known.

Under the auspices of its newly appointed consultant, Juan, the Colorectal Department had continued to function. Not quite seamlessly but with an air of calm: determined to survive, even on the most meagre of rations. Tommy Yeo was still under suspension but Clare was on the case and had high hopes of his imminent reinstatement. Light at the end of the tunnel she said to herself in rare moments of self-indulgent cautious optimism. She had even managed to get home earlier than usual one evening and had made dinner – well, bought one of those three courses for two, wine included, meals from M&S on her way home. But it had pleased the husband who had been placated and was once more long suffering and, almost, uncomplaining. It was sad about Debbie Crawley, of course, very sad, but she was in the best place now and the hospital would learn from the experience. Clare would herself keep an eye on the clinical governance paperwork, at least until she was confident that it was in reliable hands. And Juan had turned out to be nothing short of a godsend. Not good for his ego she conceded, but he seemed to be acceptable to those who worked with him on a daily basis which was all she cared about. What he did in his private life was his own business, although she had heard the stories and would not be eating Cox's Orange Pippins any time soon.

Catherine too had been feeling more optimistic. The car registration number was an encouraging breakthrough not just in the hit and run but because it had been traced to a certain Li En Yeo who had a local address, one of the large houses on the edge of the city. The sort of house that stood in its own grounds behind a wall – private, secluded and stinking rich. It was the last name that had caused so much excitement amongst the whole team. Mike had announced it with uncharacteristic jubilation in the middle of the room; Catherine had overheard from her office and rushed out to hear more. She had stood behind him as he scrolled down the database on his desktop revealing address, date of birth, clean current driving licence, no previous convictions and, disappointingly, absolutely no criminal record. Apart from routine documentation he simply did not feature anywhere on their system. They knew nothing about him apart from the fact that he was the law abiding, tax paying owner of a black Bentley, personalised registration number HLB 268. According to the eye witness account of the woman who had called the ambulance and who refused, point blank, to be named or identified publicly under any circumstances, the driver of the car could not possibly have been Li En Yeo.

“No”. She was adamant. “I've told you what I saw a million times. Why do you keep asking me the same questions? For the last time, it was a youngish man driving, not old. The passenger was quite young too but it was dark so I really couldn't say any more than that.” And she would not. It was here that Catherine's optimism began to dry up leaving little more than a patch of damp on her hopes.

“Look again. Mike. Anything connected to the name Yeo. There must be something.” Then, “All of you. Get onto it. Imports, exports, social media, the Good Food Guide. Anything. Follow up the restaurant, the Nine Gates of Heaven. Check out everything to do with the name Yeo and especially Tommy Yeo. I want to know who was driving that car, where they were going and what they were doing. Who was with him? We know he was Oriental, medium height, muscular build and smartly dressed in a dark suit. Why? Why a suit?" She stomped purposefully back to her office, calling out as she went without so much as turning around, flinging instructions behind her like resentful rice at the wedding of a rival.

"And check out all the CCTV and cameras in the city. I want to know where that car came from, where it was going, where it went. Check all the petrol stations – a car like that must eat fuel. No one goes home until we know something. Sod Christmas."

An air of glum resignation descended and settled as she shut her door and sat down behind her desk which was clear apart from a pencil and a sheet of blank paper. Catherine picked up the pencil, checked that the point was sharp by pressing it vigorously against her thumb where it left a slight grey indentation then placed it down again, neatly lined up beside the paper which she straightened. She ran her hands through her hair and began to think.

Debbie, Miss Muffat and Father had been removed by ambulance to the psychiatric hospital just a few miles out of Wyeminster. Lesley had accompanied her dear friend, although Debbie seemed to have little idea who she was and even less enthusiasm for her company.

"But she′ll know one day that I was there and that′s what matters" Lesley had said to Clare who had protested at the frequent absences of the anaesthetist from her duties.

"Do you have to?" she had almost implored. "You have important responsibilities here, at the hospital. We′re short of anaesthetists at the best of times, Lesley." Then for good measure, "Especially such experienced ones."

"Nevertheless" Lesley had beamed as she moralised, "I have an even greater responsibility to dear Debbie and I will not let her down in her time of need." So it was that the Court of Debbie arrived, in a certain amount of medical state at the converted convent set in its own (highly secure) grounds, a world away from Wyeminster Infirmary.

"You can relax here, Debbie, where you′re safe. You′ll soon feel so much better." Lesley the comforter, the stalwart, the devoted.

Debbie squinted maliciously at this short, talkative, tubby woman with the Welsh accent who seemed to know her and never seemed to go away. Father had ordered her not to trust anyone and Miss Muffat had whispered to her that she was one of those doctors who was trying to drug her. They wanted to control her mind but she was cleverer than they were, knew their game and would not be deceived. Miss Muffat was a great help. She spied and eavesdropped, reported back what they were planning and scheming: Debbie´s eyes and ears on the world and no one knew! How stupid and naïve everyone was but Father had told her to let them think that; let them think they are in control and that way, Deborah, you will always be one step ahead of them. She smiled smugly at him over the tubby one´s shoulder and he nodded back approvingly. Miss Muffat also insisted on tasting the food and drink that they brought, in case it was poisoned. Dear Miss Muffat! Prepared to sacrifice her own life for that of her mistress! This tubby one must be working with them because she kept trying to lift up the food that Debbie put down for Miss Muffat.

"You want to put your meals on the portable table that goes over your bed, where you can reach them" she told Debbie. "That´s what it´s for. The trays fit perfectly – look." And she had demonstrated. Debbie then made a demonstration of her own and flung the tray off the table onto the floor. That would show them! No one was going to poison her! Father had smiled at that and Miss Muffat purred with satisfaction. The one that called herself Lesley had then gone, in a rush, tearful and sniffly. Father had been very critical.

"Never sniff. Always blow your nose, Deborah" he had reminded her and she had agreed, showing him the handkerchief she kept tucked in her sleeve.

***

The paper on Catherine´s desk was covered in pencil marks, numbers, doodles, lines and arrows, an occasional asterisk and lots of crossing out. She had abandoned the pencil now and was invisible writing with the cursor on her computer screen, flicking repeatedly to and from Google and skimming down pages of Wiki. Now and then she added to the mess of information on the paper, circling what seemed to matter but almost always crossing it out shortly after. Suddenly she stopped, put down the pencil and examined her jottings.

"Mike!" she shouted. "Here, now."

Everyone heard the summons through her closed, paper thin door. The heavy air of resignation stirred and shook itself alert, heads went up, backs straightened and torpor lifted. Mike went immediately to answer the call, did not even knock on the door before he pushed it ajar and spoke.

"Yes, Ma´am?"

"Go out and get these." She handed him a shopping list. "And some of those ghastly doughnuts that they all like – in the box, with the different toppings. You know the ones I mean. Here." She handed over a £20 note. "Some change´d be nice."

"Yes, Ma´am."

"Then get everyone together for a briefing."

As he walked through the open plan office to the door all eyes were on him, an onslaught of unspoken questions. He merely shrugged, brandished the list and the money and picked up his jacket from the back of his chair. At the entrance he took his coat from the row of hooks on the wall and left the building. No need to gather them all for briefing on his return. They had heard the conversation. The doughnuts were unexpected and would be very welcome, but what was on the list? And why sweetmeats now? Catherine was hardly motivational and there was nothing to celebrate - was there? Catherine liked to be unorthodox but this felt like superficiality. At least it was a break from the grim, depressingly non-productive routine work under which they were drowning. When Mike returned with a large flat box of artery-stopping carbs the kettle had boiled thrice and mugs of tea and coffee were already on desks. Catherine had declined to partake of the instant ′piss′ and stuck to a small bottle of mineral water, from which she would sip for dramatic emphasis while addressing the troops. He walked back into an air of expectancy.

Catherine stood before her assembled team, mistress of the whiteboard. The doughnuts were still boxed and the contents of the Co Op carrier bag that Mike had handed to her – unopened - were on a desk close by. Beside them was an array of coloured board markers: Catherine′s props. She breathed, they breathed. She flexed her fingers and cracked the knuckles, they flinched. The performance began.

"This Tiger Bites case has been a real puzzle - a conundrum, but we′re getting there." A volley of glances amongst the audience. They were? Catherine pretended not have noticed. "It´s been complicated by the fact that there are actually two cases, but we didn´t know that at the outset. Mike." here she jumped on her unsuspecting colleague who should have known to expect the unforeseen "Outline the central issue, the Tiger Bites for us. I´ll try not to interrupt." Polite titter in audience, none of whom believed her for a moment. "Here." She handed him one of the sacred board markers. "As short and pithy as you like."

Mike took the floor, removed his jacket, adjusted his tie and prepared to begin.

"You speak, I´ll write." Interruption number one and he had not even spoken. He tried not to smile and put his board marker in his pocket. A trophy. He then stood slightly to one side so that Catherine had centre stage, the writing on the wall, and launched into his speech before she could stop him.

"Andy Barrett, aka Donald Trump." He pointed to the image of the filthy rubber mask, flaccid and sad, posted on the whiteboard. "Small time dealer and one-time user – clean now apparently but only just – has been supplying Tiger Bites disguised as sweets." Mike was a pro. Even as he spoke, he had reached for the Co-op carrier bag and tipped its contents onto the desk. Like the victor on a battlefield holding the standard of the defeated enemy he flaunted a large bag of Skittles aloft, fiery red and shook it so that it rustled and crackled. Then in his other hand he brandished a multipack of fun sized boxes of Smarties and did the same again.

"Just like these. Given to the local kids, any kids, as well as teenagers. How many of them don´t eat sweets? A visit to the supermarket, open the packets, empty out all the orange sweets and replace them with one or two Tiger Bites, depending on the price paid. Handy little fun size packets, already packaged. All he had to do was reseal and sell... Anyone want one?" Mike offered the packets out to his colleagues. Heads shook - no thanks. Not now. Mike continued. "Amateur but effective. Clever. Who´d suspect kids carrying sweets?"

"Hidden in plain sight." Interruption number two. "Sorry. Carry on, Mike."

"Andy Barrett started off at Halloween. We´re not sure why then, but he disguised himself as Donald Trump and that´s when the first casualties occurred. That´s when Tiger Bites appear to have arrived in Wyeminster. He recruited schoolkids to sell to other kids on his behalf but he wasn´t quite as clever as he thought. He put more than one dealer on the same patch and being kids, some with access to illegal knives, they fell out and had a fight. Jason Pierce died and Tyler Morgan is on a murder charge. Andy is in custody but won´t co-operate on any level which makes things difficult as we still don´t know for sure who´s been supplying him, pulling the strings. His employer, as Andy calls him. And he, or she, is the one we want to catch."

Nicole put up her hand to ask a question, which annoyed Catherine. A question was okay, but the girl wasn´t in school, asking to be excused. Mike had no such objection.

"Nicole?"

"We´ve got some suspects though?"

Catherine had to speak. "Yes, and that´s where the two cases overlap. Which is what had made this such a difficult case in many ways."

One of the team now chimed in.

"Why won´t Andy Barrett cooperate? Surely he knows it´s in his interest to help us out?" Mike picked up the baton and ran with it.

"He´s terrified. We´ll get nothing out of him. Whoever is behind the scenes has frightened him into absolute silence. He won´t say a word and is prepared to go to prison rather than spill the beans, or should I say sweets? Talking of which, we´re almost certain that the drugs are coming in from the Far East via a Chinese restaurant, the Nine Gates of Heaven, here in Wyeminster. The one on the high street; we´ve all been there."

"I haven´t." Catherine had to be different and could not stay quiet any longer.

"Thanks Mike. I´ll take over now." She had been scratching and squeaking her pen on the board as he spoke and it was now a mass of red lines linking Andy to the restaurant to the Tiger Bites to the school and the picture of dead smiling Jason.

"This is where it gets interesting." Wielding her pen, she began speaking and scrawling on the board, still in red.

"The Chinese restaurant is owned by the Yeo family – Mrs Yeo in name but it's almost certainly a family concern. It's probably in her name for tax reasons or the like – we're looking into that. This Mrs Yeo is the wife of Tommy Yeo who is a surgeon at Wyeminster Infirmary, currently under suspension for breaking medical protocols. Now." here she was planting red lines across one side of the board to the other like a junior officer taping off a crime scene. "Look at this. Andy Barrett's girlfriend, or should I say fiancée, is a staff nurse there. She's called Elizabeth Gilbert, known as Lizzie and... excuse me." She unscrewed the cap from the bottle of water and took a lengthy sip. They waited, as they knew they must. "Right. Where was I? Oh yes, Lizzie Gilbert. Well. Now we have a link with the hospital which becomes even more interesting when we learn that Deborah Crawley is a fellow surgeon of Tommy Yeo. Same department. Same team."

A triumphant look at the faces before her which were clicking into understanding. No need to remind them about the disembowelled cat, a photograph of which was stuck on the board and now joined in red to the Chinese contingent.

"Deborah Crawley has been the target of progressive, systematic intimidation. Why? Because senior surgeon Deborah Crawley is the one who brought the complaints against Tommy Yeo which led to his suspension. There is every reason to assume that she has been the victim of a personal vendetta by Tommy Yeo for blackening his name."

"Is he guilty? Of the accusations I mean?" Nicole again, but no hand up this time Catherine noted with relief.

"He strenuously denies all the accusations and it would seem from what the CEO at the hospital says, that he may well be right. The campaign of intimidation started small but escalated, rapidly. Methodically slashed tyres – remember those Nicole? Night time visitations, cryptic messages then overt violence. First her cat which was slaughtered according to some bizarre ritual as a warning and most recently, an attempt on Miss Crawley´s life. We´re looking at an attempted murder."

Dramatic pause to allow the tingle of the subsequent frisson to fill the room. Catherine basked in their reaction.

"Yes. A hit and run. Wyeminster Infirmary have confirmed that their senior Colorectal surgeon, Deborah Crawley, was admitted as an emergency from A&E – or ED as they call it – as the victim of a suspected hit and run. She was unconscious, with a broken leg and other RTA related injuries, mostly superficial. Her mental state is currently giving cause for concern and she's been sectioned, removed to a psychiatric hospital and is unable to answer questions of any sort. Which doesn't help us but we should be glad she's still alive."

"How do we know it wasn't just an accident?" It was Mike who posed the question which was met with silence from the whiteboard. "Well, it might have been," he persisted, more lamely. Catherine looked displeased. "How did they know she was going to be there at that time?"

"Opportunity, Mike. You're right, of course, to raise the question (then why did he feel so wrong?) but I think we can assume an inherent motive which took advantage of an opportunity."

"Didn't somebody call the emergency services before the witness did? What if that was someone from the car? Didn't the call handler say the man had a Scottish accent?"

Catherine was annoyed. Mike was thorough and occasionally thoughtful, but he was speaking to her as if she hadn't considered all these possibilities – obviously – and discounted them. Her neck darkened, crimson and mottled.

"Even if it was accidental, they refused to give any identification or personal details and drove off leaving their victim for dead. Failing to stop at the scene of an accident is a crime in itself so I think it's fair to assume that they had something to hide otherwise, not why stay to help?" Everyone else was relieved they hadn't been the one to express doubts. Mike simmered.

"Will we be able to question her later? When she recovers?" Nicole asked. She had enjoyed, if that was the right word, accompanying her boss to the hospital to conduct enquiries and wanted to ensure that it was she who was called upon any next time.

"I hope so. But her state of mind is uncertain and there´s no guarantee that she´ll be in a fit state any time soon. It all depends on the shrinks, and we know what that means." Glumness pushed Frisson aside and resettled itself on every shoulder. "However, we've got a witness to the hit and run. Only one, and one who refuses under any circumstances to be named or publicly testify, but a witness nevertheless." Frisson grinned and displaced Glumness. The air lifted.

"It was this witness who made the second call for an ambulance. Yes Mike, we think the first may have come from the hit and run car but as I've already said, the call was anonymous and untraceable. Although it was dark and the scene badly lit, our witness has told us that the car concerned was large, expensive and probably dark coloured. Most importantly, we have a registration number. HLB 268."

Another dramatic pause.

"Right. A doughnut for the first person to tell me how HLB 268 links the two cases. No conferring."

Brief consternation then two hands shot up simultaneously, Nicole and one of the grunt force, the backbone of modern policing - a young man in uniform with aspirations to get out of it as soon as possible into the civilian clothes of the detective.

“Anil, yes.”

“Sixteen Ma’am. Two plus six plus eight adds up to sixteen which is the number that keeps recurring with the dead cat case.”

“Go on.”

“The car belongs to the Yeos, who own the restaurant where Andy Barrett works and which is the suspected drugs centre. It’s the same car that tried to kill Miss Crawley who owned the cat and who’s a surgeon at the hospital with Tommy Yeo.”

“Give that man a doughnut.” Before the box could even be opened, she was off again. “That was the easy part. Now it gets more difficult. So, for the rest of the box, where does HLB come in?”

More consternation with conferring this time, but no more than that. No one had any suggestions to make. Eventually the room fell quiet, as Catherine had anticipated.

“Anyone? No? I’ll tell you then.” She took another sip of water, loving her moment, anticipating glory. “It’s all about the number sixteen. Miss Crawley’s tyres, the total of the times of the clock, the cooker and the white stones in her house...”

"White being the Chinese colour of death" Nicole chipped in.

"Exactly. So here our cases are interlinked because although we didn't know it, finding the answer to one was the way to solve the other. Two cases, one a drugs whodunnit and the other a hospital soap opera which have collided with devastating results. One dead, two near deaths, one attempted murder. As well as a dead cat." She paused. They all studied the photograph of Miss Muffat's intestines, neatly stacked beside her open belly.

"But why 16?" Mike voiced the question for them all.

"That puzzled me too" Catherine admitted. "So I did what you lot do, I went onto the internet. It took me a while but once I made a Chinese connection it started to make sense. In Cantonese the numbers 2, 6 and 8 are called Hei, Lok and Baat." Changing pens, she now scrawled in bright blue so that the numbers shone out from the white background. "In the 19th century the Chinese Triad – you've all heard of that – branched out and a splinter group was formed in Singapore. It consisted of 16 original members so they called themselves Heilokbaat, which abbreviated becomes..."

"HLB". A chorus from the floor.

"Exactly. 268 is their code for the number 16."

"So the car reg HLB 268 stands for Heilokbaat 16" Mike summarised. He pronounced the Cantonese word slowly, curling his tongue around the unfamiliar syllables. "And it belongs to the Yeos who employed Andy Barrett so we can directly link Tiger Bites to them."

"But we need proof of the link. It's all surmise and circumstantial at the moment and the CPS won't touch it. We have to find some evidence. I know we're on the right track but we absolutely have to be able to tie in the Yeos with the drugs and so far, we've got nothing, absolutely nothing, that will stand up in court.

It was a sobering moment.

"What did they say when we followed up the hit and run?" Nicole asked.

"They didn't. We haven't."

An unspoken 'why not?' reverberated around the room, written on every gawking face.

"I didn't want them to know we were on to them." Catherine replied. "My decision. Didn't want to frighten them off. I want to get the whole operation - a sprat to catch a mackerel and break the drugs ring wide open." She went on, ignoring the glances of surprise in front of her. They were not convinced and it showed. She pressed her point.

"The Yeos are distributing the drugs, using the Nine Gates of Heaven as a front. They're extremely professional and very dangerous. Look at what they've done to Debbie Crawley. Who knows what they're capable of? No wonder Andy Barrett is terrified. I would be too."

“What about the Fentanyl from the hospital that was stolen by the nurse, the girlfriend of Andrew Barrett?” someone asked.

“A red herring, I think. Connected but not significant. Andy wanted it for personal use although I suspect he sold it on the street and used the money to help finance his Tiger Bites enterprise, or feed his habit, who knows? After that he was working for the Yeos - the HLB - so we’ll never find out what happened to the Fentanyl because he’ll never tell us.”

“The boy that died was 16.” Another question from the one of the team whose combined creative juices were beginning to flow, to run with the theme.

“Yes, that threw me too, for a bit” Catherine conceded, “But much as I don’t believe in it, I think it was coincidence. Sixteen-year old kids don’t need Chinese number patterns to get into trouble, especially where drugs and knives are involved.”

“Any more questions? ... No? Right. We need to pay a visit to the Nine Gates of Heaven and the Yeos’ homes and turn them inside out. I want evidence. Now. ... Doughnuts when you find it.”

In a moment the room was emptying, abandoning doughnuts and the permanent office staff in a flurry of coats, jackets, frisson and expectation. This was sexy policing, the sort on TV that in reality hardly ever happened and when it did, was impounded by paperwork after the event and endless debriefings. Uniform would be there when they arrived looking the part in bullet proof vests – they always wore them, even when it was obvious they weren't necessary. But on this occasion, well, who knew? Wyeminster Constabulary had never dealt with a Chinese Secret Society before. Armed back up? Yes. Personal involvement of the Chief Super? Definitely. He had been briefed, the paperwork had been cleared and it was operation go. Catherine showed mercy and called to Anil, he of the stationary office staff.

"Anil. Go with Mike to the Yeo house. Watch and learn but don't get in the way."

They were gone.

The streets of Wyeminster shook and rattled with the noise and vibration of the cavalcade heading into town to the Nine Gates of Heaven. A confusion of speed and colour, shrieking through red lights, on the wrong side of the road, intimidating and bullying ordinary traffic to move aside, to climb up kerb edges onto pavements, anywhere but get out the way. And not just in the city centre either. A second contingent, aggressive and loud was clattering its way through sedate suburbia to the large, walled edifice around the Yeo's mansion while yet a third was heading towards Tommy Yeo's home nearby, smaller but no less select. A combined raid of proportions unknown to sleepy Wyeminster, now rocking on its heels, chattering to strangers, speculating wildly and driving the local Press into a frenzy of curiosity. As fast as the police were travelling, they were being pursued by the Press and the flicker-clicks of mobile phones recording the event for posterity and possible financial gain. Who knew which would be the defining photograph of the moment? How much the Press might pay for it? Maybe even the national Press, the Big Boys, who would surely be back after so much action? Excitement bubbled and frothed behind the tidal surge on Wyeminster's unsuspecting streets.

Outside the Nine Gates of Heaven, firmly closed, solidly locked against all invaders, the cohort screamed to an abrupt stop in a smelly turmoil of hot brakes, tyres squealing like pigs in an abattoir, doors opening, closing, cleaving open again, engines being cut and heavy constabulary feet pounding into position. The vested and helmeted vanguard thundered ahead, Catherine and her team watching, tense, hovering. The heavy doors remained shut, defiant, unassailable. Silent. No way of getting in from outside unless by force. So be it.

"Break it down." The pneumatic batterer slammed against the doors one, twice – they were impressively substantial. On the third attempt however, they surrendered, splintered with a thousand raspy sighs and opened with a snort and a rumble as the locking mechanism collapsed and the wood rattled out its dying breath. Flung aside, mocked by the gaudy pillars standing intact but helpless at their side, the marauders of law and order swarmed into the unlit interior of the Chinese Restaurant.

It was utterly deserted. A surreally calm collection of immaculate tables laid ready for the lunchtime rush with chairs waiting patiently and neatly below them for a clientele that would never arrive. It felt like a film set when everyone had gone home. The sudden movement of black clad, armed helmeted men threading their way between the furniture seeking out dangerous criminals was the theatre of the absurd. The carpeted floor dumbed the sound of their moving feet: a silent movie in subdued monochrome which came to coloured life when the lights were suddenly activated by one of the dusky invaders who then stood upright at the far side of the room.

“All clear, Ma’am.”

“Damn.” Catherine wanted to say worse – far worse, but she was in public and had an image to maintain so she kept the expletive polite and contented herself with spitting it out. She tried not to let her disappointment show but failed. “Someone must have tipped them off.” She was angry but there was a job to be done.

“Alright. Turn it over. Take it apart. Get the dogs in, forensics, whatever it takes. If there’ve been drugs here, I want evidence. Cold, hard evidence.” … “Well? What are you waiting for? Get on with it.”

She turned around and retraced her steps back through the tattered doors and returned to her car, where she stood for a moment inhaling deeply. If she still smoked, she would have sucked on a cigarette now as life-restoring elixir. But she didn’t – had given up when she took out her first mortgage over twenty-five years ago and had to choose between a home or a nicotine addiction. The promise of a solid long-term financial investment had won, easily, but at times like this, God, she was tempted to light up and drink in the heady fumes. She earned enough now to pay for both. Then she remembered her gambling losses.

The news from the Yeo's homes was no more encouraging. They were empty, forsaken and deserted, just like the restaurant. Tommy Yeo's kids had not turned up for school that morning – no explanation given and the secretary had been unable to contact either Mr or Mrs Yeo when she had tried to call. Catherine's team back at the office were orchestrating the search and though sedentary, were extremely efficient and she was proud of them. If they'd eaten the doughnuts she wouldn't have blamed them. They had contacted employees of the restaurant who had all, to a person, been texted within the last twenty-four hours from an untraceable pay as you go phone to say that the restaurant was closed until further notice and that their services were no longer required. Any monies due would be paid into their personal bank accounts and that was that. They were unemployed. Just in time for Christmas. They were livid.

"You've tried all the Yeo phone numbers? Every single one?" Catherine insisted.

"Yes, Ma'am. Repeatedly but there's nothing. No response to any of them. They're all switched off or unavailable. It looks as if the batteries and SIM cards have been taken out."

"Phone providers?"

"Nothing they can do if a person doesn't pick up and tracking won't work if the devices are disabled."

"They've probably dumped them by now."

"It looks that way."

"Put out an alert on ports, airports, the Tunnel, the lot."

"Done it, Ma'am."

"Oh. Well, good. Good. They're probably out of the country by now though." She swore vehemently under her breath. The officer at the other end pretended not to hear.

"I'm going to the Yeo's house – the big one, the one belonging to the parents. Keep me informed of any developments."

"Yes, Ma'am." But by this time Catherine's phone was punched off and she was sitting in the driving seat of her car, missing the girls and accelerating out of the melee of police vehicles on her way to the outskirts of Wyeminster.

The imposing outer wall had been breached, the gates split apart by a combination of impatience, desperation and pneumatic force and the large, salubrious house strangely exposed - vulnerable. The techies had arrived too late to disable the electronic security systems – the previous incumbents had already done it, erasing all potentially incriminating footage so that the forces of law and order were left with an empty stage, a blank canvas. Pea gravel squirted from Catherine's wheels as she swung into the drive and then hit her brakes with a heavy foot and loud obscenities to avoid smashing into the back of the police vehicles banked up in rows outside the house. Abandoning her car, leaving the driver door open behind her she twisted in between the flashing obstacles and hurried bulkily up to the front door which was open wide and undamaged.

"Mike?"

"Yes Ma'am." He emerged from the shadowy interior, blinking slightly in the light, a kind of Gollum in a suit and tie.

"Well? What have you found?"

"Nothing, Ma'am."

"Nothing? What do you mean, nothing? There must be something. Somebody? Where have they all gone? How hard have you looked?"

Mike ignored her final question and simply stood aside to admit her so that she could see for herself. And she could look as long and as hard as she liked he grimaced as she strode past him into the ornate black and red hall.

"The door was unlocked when we arrived. Closed but not sealed – it opened the first time we tried it." If Catherine heard she did not answer but Mike continued regardless; she had this uncanny knack of seeming not to hear but then repeating it back to you later on so those in the know were always extremely circumspect about what they said aloud. Good thing she couldn't read minds, though sometimes he'd wondered about that too.

"Is the car here?" The question was barked at him as she was moving ahead but after years of working in her team, he knew exactly what she meant.

"We found it parked in a garage round the back. Several garages actually, with the cars still in them."

"It's the hit and run vehicle? HLB 268?"

"Yes, it looks like it. Forensics are all over it at the moment but the reg. number is the right one and there's damage on the front bumper which fits with the collision."

By this time Catherine had worked her way across the parquet floor, once so immaculate but now scuffed, soiled and scratched by the battalion of heavy boots and footwear that had tarnished its hallowed surface. She was working her way through the double doors, majestic, tall and imposing but now strangely emasculated – redundant – into the ante room towards the Mah-jong table. The four chairs had been pulled away from the square table and carefully placed two feet from each side, as if designed to make it easy for a spectator to approach the table and read its story. If a game had been in progress it was now over. Most of the ivory tiles were neatly put away in their rosewood box. Everything in order, tidy, orchestrated.

Three of the tile holders were empty, staring blankly at the unoccupied chairs of the players no longer present. Only the fourth holder contained any tiles – the Four Winds. North, South, East and West, elegant, lovingly painted with confident lamp black brush strokes cradled in the creamy whiteness of their background. Beautiful. Simple, artistic and eloquent. In the centre of the table a single tile had been carefully placed, face down. Putting on a latex glove from her pocket, Catherine reached out and turned it over, tenderly, almost reverently. It was the West Wind.

"The bird has flown." She spoke to herself but then, aloud, to Mike,

"They've gone. We've lost them."

Chapter Twenty-Seven

The Week before Christmas

Debbie sat in her room in the psychiatric hospital and stared unseeingly out of the window. She looked beyond the white painted bars, attempting but failing to be discreet. She never really noticed them now as she watched the meagre winter light scuttle uncertainly across the scrubby gardens and out of sight into the trees beyond. It all looked so barren, so cold, so colourless. She looked more or less the same but her eyes were steadier, flickered less and trusted more. Her hair had been cut and trimmed, finally putting the split ends out of their torment, releasing them from their elastic-band chains and Debbie's endlessly plucking and fiddling fingers. Still grey and threadlike, her revamped hair now bumped against her bony shoulders with wide eyed energy, as a battery farmed chicken released into an open yard. Eventually it would gain confidence and might begin to swing against her neck, but that would take time.

Father and Miss Muffat had left with the split ends, quietly and unobtrusively. One day they just were not there any more but Debbie did not seem to notice. She took her oral medication now without demur; the cannulas had been removed and her leg was mending well inside its plaster cast although the itching was maddening. The doctor had said that was normal and she remembered something about that being the case, that it was a good sign – or was that when you had a cut and it was healing? She really could not remember. So much she seemed to have forgotten. Was it the drugs? She shrugged and thought of other things.

"Debbie, my dear friend! How are you feeling today?"

"Lesley! How nice to see you. Very well, thank you."

"Is the leg still itching? I hope not. But if it is, we can get something to help." Not a knitting needle to poke down and scratch it with though Lesley thought, even as she smiled brightly and encouragingly. You're better, but not that much better. I wonder if the flowers are still talking about you?

"Lovely flowers, aren't they? Juan sent them. He's been sending you the most beautiful bouquets ever since you became ill. Such cheerful, bright colours on a winter's day. I don't know how he does it but he always seems to find spring flowers in the middle of winter, just when we all need cheering up the most. But that's Juan for you; always so kind and thoughtful. Such a gentleman. He's doing an excellent job at the hospital I understand. Not as good as you, obviously" she added, a little too hastily, "but coping remarkably well in such a responsible role. Difficult shoes to fill. A hard act to follow." She smiled ever more brightly. Debbie smiled vacuously back, nodding agreement, perfectly content. Lesley inhaled deeply and set off again at a sprint.

"What do you think of the flowers, Debbie? Goodness, how they light up the room! When I think how much they cost! Perhaps he has a contact? Juan seems to be so well connected..."

Debbie intervened, turning the sound off.

"They're very pretty, yes. From Juan you say? How kind." Now she was struggling to visualise Juan. The name was familiar but his face was a blank, however the flowers were very pretty and certainly brought colour to the room's pale cheeks. There had been a time when the nursing staff had had to remove bouquets, pot plants and especially fruit because Debbie had been convinced that they were plotting to cause her harm. That was the time when Father and Miss Muffat had been with her. The fruit had been particularly aggressive as well as a certain carnation that refused to stop staring at her. Eventually she had thrown her lunch at it. It was only in the last week that Juan's floral offerings had once more made an appearance in her presence to the disappointment of the nurses who had loved having them in their office at the end of the wing.

"The good news is that you'll soon be well enough to go home!" Lesley announced like a vicar reading marital banns for the third and last time. "Won't that be nice? Just in time for Christmas!"

Christmas. Despite the pressured preparation and commercial hysteria it always seemed to arrive in a rush, ahead of time. Forever something still to be done or left until the last minute, or forgotten until too late.

It never seemed to matter in the end, however pressing it had been until the day itself. And there would always be a shop open somewhere, at a price. In the hospital there was that uncomfortable, peculiar annual spirit of festive-reality, colourful jollity combined with gore, fear, bodily functions, pain and haste. Doctors wore Santa hats with their stethoscopes, consultants brandished cheery light-up ties that sang synthetic carols or said hohoho if squeezed. Nurses flaunted tinsel in their hair or had earrings that flashed on and off to the discomfort particularly of the more confused patients who wondered if they now had defective eyesight in addition to their hip/knee/digestive/bowel complaints. It was all so very unsettling. Even the food seemed to be different and why was the porter dressed as a snowman? A tree on the ward – call that a tree? -was all very well, but how did that alleviate constipation or ease their stomach pain? Once the sad little artificial tree had received its ritual PAT and fire safety inspections, intimately examined by cold hands in the name of infection control then finally pronounced fit by Health and Safety, it tried hard to shine and glow. Once silver but now grey, middle aged and thinning on top as well as all along its spindly branches, its dilapidated plastic ornaments hung suicidally towards the linoleum floor. Old friends, annually reunited, there was nothing left to say after so many years together so tree, lights and decorations sat lustreless in the corner of the ward, watching and listening like an old married couple at a restaurant table. At least it was not Women's Surgical this year. Nothing so depressing as the elderly women left in the ward over Christmas because they had nowhere else to go. All the bonhomie and carol singers in the world could not revive the thin slices of reheated turkey and decomposing sprouts pinned to the plate by something brown disguised as gravy. Once upon a time over thirty years ago, patients on every ward had received cheerfully wrapped presents and one of the consultants had arrived accompanied by his family – even the teenagers – to ritually carve the ward's whole turkey and spread the good news.

Not all the staff were jovial. Nigel never changed his sombre demeanour, spoke little, smiled only rarely and then only tight lipped. Debbie was often on his mind but he kept that to himself. For once he was the envy of his colleagues. He did not deign to wear silly hats or gimmicky neckwear, declined all festive food and did not drink on duty thank you. This released him from the annual torment of the staff party or night out, a ghastly forced good time at a local hotel or restaurant where the food was cooked on an industrial scale and had all the appeal of a bowel screening. Doctors and consultants who spent the whole year being personable and approachable paid a heavy price: they found themselves compelled to attend. They pulled crackers, wore paper hats and disco danced with dogged smiles. The miserable gits like Nigel were exempt. He managed to look quite cheerful when coughing up the obligatory cash for the wine to accompany the meal, traditionally paid for by the consultants, knowing that he would neither have to share or drink it. Money well spent in his book, as he drove carefully home or tucked himself up in his office for the on call that no one else wanted. Situation normal then, everyone said about him and steeled themselves to the task of having fun. Some of them really did; actually enjoyed it. No reason why you couldn't do your job and have some fun once a year; God knows how hard it could be for the other 51 weeks. Sesi loved the atmosphere of goodwill and peace to all men, even in ED when the pubs had closed and the drunks arrived in all colours of inebriation. The downside was that tragedy, always difficult, became doubly so at Christmas. It was a time of healing and hope, when people went home, not came into hospital, when families were together and happy. She had chosen to work over the holiday period so that those with kids could have the Day with them. It was a surprise to find that Rohan would also be on duty but she did not ask. He had been so much more subdued recently. Still plump and soft-fleshed with sweat patches under his arms even in cold weather, he seemed somehow smaller. Not thinner yet reduced. What was even more disconcerting was that he seemed to have stopped flirting – with everybody. Where once no female had been immune, now they were all ignored and, sad to say, resented the neglect. Lorna on reception was quite put out.

"Of course, I never believed it, not for one minute, but it was nice to be appreciated. Cheered me up no end, 'specially in here" she had grumbled, indicating the crowded waiting room with a disgusted flick of her head. Sesi was more concerned about Rohan himself. He mooned about the department, still clutching his piece of paper, drifting between patients and the operating theatre with an unchanging whipped dog face. He never mentioned his home life or his family and Sesi chose not to ask, but smiled at him whenever she could. He did not smile back.

Analyn from the agency had become something of a permanent fixture in the department since Lizzie had left. It was all very mysterious. Without warning, Lizzie had just not turned up for work and appeared to have vanished. Her phone was unavailable, no one had set eyes on her anywhere in the city and the house where she lived was a building site. The rumour machine went into immediate overdrive. It was common knowledge that Andy, her fiancé, was being held on remand but what had that to do with Lizzie? It was impossible to imagine but not to speculate. She and her enormous diamond ring had disappeared from the face of Wyeminster... she must have been involved or she wouldn't have gone, would she? Andy was supposed to have been involved in those Tiger Bites drugs and someone had ludicrously suggested that he was the Donald Trump lookalike. But that was absurd; not Lizzie's fiancé? Surely? But if he was, what did that make her? Drugs runner? Accomplice in crime for sure. Accessory to attempted murder? Who would have believed it? She had always seemed to nice, so honest, so good at her job. Well, you could just never tell. And they all shook their heads in exultant disbelief and shocked dismay and forgot about her.

In the Colorectal Department Juan had managed to achieve the impossible – he had successfully combined Christmas levity with all the sophistication and decorum of a senior consultant which he was now carrying off with style and aplomb. Only he could have found a silk tie that reflected festive cheer yet had panache and perfectly complemented his bespoke suit, the jacket of which he always wore, especially when doing his ward rounds. Perhaps it was in his aftershave – a special holiday aroma maybe? Whatever, he exuded bonhomie and gravitas in well balanced measures, inspiring confidence in his male patients, a flutter of the heart in the ladies (never women, always ladies) and incredulous admiration from the mostly female medical students who clustered in his wake. Juan's harem as they had become known.

In addition to the usual trials of her CEO responsibilities, Clare's Christmas was full of very unseasonal staffing problems. Couldn't God have given her a break over the holiday period? It was his birthday after all. So much for regular church attendance and devotion. Then she felt guilty; she was healthy, she had a family to go home to and there was always a solution if you made enough effort. She pulled herself together, resumed her inner Head Girl and got on with the job. Poor Debbie Crawley. Clearly there was no question of her returning to work in any capacity. She would be retired on medical grounds of course – full pension, recognition of long service, blah blah. The hit and run had been opportune in some ways (guilty feeling: shocking way of thinking; sorry, God). It was true though and Debbie would benefit. All doubts about her professional conduct and competence would be quietly laid to rest and she would leave the hospital with dignity and respect. Juan could be made substantive – no problem there. He had shown how well he could run the department. Recruiting would have to start at once to fill the gap left by Tommy Yeo but they could manage in-house for the moment. No reason why that young man whom Debbie had found so objectionable, the one from Dorking (what was he called?) couldn't be moved up to fill in some of the gaps. He seemed capable and well qualified enough; it was only Debbie who'd had a problem with him.

Yes, she was starting to feel better. The revelations about Lizzie Gilbert had been a real shock and hugely disappointing. She had seemed so ... honest. Like that Rohan Patel, who would continue to work for the infirmary but would never progress beyond his current level. Clare shook her head. You could just never tell. Lizzie had, of course, been immediately suspended and had sensibly resigned before she could be officially dismissed. What the police decided to do about her was none of the infirmary's business. Out of sight, out of mind and good riddance. One less thing for Clare to worry about. However, she retuned into the one thing that puzzled her most. Where was Tommy Yeo? What had happened to him? And his family? It was the oddest thing. She had received a hand delivered, word processed, personally signed letter of resignation from Tommy and that was all. No address, no contact details, no apology or explanation. The unmarked envelope had manifested itself on her secretary's desk a day ago and that was as much as they knew. How it had got there was another mystery. The police had been informed, as requested – anything to do with the Yeos had to be reported to them as a matter of extreme urgency, but they seemed to be as perplexed as Clare. In fact, they just seem perplexed. Apparently the whole Yeo clan had left the city. Their restaurant had closed without notice to the extreme annoyance of those who had booked en masse Christmas celebratory meals, the Colorectal Department included but, Clare reasoned, as they hadn't got much to rejoice about perhaps it was a good thing after all.

She felt very much better. Lizzie could be replaced, Rohan would not transgress again of that she was sure, Tommy and Debbie were no longer her problem, Juan had stepped up to the Colorectal plate and she would get him to organise Debbie's leaving do. Christmas was coming. She should even be able to squeeze in some present shopping, to make up for last year.

Lizzie was dreading Christmas. How could this have happened? Where had it all gone so wrong? She had resigned from the hospital and left Wyeminster the day after she had been interviewed by the piebald detective. Obviously the police had had to have her contact details and she had given them her cousin's address in Bristol as her place of residence - refuge. It was a relief to be anonymous in a large city. Andy was on remand nearby but she would have nothing to do with him – no contact, nothing. Which to be fair, was not of her choosing. He had made no attempt to get in touch with her in any way which had hurt almost as much as his betrayal on, oh, so many levels. She had no idea what action the police would take against her or if the infirmary would press charges but of one thing, she was absolutely certain: the diamond ring had to go. Its once glorious, faceted sparkles were now crystal spikes dissecting body and mind, every glimmer a punch in the stomach. All it meant to her was the amount of money she could raise. After first trawling a number of reputable jewellers and then resorting to pawnshops in less salubrious parts of the city, she eventually found a take it or leave it, cash in hand, no questions asked buyer who gave her less than she hoped but more than she expected. A thousand quid was less than it was worth she knew, but in view of its dubious provenance she counted herself lucky to get even that much. It would be enough, just, if she was careful, to set up as a tattoo artist. There was a 'studio' - not a shop - in Totterdown where she could get work. Her tats had impressed the guy that ran it but not as much as her nursing credentials which he said would,

"Give 'im 'n 'Elf 'n Safety edge over 'is rivals" so "yeah", she could start work there, minimum wage, free tats, as soon as she liked.

Her cousin had said she could stay as long as she paid the council tax, internet, half the leccy and her own food. Oh, and either went out or kept to her own room on Tuesday and Saturday nights. All night. She did not say why. Lizzie had agreed; it was a sweet deal and she messaged as much to Taya, the one person in Wyeminster with whom she had kept in touch. Taya and her foster mothers had proved to be unlikely rocks in tempestuous seas. Lizzie did not know if they knew about the Fentanyl and she was careful not to tell them, but their sympathy over the demise of Andy was little short of magnificent. He was scum, deserved to be locked up, had at best exploited Lizzie and at worst, abused her. Either way, it was outrageous; behaviour not to be borne and whatever they could do to help they would. Always a place for her with them but of course they understood why she wanted to get away from Wyeminster; great decision. Put some distance between herself and the scene of such pain, such misery. Men! Taya was bemused but relieved. She had become very fond of Lizzie. What was more, Annie and Ella approved of the friendship and encouraged it. Lizzie was a professional, sensible, had a nursing degree; she could deal with any emergency in a calm and mature manner. A marvellous person to know and such a good influence. It was the person beneath the tattoos that mattered. She was also neither Kezia nor Courtney which sealed the deal. If Taya wanted to go and visit or spend time in Bristol with Lizzie, that was fine, as long as she never went anywhere without her. A trip to Bristol after Christmas? Yes, why not? While

Taya was with her friend, Annie and Ella could visit Clifton and the suspension bridge. Hadn't been there for years. Apparently, the Waterfront was wonderful these days and the post-Christmas sales would be on. What could be nicer?

Debbie returned to her house a few days before Christmas. It was a difficult homecoming: no Miss Muffat but her hairs everywhere, a ghastly reminder of what had happened. Lesley had attempted to clean before d-f-D crossed the threshold but had retired defeated, overwhelmed by the amount of hair by/in/on/under every surface. The hoover had blocked; spluttered, coughed, choked and died. The house was also neglected but not just in need of redecoration – it was dirty.

"It's awful, Nigel. She can't go back into that. I don't know what we're going to do." She began to hum. Nigel took the hint. "I'll get a cleaner."

Lesley was astonished into silence, for a moment, then exuded.

"What a good idea, Nigel! Someone to come in on a regular basis and keep everything in order, clean and tidy, that sort of thing. Maybe do some laundry? I must say, I'm surprised by the state of the place, Debbie being a senor consultant with so much experience and all that but then she's always been so devoted to the job, no time for herself and things like housework I expect. Even so, I was surprised. But Blue Persians are renowned for shedding hair – such luxuriant coats – what shall we do with all Miss Muffat's belongings do you think? Her cushions and bowls and ... oh dear, I really mustn't cry."

"No. Don't. I'll deal with it."

Nigel had already decided what had to be done. He was there when Debbie was delivered to the door by patient transport, unloaded in a wheelchair and deposited outside the front door, clutching a carrier bag on her lap. Her own trusty, Colorectal Convention carrier had been hung up on one of the hooks by the door and would stay there for time immemorial, gradually drowning under the weight of the coats and jackets piled over it in the years to come. A sad end for so much service.

Debbie was nervous. The new mat on the door step was a relief; the glass in the front door was clean which made a pleasant change and the CCTV camera was angled reassuringly towards her, on guard, wide-eyed, vigilante. Lesley opened the door with as much flourish as her robust frame and a narrow hallway would permit and hailed the homecoming voyager – a fat Penelope welcoming skinny Ulysses with a broken leg.

"Welcome home my dear friend! Home sweet home!" She sounded like a sentimental greetings card. Debbie blushed. Nigel, standing further back in the hall, winced. Time to act.

"Let me." With reprehensible invasion of Lesley's immoveable personal space, Nigel managed to squeeze past her to manoeuvre the wheelchair over the step and into the house. He pushed Debbie into the living room. All traces of Miss Muffat had gone. Not just one cleaner, but a team, had been through the whole house and even Nigel had to admit they had performed if not a miracle, something holy close to it.

“Blimey, my love” the sweating leader of the track-suited cohort had confessed to him as she wiped her forehead like a finalist at Wimbledon, “never seen so much bloody hair. How many cats did you say? What? Just the one? Never!”

Debbie stared at the chair which had previously enthroned her darling. No trace. No cushion, no softly flattened patch on the dralon where a cat had nestled and curled but just a brushed, empty armchair.

“A nice cup of tea, Debbie, don’t you think? You must be parched after all the upheaval. Here, allow me.” As she spoke Lesley attempted to remove the bag from Debbie’s thin lap but scaly chicken’s feet hands clung onto it. Nigel mouthed above Debbie’s head

“Miss Muffat’s collar and Father’s dressing gown cord.”

“Ah. Oh. Well. Of course. Sorry! Didn’t know.” Lesley discomforted into broken speech was a rare sight and Nigel was tempted to smile. However what else he had to say might even render her fully quiet and that would be the moment to cheer. He settled Debbie into the armchair, pulled up a foot stool to support her leg and followed Lesley into the kitchen.

"I don't know how dear Debbie is going to manage, Nigel. What about shopping and cooking and cleaning, getting up and down stairs, washing and bathing and all that sort of thing? And at Christmas! When everything's closed, how will ..." She had opened the fridge in pursuit of milk she did not expect to find.

"It's full! But how?"

"I did it. Debbie'll be fine. I'm going to stay with her until she's back on her feet."

"What? Here?"

"That's the plan."

Nigel grinned. Lesley gaped and searched for something to say.

***

Catherine stood uncomfortably in front of her boss. The Chief Superintendent had required her presence at a mutually convenient time, to be arranged with his secretary, as soon as possible within the next twenty-four hours. So, here she was. His office was utterly devoid of Christmas. Deliberately, she thought, resentfully. He might have made some effort at least. Even her team had hung cheap paper decorations tastelessly across the ceiling, stuck onto the exact same Sellotape stains of previous years. The chains drooped miserably under the harsh strip lights, joyless and depressed in sympathy with the humanity below. Since the fiasco of the failed raid on the Yeos, dejection had settled over the entire floor and showed no signs of lifting, not even for Christmas.

"I'm waiting."

Catherine tried not to sigh and stood a little straighter. She had not even been offered a seat. Truth to tell, she did not know where to start but fortunately the Chief Super's fury outweighed his patience and he seized the initiative.

"Am I to understand – correct me if I'm wrong – that there is no chance whatsoever of a conviction of any description related to the drug cartel that has decimated our city and our young people? That the Yeos have gone and no one knows where? That they have completely disappeared? That no drugs of any description have been found? That you do not even have an arrest for the hit and run that nearly killed a senior consultant at Wyeminster Infirmary? Not even CCTV footage of the break in at the same consultant's home which might have led us to the drugs? Why is that by the way?" This was a question Catherine had really been hoping to avoid. She knew how it would sound – the faces of her team had said when she had explained it to them.

"It seems that the firm that fitted the security system required specialist expertise for the job which was supplied by someone connected to the Yeos. He came by personal recommendation, was immediately available and did not cost the earth. The owner of the firm, which is local and not used to such high-tech projects, leapt at the offer. Obviously."

"So, you're telling me that the Yeos had access to the security system and could control it as they chose? Obviously." Really, the Chief Super could be quite sarky when he chose. She kept quiet, let him twist the knife yet deeper. "Let me understand this clearly, D I Scott, just in case I've got it wrong. In addition to one dead teenager, two near dead teenagers, one hit and run, assorted break-ins, hate crimes and a ritually slaughtered cat, we have not one but two – two – serious crimes that will forever be filed as unsolved even though we know perfectly well who committed both of them?"

"We do have the man responsible for distributing Tiger Bites in custody."

"A man disguised as Donald Trump? The most insignificant link at the end of the chain who was selling Tiger Bites disguised as sweets to kids and used kids to sell to other kids? Who won't talk? Who refuses to tell us anything we really need to know so that the secret society behind the entire operation has simply upped and offed? A secret society, Detective Inspector Scott, in Wyeminster! Which we could have had. We knew who, and what, and where, but you lost them! Let. Them. Go." He glared and continued. "Why the hell didn't you arrest them after the hit and run? It was their car! At least we would've had someone."

"I didn't want them to know we were on to them in case it jeopardised the drugs set up."

"Oh, that worked well, didn't it?" He leant back in his chair as she continued to stand, wanting to shift her weight from foot to foot but not daring. "We are a laughing stock, an absolute laughing stock. Every police officer and criminal in the country is jeering at us. We are the constabulary that had a Chinese Secret Society within its grasp but let it vanish, without trace. And I blame you. Not your team, not uniform or forensics or the drugs squad but you, and you alone."

Catherine kept her head up and stared at a point above the Super's head. Say nothing she decided; let him vent; accept it and move on. She would weather this one, as she had so many others. He vented on.

"Are we absolutely sure that it was the Yeos and that they've gone?"

"Yes." At least she could now supply evidence, of a sort. "There was a message left at the home of Li En Yeo, in the Mah-jong tiles."

"Go on."

"The tiles left out for us were the Four Winds. There are four tiles of each wind in a Mah-jong set. Four times four equals 16, the symbolic number for the Heilokbaat. The Four winds are inscribed with the Chinese characters for the four compass directions north, south, east and west, so they represent the whole world. Each wind is associated with a time of year, a colour, a constellation and an element. Because we are in the western hemisphere we are associated with the West Wind. Our season is Autumn – Halloween - our colour is white, like the stones at Miss Crawley's house and our constellation is the Tiger. Tiger Bites. Our element is metal, which I interpret as money. The message is simple: like the winds, Heilokbaat are everywhere. Universal. They have gone from Wyeminster yes, but who knows where?"

The Chief Super looked thoughtful as he assimilated a type of evidence that seemed to him more like a cryptic crossword than policing – something out of a Colin Dexter novel, not a provincial city which did not even have a university. Shedding this like a wet dog shaking itself, he returned to more tangible issues.

"What I don't understand is how they knew when to leave? Not just the Yeos but all of them – everyone who worked for them or was directly involved with the family. You're not going to tell me that Mr Yeo, a man in his mid-70s, did all this on his own? Did someone tip them off?"

Catherine lowered her gaze to face her opponent. This was an unexpected turn in the encounter which she had not anticipated and it had taken her by surprise.

"Tipped them off, Sir?"

"You heard the first time. How did they know to leave Wyeminster when they did? Just in time to escape any kind of discovery or arrest? It does look rather suspicious, wouldn't you agree?"

"I suppose so, yes."

"You 'suppose' so? Who knew what was being planned apart from you?" She did not reply.

"Let me put this another way. Who's Hippocrates?"

For the first time in her life, Catherine's face appeared a single shade of white. Ashen. Even her eyes seemed to have been bleached of colour.

"Hippocrates?"

"Yes, Detective Inspector."

"I don't actually know. Just a name for a ..." she stalled.

"Gambler? An on-line Poker player? To whom you owe a considerable amount of money I understand?" Unable to speak she stared in disbelief and fear. "You look surprised. You shouldn't. I make a point of knowing what goes on in my station and it was drawn to my attention very recently that a computer in this building was used to contact a gambling site called The Poker Parlour. You may not realise that I.T. do regular routine security sweeps of all the hardware on site and when they discovered that such communications had been taking place from your IP address I asked them to investigate further. Much further. According to your computer history it seems you made some attempt to cover your tracks, but you didn't do a very good job."

"The money has already been paid, Sir. I owe nothing. All I was doing was permanently terminating my connection with the poker website. I've given up gambling for good. Never again."

"You've said that before, I believe."

"It was a single lapse, Sir. The first in years. It'll never happen again. I give you my word."

"You are aware that Hippocrates is a pseudonym for Tommy Yeo?"

The breath left her body with a gush and she wanted to faint.

"No! I had no idea!" Now it was his turn to stare. "You must believe me! I didn't know. Hippocrates was just the name of a poker player; we all do it. Did it. Mine was The Mathematician but no one would know it was me. How could you find all this out?"

His laugh was incredulous and patronising.

"For God's sake, Catherine!"

Human after all, she noticed when he used her first name, but would it help? "We're a police station! And online gambling sites can be extremely helpful if you talk to the right people. I didn't know that the debt had already been paid though and I'm glad about that. It means we won't have to probe too deeply into your finances - again. But you must see how this looks? In debt to Tommy Yeo – Hippocrates – then he and his family know just when to leave Wyeminster to escape justice in an operation in which you have control? You know you haven't heard the last of this? After what happened before? There'll have to be an inquiry and the PCC will have to be involved, especially in the light of your previous warning from them. What were you thinking of? You do realise that you face disciplinary action and that I'm going to have to suspend you with immediate effect?"

Her white face began to flush patchy red and pink as the blood infused her complexion; her neck was mottled and the room airless. She gasped for breath.

"Would you like to sit down, Catherine?"

"No, thank you. Sir. But for the record and because I want you to know the truth, I did not tip off Tommy Yeo. Or his family or anyone connected with him. I have no idea how they knew when to leave, any more than I know how they brought in the drugs or what they've done with them. But I do know that the organisation we have been dealing with is international, universal and extremely professional. We never stood a chance. We were completely out of our depth and I think we still are... I'm very sorry. I wanted to solve this case – both cases, as much for the dead boy as the drugs and what happened to Miss Crawley's cat."

"I'm sorry too, Catherine. God only knows what I'm going to say to the Chief Commissioner."

Is that all, Sir? I need to get home to my dogs."

"Your dogs. Of course, you do. I advise you to contact your police rep. as soon as you can. Leave your warrant card with my secretary who will see that you receive the appropriate paperwork."

"Thank you, Sir." Not quite sure how, she turned to leave and began walking towards the door only to halt, momentarily to register his parting shot:

"Happy Christmas, Catherine."

Chapter Twenty-Eight

Christmas Eve

Not a white Christmas on the horizon but a cold one nevertheless. Debbie and Nigel were sitting in her beige living room in front of both bars of the electric coal effect fire. Orange light mingling with the grey afternoon invading dark brown corners and camel walls but one splash of colour from a crimson Poinsettia, perched bravely on an occasional table, absurdly resplendent and festive amidst the gloom, shouting out into the silence. Debbie's leg in plaster was perched more comfortably than bravely on a footstool. Beside her another table was festooned with reading glasses, magazines, tissues, pens, word searches and a glass of red wine.

"Oh Nigel. Do you think we should? So decadent! Drinking in the afternoon. Whatever would people think?"

"Christmas Eve, Debbie. It's not as if we make a habit of it. Seasons' greetings." His glass was raised; she did the same. The doorbell rang, sonorous, slow and as world weary as ever, even at Christmas. Especially at Christmas.

"Goodness! Whoever can that be? At this time of day?" Debbie, guilt ridden and shamed, abandoned her untasted wine and began to fret. Nigel sighed, rose reluctantly from his chair, regretfully put down his wine and headed towards the front door. Impossible to tell who the intruder was through the frosted glass but really, it was Christmas Eve afternoon. People were so inconsiderate. Shouldn't they all be at home with their families, loved ones, significant others, whatever they called themselves these days? Even Lesley was not expected until Boxing Day. Surely not a delivery? They were not expecting anything so if it was a merely an enquiry or a wrong address, he would be extremely annoyed. Might even have to say something.

It was Juan.

"Good afternoon, Nigel. Lovely to see you. May I?" He was already over the doorstep so Nigel had little choice but to stand aside. Juan, dark, suave, suited and conspiratorial was holding a large box.

"Shh" he whispered. "Surprise for Debbie. Don't say a word." Nigel had no intention or even the capacity to utter so much as a syllable. He followed the unexpected deliverer of gifts into the glow of the sitting room.

"The compliments of the season to you, dear lady" Juan boomed. Nigel half expected to see him pull out a Santa hat and beard and maybe ring a bell like some Scandinavian town crier. Debbie turned to face him as much as her plastered leg would permit and blushed.

"Juan! What a surprise. I didn't expect to see you."

"No, my dear, which is all the more reason to be here. I've brought you a small gift. Which I think you'd better open immediately." The box had begun to move as he spoke. It gave off a sound of vigorous scrabbling and scratching and bounced as it was placed on Debbie's spindly thighs.

"Whatever is it?" She seemed almost frightened.

"Open it and see. It won't hurt you." Juan, reassuring, in control, covering Debbie's back, just as he always had. Stepping forward he prised the cardboard wings apart so that Debbie could peer into the box. She started to cry.

"There, there my dear. I'd hoped she would cheer you up!"

"Oh, Juan." Debbie was weeping copiously over a kitten, all eyes and ears and ginger fluffiness rapidly being streaked flat by watery tears. "She's beautiful."

"Not a Persian Blue I'm afraid, but less hair to worry about." Nigel looked relieved.

"Glass of wine, Juan? To celebrate?"

"Thank you, Nigel, but no. Driving." Juan the ever tactful who would rather have drunk water than Nigel's supermarket plonk, however festive or well-reviewed.

"Does she have a name, Juan?"

"Not yet, Debbie. That's up to you."

"What would you suggest, Juan? I think you should choose."

“How about Pippin?”

Debbie beamed.

“Pippin! Yes. Perfect. I love it. Pippin it is.”

Nigel, who had heard the stories, avoided Juan and headed for his glass of wine.

Chapter Twenty-Nine

Singapore 2018

A city in the sky. An economic miracle island - platinum, steel, glass, air conditioned, afloat on itself. Sampans on a brown river have become sleek liners in the air, gazing down to the sea and the concrete clad banks of clean water edging around commerce on its way home. The past is insignificant white - the Raffles Hotel, the cathedral and cricket pitch green only splash, a passing memory. It is dwarfed by the present and the future, fertile bed mates spawning the forever new. Once a colony, now colonising the world's money, Singapore city is the perfect operating theatre. Sterile clean, litter free, tobacco free, temperature controlled, filter aired, a technological temple of futuristic machinery designed to repair, remould, excise and rebuild. A centre of excellence and expertise in the very best hands: the most accomplished, the risk takers, the experienced, the theorists, those who want to learn and make the future. Everything is judged by outcomes. Success. Profit and loss, the bottom line, the quality of life.

At the top of one of the tall elegant modern fingers in the sky, ringed with glass eyes, four men sit around a table playing Mah-jong. They wear short sleeved shirts without ties but are crisp and sharp, pressed and one at least, starched. An inky tiger bites the inner crease of each right elbow with every arm movement. There is no noise, within or without, apart from the gentle hum of the air conditioning and the chattering of the tiles. The room is wide, light and open, all white and grey and ultra violet proof. The sun watches from outside, a solitary witness. Clouds are building for the afternoon downpour, too busy to take notice of what is happening in the hard towers that block their path across the sky. Such unwelcome intruders, unavoidable, ever present and ever taller. Only the sun will see what happens in the apartment at the top of the tower, unless she is blocked out by the dark rain which will mass, deepen, explode then run out of breath and end all at once, exhausted.

Li En Yeo has come home. It is a different place, yet remains the same – so much more than sweat, heat, noise and pollution that he once knew. No kampongs on stilts over marshy ground, licensed bicycles fighting for survival on the Bukit Timah road flowing through the stench of the Amoy soy factory, flooded with open windowed cars with white cotton seat covers to protect flesh from the searing humidity. Orchids that grew as wild flowers, the slap slip of plastic sandals on hot, hard pavements, a thousand bicycle bells arguing with car engines and teak laden trucks and taxis, taxis, taxis. He is back in the place that his heart never left, with his language, the climate of his youth, his past and his people. So, he plays this game with devotion and love knowing he will never have to leave again. Now it is the turn of another. Sitting with him at the other three points of the table, north, south and east, are his son, Tommy with Lee and a man he does not know, a stranger to this story. Who will be the chosen one? To carry on their work?

The tiles would decide.

Acknowledgements

We both owe so much to so many. Thank you.

Huge thanks are due especially to our families for their patience, humour and honesty. Nick, Alipops, Pippa, James, Alexis and Lucy for Fionn and Fiona, Jack, George and Doug for Simon. Thank you to all those who have advised, proof read, commented and supported: Jo, Margie, Shayna, Chris, James, Caroline, Lynne, Estelle, Jo, Carolyne, Jennie, Daisy, Charley, Julie.

And very special thanks to Simon, without whom Fionn would not be here and to Fionn from Simon, for helping keep me sane.

25907607R00194

Printed in Great Britain
by Amazon